Weird Tales of Argana Zeit Volume I

by

Owain Oakwood

For Jessie
Thanks for all the help
Much Love
— Owain Oakwood xx

Copyright © 2021 Owain Oakwood All rights reserved

The characters and events portrayed in this book are fictitious. Any similarity to real persons, living or dead, is coincidental and not intended by the author.

No part of this book may be reproduced, or stored in a retrieval system, or transmitted in any form or by any means, electronic, mechanical, photocopying, recording, or otherwise, without express written permission of the publisher.

Argana Zeit and the Haunted Busker

"You call that a shopping stampede? It's just one guy, making bull horns with his fingers, charging bystanders!"

Argana Zeit tried not to laugh at what she described in the CCTV still image, but all the same she let out a cackle that would put a witch to shame.

"This is serious," insisted Constable Fred Berkshire, who was showing her the tape.

"I daresay. But it doesn't look like anyone was hurt."

"One woman broke her arm."

"OK then, not hurt *badly*," she conceded. "Or robbed."

"Two teenagers had to abandon their shopping to escape."

"Well, that *is* unfortunate, but I'm not sure it's a robbery. Go on, run the whole thing."

Berkshire complied, his mild annoyance twitching his abundant moustache. His office was tiny, piles of folders forming miniature skyscrapers. Argana yawned, the fluorescent light-strips of the windowless room doing nothing for her alertness. Trotterwell was far too small a town to have its own paranormal investigator on the force, so they made do with her instead whenever they needed one. It was OK; it beat the day job.

"Here we go. This is another camera, a better angle," said the policeman.

The tiny monitor fritzed its way into soundless life, stuttering away at a steady but unimpressive five frames a second. Each individual image was clear though, starting with a view from high up above a corner on Arbor Low Way, just off the high street.

A busker was visible, a frizzy-haired young woman known as Mad Alice, wearing the kind of luminous patchwork trousers that Argana associated with poor quality storytellers. Shoppers trundled by, all giving her a wide berth on account of her chosen instrument.

"Are those bagpipes?" Argana asked incredulously.

She tried to imagine the tune, but instead imagined the sound of three cats in a tumble drier, one of them on heat.

"Cacophonous things," she added conversationally, "invented by the ancient druids as a weapon of war, not as a substitute for effing sax solos."

"I wouldn't know about that," said Berkshire, "but Mad Alice here has only just started with them. Last week she had a guitar."

On the screen, a small child had their hands over their ears while their embarrassed parent tried hard to pretend that they could not hear anything. But Argana was concentrating on the bagpipes. They consisted of bellows tucked under the busker's arm, a handful of wooden chanter pipes hanging over her shoulder and a smaller pipe into which she blew. The pipes were all wooden, with a mouthpiece made of a white, translucent material. Bagpipes, to Argana's mind, should be tartan, but the fabric of these was adorned with some kind of face, daubed in black marks on white. A mere outline with close set ears and a pointy beard.

"Here's our man," said Berkshire, jabbing a finger at the edge of the screen.

A middle-aged gentleman in a sweater, carrying a reusable shopping bag full of vegetables, appeared from a side street. Argana stared at the screen, recognising the perpetrator for the first time.

"That's my uncle!" she said. "Mr Lovegreen. He's the last man I'd expect to be violent. He's a sweetheart, runs the greengrocers. They do vegan pies!"

"Not today he doesn't. Keep watching."

Mr Lovegreen moved toward the busker to put a coin in her empty hat, but as he got closer, he started to move in a jerky, twitchy way, as if he was suddenly unsure of the lengths of his limbs. Argana recognised the body language from her remote study course with the Astral University of Tibet.

"That's a possession!"

On the screen, the hapless piemaker dropped his bag. Vegetables rolled away to the surprise of other shoppers and the disappointment of a Labradoodle that mistook a hunk of beetroot for something more interesting. Mr Lovegreen bowed, lifting his hands to either side of his head, pointing his index fingers forward like horns next to his cheekbones. He stamped his foot twice, ducked his head and charged a matriarchal-looking woman in a sari. Engrossed in her phone, she didn't see him coming and was knocked uncomfortably to the cobbles.

He proceeded to rampage to and fro until the street was clear. Mad Alice gathered up her hat and backpack and ran for it, the bagpipes bouncing against her shoulder like a lamb given a fireman's lift. Constable Berkshire stopped the video.

"About twenty seconds later, Charlie got cuffs on him. Now he's in cell number 3. He's been ranting in a barbaric tongue since we brought him in, making no sense. That's when we called you."

Argana bit her lip and thought of dear uncle Lovegreen. He was forever buying her little ceramic dragons that she had loved as child, although she couldn't stand them now. She felt suddenly guilty about the freakishly high proportion of them that had 'fallen' from her flat window.

"You didn't think to tell me it was my uncle?" she demanded.

"You can't treat this personally. You've got until tonight to prove spirit involvement, or the county will have him sectioned. Or we'll charge him with assault. And I don't want to see either of those happen to an innocent man on my watch."

"Can I speak to him?"

"Unfortunately not. I mean, you're not *actually* a cop, Ms Zeit, and we do have rules."

"That doesn't mean you have to follow them, moustache boy. Fine, I'll go and see what I can get from Mad Alice."

"You think she's the source?"

"More like the pipes are, as they're new. I'll have it all wrapped up by lunchtime, I'm sure. You get on to the catholics and order up an exorcist."

***

Mad Alice would be easy enough to find. It was a small town; everyone knew her and either liked her or made allowances. Argana tended toward the 'making allowances' end of the spectrum, on the grounds that Alice should sort out her huge tangle of hair into a more manageable style. That this was entirely hypocritical was not lost on her, but you could waste a lot of time finding a genuine reason to dislike someone.

Argana drove past her flat to pick up Max, who she thought of as Dr Watson to her Mister Holmes. They drove over to where Alice lived in a shared house on Grindleford Road, a ramshackle terrace with a rotating roster of housemates with names like 'Leaf' or 'Vermillion'. After parking her battered blue Micra haphazardly across the hammerhead at the end of the road they walked down, her faux-blonde hair shining in the sun and Max unrepentant in his choice of black and tan coat. At the house they were saved having to enter the hippy lair by that fact that Alice was in the front yard, trimming roses with a pair of kitchen scissors.

"Many blessings," smiled Alice.

"Good Morning Ma— Morning, Alice," said Argana, far too courteously, feeling her sense of propriety rise to match Alice's levels of faux-spiritualism and resenting herself for the sensation.

Max, as always, seemed unfazed, first poking his nose into the roses and then wandering down the pavement to check the lampposts for fresh news articles.

"I'm investigating the assault on Arbor Low Road; it looks like a possession case. My working theory – and I'm rarely wrong – is that your bagpipes are cursed. I'm sorry, Alice, but I'm going to have to take them off you."

"They're *smallpipes*, not bagpipes," insisted Alice, "and you may style yourself as an investigator, but you're not really with the police.

I've never heard anyone call you Detective Constable Argana, have I? If people call you anything, it's Mad Argana."

"Mad Arg— no they don't! If anything, it's you that – oh never mind, I can get a warrant from Constable Berkshire. Look, I'll give you a receipt, take the cursed thing back to my flat and run some, er, experiments. Then you can have it back. Probably."

Alice put her hands on her hips.

"Black magic, you mean. I'm not up for that. I'm keeping the pipes."

"Oh," sighed Argana, disappointed to discover that outthinking Mad Alice didn't seem to be in her repertoire. "Well, at least tell me where you got them."

"That's better. Sharing is caring, isn't it? Naturally I can be generous with my time."

Argana considered biting back her intended reply to be equally generous.

"It's a marvellous story, really. I got them for a song on Gumtree," continued Alice. "They'd been in storage for nearly four decades after some guy got imprisoned. It's sad, isn't it? We should rehabilitate people, not imprison them. But he was a poacher, and I don't suppose anyone who hurts animals should be forgiven, ever. Pass that on to your Constable Berkshire. The smallpipes were packed up with their original letter of commission though, and it turns out – how exciting is this – that the cloth the bellows are made out of was a shroud. A shroud! From a catholic saint!"

"Cool," said Argana, getting interested despite herself. "Which saint?"

"Saint Tukesburg, the note says. The smallpipes were originally commissioned by Sir Samuel Brink, who owned Brink Hall at the beginning of the twentieth century."

"Thanks. Oh, and Alice?"

"Yes?"

"Playing a set of pipes with a saint's face on is definitely cultural appropriation."

Alice looked suddenly ashamed.

As Argana walked back to the car Max looked reproachfully at her.

"OK, I know. That was a dick move."

Back in her car she rang Constable Berkshire.

"Fred?"

"Hello?"

"Yeah, it's Argie, I've got this whole thing wrapped up. The cloth was cut from a shroud, some catholic dude who got wrapped in his cloak when he went to join his master in the sky. I can't get hold of the pipes, but I'm sure his spirit is hanging around them haunting people, so now your exorcist will know who to deal with. Case closed."

"Saints are famous for haunting people, are they?" said Berkshire sarcastically. "I thought their souls went straight to heaven."

"You're completely misunderstanding the metaphysics of this," grumbled Argana.

She put the phone down, ecstatic with her victory. Hours still to go; way to smash it out the park.

She turned the keys in the ignition, flicking her eyes quickly to the rear-view mirror. No cars in the road, but Mad Alice still pruning her roses. The busker's hair was as ridiculous in profile, her ear like the bullseye of a big frizzy target. Something uncomfortable occurred to Argana about the distance between Alice's ear and her nose, between anyone's ear and their nose. She thought of the face she had seen on the bagpipes, the ears flat to its sides. She turned the ignition off and rang Berkshire again.

"Hello, Constable Berkshire," he answered.

"Er, Fred it's me again – slight problem. If the shroud were genuine, the markings would be on different places. If you wrap a face in cloth and mark the positions of everything, the ears end up a long way from the rest of the face. Try it now – put your thumb on your ear and your finger on your nose, see how big the span is. But in the image on the pipes, the ears are face on. It's a fake, in the same way as the Turin Shroud. So… it's likely to be something else."

"That's disappointing," said Fred calmly, "but we've still got a little time. There's an exorcist already on his way over from Liverpool, one Father McGillycuddy, approved by the Bishop. If you can find out the exact nature of the possession, he can cure Mr Lovegreen and we can release the poor man. Just make sure you've got this thing straight before he gets here."

"Yeah… I'm going to the library, hit up their internet, do a little research."

"No messing about, you know, right now you're on the taxpayer's dollar."

"*Pound*," she said.

"It doesn't sound the same. Seriously though, you're just going to google everything?"

"Ghosts don't like Google, Fred. The level of certainty collapses the quantum parallel field that they require just to exist."

She was sure she could hear him raise an eyebrow.

"OK, I made that up", she admitted, "but they don't like Google. Search any ghost you've ever heard of, and you won't find definitive evidence. No, everything I need is on the dark web. The *daaaaark* web."

"Where I conveniently can't verify it?"

"That's right, Berk."

"Berk*shire*."

* * *

The library was a purpose-built stone relic on the edge of town. Most of it had long since been sold to a coffee chain, leaving only the dregs to house books and the purveyors of information. On the way Argana had dropped Max back at her flat. While his instincts were always keen, his talent for operating a laptop was strictly limited.

Argana always found this bit the most tedious, and the most difficult. Finding information wasn't hard – she was doing a remote diploma, after all. But keeping her mind on the task as each connection was made, as each file downloaded, as each specialised script scrounged information, was next to impossible. Whenever she didn't actively pay attention to what she was doing she would miraculously discover that she had spent the last ten minutes reading an article on whether anyone made Wellingtons for ducks. It turned out they did, and that she could buy them on Etsy.

Soon enough she retreated from the library to the coffee shop, although she piggybacked the library's Wi-Fi. Among other things she drank six expensive cups of tea, ate a whole carrot cake that she had intended to give to her mum at the weekend and got bored enough online to order an ornamental elephant to keep toothbrushes in.

But at last, she found enough to justify ringing Constable Berkshire.

"Hey Fred, I've got some info to be going on with."

"Thank goodness. We're on the clock here, Ms Zeit; if we can't exorcise Mr Lovegreen then we're either charging him with assault or passing him onto the funny farm. Sorry, sensitivity training; having him sectioned to a psychiatric ward."

Argana's nose twitched. On her course sensitivity training meant something quite different, mostly involving cards with squiggles and a healthy dose of meddling-with-that-which-man-was-not-meant-to-know. Or that woman was not meant to know either, although that never came up in the fine print. Hopefully, if she ever inadvertently stirred up that-which-man-was-not-meant-to-know, it would turn out to be a disciple of pedantry.

"The bagpipes – smallpipes, apparently – have an epic history. All their owners are dead, but I've got a bunch of heirs and relatives to look up. Some guy called Thomas Turpentine had them last before Alice, but I'm going to start with their original owner."

"Sounds promising," said Berkshire, sounding relieved.

"See, I've got this. Anyway, about my uncle – about Mr Lovegreen that is – you can't just bend the rules a bit, keep him a bit longer? You are a constable, after all."

There was an exasperated sigh from the other end of the phone.

"You don't seem to appreciate this, but there's some people down the station who outrank me."

"Who?"

"Pay attention Ms Zeit – literally, *everybody*."

"Even the canteen lady?"

"We don't *have* a canteen lady. You've been down to the East Street station; you know how small it is. Just hurry it up for the sake of Mr Lovegreen. Plus," he added sheepishly, "I want to leave early today."

* * *

It took Argana thirty nerve-wracking minutes to thread the narrow roads out to Brink Hall. Off the ring road and down into the low ground over the marshes, over the zigzag bridge, on to the half-dozen blind summits on tree shrouded hills. Not nerve-wracking to Max, his happy face pressed against the glass with each swerve of wheel or road. Not nerve-wracking for Argana, who had gained her license from the Dunning-Kruger school of driving. Nerve-wracking however for every tractor driver, cyclist, horse rider and occasional prodigal sheep that they startled along the way.

Brink Hall driveway sported automated gates of the kind where the password is neither 'open sesame' nor '1234'. So she left the car half in a layby, half in a ditch a hundred yards down the road. Max stayed with the vehicle to guard it, like anyone would want to steal it anyway. Not unless they really dug 70s inspired bead coverings on their driver seats. Ages were funny things; born in the nineties she didn't feel old, but her automobile of the same era seemed decrepit. Well, at least she didn't have structural rust or backfire when cornering. Not yet, anyway.

She hopped the fence and continued to the hall, a sprawling eighteenth-century tribute to just how much money a team of stonemasons could make out of someone else's sense of self-importance. One wing presented a substantial door accompanied by a stone lion with a buzzer in its mouth, and she buzzed it.

A tactically unkempt man in his thirties opened the door, wearing paint-spattered jogging bottoms and a Metallica t-shirt. He didn't say anything, he just blinked at her. A dozen sensible things to say popped into her head, but his general confusion was just too hard to resist adding to.

"Have you heard the good news about our octopod overlords?" she asked, straight-faced.

"What?"

"OK, never mind. Here, I'm Argana Zeit, a licensed psychic investigator," she said, waving her student ID for the Astral University of Tibet Parapsychology Diploma. "I'm interested in a set of haunted smallpipes – I'd totally like to talk to the descendants of a Sir Samuel Brink?"

The man chirped up a bit.

"Mate, now you're talking! I know all about them. They sold up the hall twenty years back. Some bozo banker had it for a while, and now it's mine."

"And who are you?"

"Oh, Akira Pixels. *The* Akira Pixels."

Akira Pixels, possibly not his birthname, executed a bizarre swooping handshake as if he was a rock star, starting with his hand high and twisting it as it came down. Caught off guard, Argana somewhat fumbled the receipt. His thumb audibly clicked out of his joint. Figuring that somehow apologising would make things even more awkward, Argana ignored it and he ploughed on as if he were still the coolest guy in the world.

"I made a ton in bitcoins early on, bought this place, put up a bunch of solar panels to run ASIC farms to make more coins. Know what one of those is?"

"So you *don't* know anything about the Brink family?" Argana said, blatantly changing the subject.

"I imagine you're after the old ghost story, Argana. *I* don't buy it one single bit. But plenty of other people do. Sadly, because this is England, the solar panels don't work that well. The last big spike in coin prices came in winter and I missed the lot because my miners were hibernated. So here's me and a few of my mates sitting on a big ass loss with a big ass hall to maintain. We're converting it into a luxury BnB with the remains of the money. Me and my mates. A BnB with a ghost, and we'll tell the story to everyone who stays."

Beyond him, through the doorway, many of his 'workers' were visible. To be sure, there were plentiful piles of tiles, cement, cartridge guns and untouched toolboxes. The workers were less inspiring, each one of them slumped in a different corner feverishly playing on handheld consoles.

"They're on breaks," said Akira defensively, seeing her expression.

"Regale me this story," Argana put on her best smile. "It will be good practice."

Akira Pixels shrugged.

"Sure, why not. Come on in."

He ushered her into the hall, with its damaged Victorian flooring, past the worker-slackers and into a grand wood-panelled ballroom. Someone had prized out a dozen priceless Edwardian fittings to run cables through and left them dangling. They hadn't got as far as ruining the ceiling yet though, so she let her eyes drift across that as he spoke, his voice taking on a faux gravitas.

"Sir Samuel Brink procured an occult instrument that he intended to be the centrepiece of his new band. He was an amateur musician, don't you know, frequently playing at The Coach and Horses over on White Street."

"Naturally. He was an avid fan of the occultist Aleister Crowley in the inter-war years," interjected Argana.

"Absolutely. You've done your research. So, this artifact…"

"The smallpipes."

"If you don't want me to go on, just say so. I've got things to do."

"So have I – that's why I'm driving you to the point."

"But you seem to know everything already!" he said, visibly crestfallen.

"Not so. I've heard already that he had the bellows made from the shroud of Saint Tukesburg. But there's something else, isn't there? There has to be, because the shroud was fake."

"None of it is real, Argana."

"Humour me; I bet I'm missing the best part. And your speaking voice is sooooo relaxing."

"Lord Brink ordered the chanters – that's the pipey bits – made from gallows' wood. That's wood taken from gallows. He wanted to claim that they were cursed, to impress his friends. Here's the best bit though. He couldn't just order that stuff up – it's not like they had Alibaba back in the black-and-white era. So, he put a couple of no-goods up to the task. A pair of graverobbers sorted him out, got him what they claimed was the scaffold that was used to hang a renowned criminal. The pipes were whittled out of that scaffold," Akira said, the gravitas of his storytelling voice giving her goosebumps.

"Really?"

"Absolutely. And, you see, Sir Samuel Brink played those pipes; he played them day and night. In his house, in the pub, in the street. He was obsessed with them. But his friends and family noticed a change in him; his mood became darker and he withdrew from the world. Finally, he drank arsenic, and played the things as he died."

"Wow," said Argana, her green eyes wide. "Why'd he do that?"

"You see, the thing that Sir Samuel Brink didn't reckon on is that his no-goods flat-out lied to him. They didn't get the gallows' wood from an old murderer. No, they, haha, they, oh, this is good… they got it from a hanging, alright, but it was a suicide. Man hung himself from a tree, and they used bits of the tree to make the chanters."

"How sad. What happened to the smallpipes?"

"His eldest daughter inherited the hall. She put in the maze out the back; there's bodies under it, they say. I can take you on a ghost tour of the maze. We're going to add little pictures for the children to hunt, maybe a fairy grotto at the end of the garden. "

"And the smallpipes?" she insisted.

"Oh, those?" Akira said, his voice returning to its previous nasal register. "They sold them on. The daughter didn't like the dreadful things, so she gave them to Buxton Museum."

"You've been very helpful, thanks. I've got to go."

He led her back to the front door. She had to duck under two of his nerd labourers ineptly manhandling a stag's head onto the wall, nearly skewering her on its prodigious antlers.

"Hey!" she objected.

When they froze, she impulsively patted the decapitated stag on the nose.

"Don't mind Morris," said Akira. "Not all Sir Samuel's stories are ghost stories – the old rogue kept illegally shooting his neighbour's livestock and mounting his trophies."

"Outrageous. Thanks again!" Argana skipped out into the expansive, expensive driveway.

"Hey, no problem!" he called after her, "Tell everyone you met Akira Pixels, leave me a comment on my YouTube channel!"

Back in the layby, she kicked the car and Max woke up with a start and an extravagant yawn. He didn't have the decency to be ashamed and instead fixed her with a – well, it was not a smile exactly, but it was not far off. He had such soulful blue eyes it was hard to stay mad at him. She sidled into the driver's seat and called Berkshire.

"Constable Berkshire here – oh, it's you," said the voice on the other end. "Did it check out, whatever your hunch was?"

"I went to Samuel Brink's gaff. He's the guy who had the smallpipes made in the first place. I couldn't interview him of course; he's been dead 60 years. I got some deets anyway – the chanters, the wood they were made from is cursed. A suicide from the 1930s, his doomed spirit crying out for vengeance."

"Less drama, more facts. You're sure this time?"

"Absolutely. All wrapped up. Is the exorcist there yet?"

"No, still on his way. But I'm expecting him soon, and I don't want to keep him waiting. Anyway, I want to get off, I've got a date."

"You've got a date?" exploded Argana, tears of laughter filling the sudden crinkles at her eyes.

Max turned toward her and lifted an eyebrow. He didn't look impressed.

"What? You think I like him? I'm not interested," she told him.

"Hey, you what? I didn't catch that," asked Berkshire uncertainly over the phone.

"Nothing, I was talking to Max."

Max grunted and went back to rummaging for treats in the glove compartment.

"When Father McGillycuddy gets there, tell him he's looking for the spirit of a suicide, a man who hung himself in the 1930s. They used his doom-tree to make the wooden parts of the pipes," said Argana.

"And now he's possessing shopaholics and getting them to attack people."

"The dead do all kinds of crazy things. Have a good evening, Constable. I'll chuck my invoice in tomorrow."

She revved up the car and pulled out of the layby, filling the non-existent mudguards with lumps of newly excavated turf.

She caught Max's expression out of the corner of her eye.

"Of *course* I'm certain, you duffer. Cut and dried. Fred can make his date and breathe a sigh of relief. I'd bet my freckles on it."

A speed bump as they passed through a village bounced the entire car, near mortally surprising the suspension.

"Breathe a sigh of relief," she repeated to herself, "a thousand curses, Max. Sir Samuel's last breath – that's it, we'll have to check that out too. Deadlines, shmedlines."

They took an erratic left at the next crossroads and bounded away down a track lined with high hedges.

* * *

Another memorable parking expedition found them in the cul-de-sac of Thomas Turpentine's last known address, a three-bedroom semi on the rainy side of town. According to Argana's earlier research, it now belonged to one Janet Turpentine, who her keen investigators instincts suggested might be a relative.

"You'll be wondering," she said to Max, "who Thomas Turpentine is? According to my research, he's the fellow who got the smallpipes after Sir Samuel Brink turned up his extravagantly upholstered toes."

The front door opened before they had even set foot on the path, Argana having phoned ahead. She cast her trained investigator's eye over the woman who opened it, and immediately forgot every impression of her apart from her greying hair and considerable bulk.

"You must be Ms Zeit," said the woman. "Come on in, then."

"Hi, Janet, is it? Thank you, we shouldn't take up too much of your time," said Argana, although her internal monologue continued, "because if I do, Fred will have kittens."

"He's a handsome one, isn't he?" said Janet, looking past Argana at Max. "You want to come in too, love?"

"I wouldn't, he's bloody scruffy. He's been gardening."

Max's eyes looked big and innocent, although his mud speckled coat gave the lie to that. He barged past Argana into the hall leaving a trail of dirt behind him.

"I'm so sorry," said Argana.

The crowded hallway gave way to a front room that had been decorated in a careful homage to the 70s, all yellows and browns. A lava lamp gurgled in slow motion next to a tank of tropical fish. Miss Turpentine gestured Argana into the armchair and sat herself down at one end of the sofa. She looked at Max and patted the cushion next to her, saying, "You too love, come over here."

Max looked uncertainly between the two women, as if sizing up risk and reward, before settling for hovering awkwardly near the fireplace.

"What's this all about?" asked Miss Turpentine. "You said on the phone you're a licensed psychic detective?"

"Investigator," she corrected as she started to pull out her ID.

"Don't bother with that, duck."

"It's about Thomas, your – er—" Argana floundered. "I'm going to say your husband."

A slight tremor of sadness passed Miss Turpentine's face, and then rippled out and dissipated amid her curls and jowls.

"Father. He was my *father*. I couldn't possibly look that old, could I?"

"Er, no, not at all. I know it's a small detail, but I wanted to ask you about some smallpipes that he owned."

"Oh, those. He changed after he bought those stupid pipes. He picked them up at auction during a museum clear-out; used to play them all hours. Mother banished him to the shed in the end. She couldn't stand the noise. He stopped taking holidays with us, used to go alone to Zimbabwe. Just after it stopped being Rhodesia. He wanted to kill things, like he never did before."

"Constable Berk – Constable Berkshire tells me he went to prison."

"That's right. They weren't running enough tours – shooting tours, that is – for his liking. He'd go out there and think he was a big man with his big gun, taking potshots at big game. Lions, tigers, rhinos, elephants, he wanted to do it all. I can't say we approved."

"There's no tigers in Zimbabwe," said Argana.

"Once he got an idea in his head, there wasn't any shifting it. Facts be damned. That's why he was stubborn enough to be bribing officials. He got mixed up in something off the back of that, went to prison over it. By the time he got out, we were estranged. Some of the guns he wanted he had to smuggle into the country, and when they caught him they thought he was running them."

"What a sad story. And such a sudden personality change."

"Yes, Ms Zeit. We had our happy times, but it was going bad even before he went to prison. After he went on holiday at Her Majesty's leisure, we threw all his stuff out, stupid knickknacks, lumps of ivory. Look, I keep one of his bragging photos, just to remind me why he and mother divorced if I find myself wistfully thinking of the happier occasions."

Miss Turpentine passed Argana a polaroid photograph. It showed a man in what he obviously thought was colonial hunting gear, his garments incongruous in his suburban living room. He cradled a giant hand-cannon – Argana had never been hot on memorising the names of guns – lovingly in his arms. Behind him was a mantlepiece covered in small carvings of African wildlife, and above them in pride of place a pair of crossed tusks mounted on the wall.

The photo had been framed badly – taken long before the days of digital – and a chair filled with hastily cleared clutter could be seen in one corner. The clutter included the smallpipes, an instrument that would have happily looked untidy and tangled all by itself. Another broken wooden tube was next to them, very much in the same style as the chanters.

"There's a second mouthpiece, but it's bust," said Argana, surprised.

"Yes, dear. The very first time he played the pipes, stupid man, the noise panicked him and he dropped them, snapping off the mouthpiece. He got it repaired soon enough, but he kept the old bit around because he could never bear to throw anything away."

"You saw him panic?"

"Oh yes," said Miss Turpentine, looking into the distance, "the very first time he played them they shrieked like a banshee, and he jerked like a mouse caught by a cat. He went very, very pale, shut himself in the study for hours."

"I'm sorry to tell you," said Argana in a gentle voice that hid her excitement, "but I think your hus— your father was possessed in that moment. In all the time that the pipes lay in the museum, they harboured the last breath of their previous owner."

"I don't know about that; some people just go bad."

The silence that followed was awkward.

"Are you staying for a bit, love?" said Miss Turpentine finally, in a voice that suggested she hoped not. "I can put the kettle on. I can put some food on too, if you like, I've got lamb chops. You like lamb chops, handsome?"

Max licked his lips.

"We will decline," insisted Argana. "We'd better be going. Thank you *so* much for your time."

Miss Turpentine saw them out, giving Max an affectionate pat on the rump as he passed.

"She was all over you, don't think I didn't see that!" Argana said disapprovingly as they got back in the car. Max stared sadly out of the window.

"It sounds a lot like poor Thomas Turpentine was possessed too, I imagine by the spirit of the late Sir Brink. His dying breath was surely trapped in the bellows. Fred isn't going to like this much."

She rang Fred. She wasn't wrong.

"What is it this time? Father McGillycuddy is nearly here, and I'm already changed to go on my date," said Berkshire.

"It's barely the afternoon," she scoffed.

"It's a very respectful first date. And stop changing the subject! I need to go, what is it?"

"The case – it's more complicated than I thought. There's at least one more ghost that's possibly involved."

"Oh my heavens! Why do you always do this to me?" he roared.

"Me and Max are going to go back to my flat and think it over."

"Can't you come down to the station—"

"Nah, the tea at the station is rubbish. I'll call you in a bit."

"Don't hang u—"

She hung up.

* * *

Argana Zeit's flat was an untidy affair in the top floor of a converted Victorian terrace, one of the ones pointy enough to be ambitiously and erroneously called a villa. Studio living didn't suit her, leaving no bulwark for her mess. Occult tomes sat side by side with unfinished knitting, tins of beans and the endless, unwanted ceramic dragons.

This was the domain that she surveyed as she reflected on everything she had learned. She sipped on her well-brewed tea – some things were worth doing right – as she mused. Max just drank water; he didn't like tea. Max was an idiot.

She was interrupted by the doorbell, and Constable Fred Berkshire was there looking out of breath and exasperated. He sounded exasperated too.

"Time's up, Ms Zeit! In ten minutes they're going to charge Mr Lovegreen with assault and throw away the key!"

"You're exaggerating, Berk. They won't throw away the key. He's an alright bloke – he'll end up with community service."

"Please tell me you've got something. I've just cycled all the way here!"

"Wait, you cycled?"

"Sergeant Cianciolo has the squad car, and you know what she's like. Anyway, that's beside the point. The bloody exorcist is at the station already. We need to be able to give him *specifics*. And I can't tell which of your theories you're currently backing!"

"Relax, I've got it all worked out," she fibbed, playing for time.

He paced up and down, frantically picking a path through the mess. Max eyed him suspiciously but said nothing. Fred caught the look and stared back. Max always knew when Argana was lying, and he had a tell too, tapping a nail three times whenever she was. Unconsciously he was going rat-tat-tat, rat-tat-tat on the surface in front of him.

"You haven't got a bloody clue, have you?" snarled Berkshire, seeing the gesture.

"Is that any way to talk to a colleague?"

"The amount of time you've wasted, you'll be fired."

The doorbell rang again. Max was up in an instant, keen to see who had arrived. But all the same he waited for Argana to open it.

"Miss Zoot?" asked a gangly youth in an oversized red uniform.

"Close enough." She took the package from him, and he left.

"Are you serious?" Constable Berkshire asked. "Put that down and tell me what you're thinking."

"This should be a new Tarot deck I ordered. We can read…"

Constable Berkshire rolled his eyes.

"Oh!" gasped Argana when she took off the wrapping.

It was not the Tarot at all. Instead, peeking out of a half-roll of bubble wrap, it was the ceramic elephant she had ordered in her frenzy of internet surfing that morning. It had a curled pink trunk, mock gemstone eyes and short blunt tusks. Finger-shaped tusks.

"I've got it!" she exclaimed. "To the station, I'll explain when we get there!"

"Can't you explain on the way?" he groaned.

"Nonsense. You don't want me distracted while I'm driving, do you?"

Constable Berkshire paused, clearly thinking of the dents in Argana's car, of the missing wing mirror, and swallowed nervously.

"No, I don't," he conceded.

* * *

Arriving at the police station, Argana hastily parked the car in a bush at the roadside. It made a scraping sound against the that-boat-has-sailed-anyway paintwork. Argana jumped out, at once followed by Max, who had been on the back seat, but Constable Berkshire found his door was pinned by an angry rhododendron. He clambered across the handbrake and out of the driver's side.

"Wait up!" he yelled,

"No time!" called back Argana, physically sprinting ahead of him.

Max had no such sense of haste, and was investigating the snapped foliage with a determined glee. The cause of the urgency however was obvious; an ambulance outside the station, the stencilling on the side announcing it as belonging to the psychiatric hospital.

The proverbial men in white coats were coming to take Mr Lovegreen away. There were two of them, a man and a woman, going up to the revolving doors when Argana barged through.

She got inside, Constable Berkshire breathlessly catching up behind her. A man in a black dress was sitting on a chair outside Berkshire's unoccupied office. Father McGillycuddy, the Vatican-approved exorcist. He looked up.

"Yes? Oh, it's you," he said with disappointment.

"Don't worry, this isn't anything like what happened in Salford."

"The state is paying me for my time, exorcism or no, so if you've no idea what did this to your client—"

"He's not her client, he's my prisoner," objected Berkshire, who had caught his breath.

"Still, if you've no idea what happened to him, then I'll be getting back on my train and going home. I can be drinking sangrias at Albert Docks by teatime."

"We'll be taking him now," said a new voice, the white-coated woman coming through the revolving doors. Her colleague was just behind, although Max had made valiant efforts to block him.

"We've got paperwork and everything," she said.

"Stop right there!" shouted Argana. "I'm acting paranormal investigator Argana Zeit, and if I can demonstrate who or what possessed the prisoner, then you can't have him!"

The two psychiatrists glared at her, but they stopped their advance. Berkshire moved himself subtly between everyone else and the door to the holding cells.

"Go on, Ms Zeit," he said.

"Mr Lovegreen suffered an occult attack of the sonic persuasion, emitted from a set of smallpipes unwittingly wielded by one Mad Alice. These pipes were commissioned by Sir Samuel Brink in the 1930s, as you possibly know. He spent far too much time wanting to be the next Aleister Crowley, and in an act which I'm going to describe as 'occult signalling', he had the pipes whittled from cursed wood. That is, wood taken from the gallows at which a criminal had been hung."

Argana shook as she faced down the psychiatrists, but she carried on:

"Brink practiced the instrument in private, and it did him little good. The hanged man had committed suicide, and his ghost hung around in the instrument. It possessed Samuel Brink, and when he killed himself, his last breath was trapped within the instrument forever. It wasn't until the unfortunate Thomas Turpentine bought the instrument in the 1980s that it was played again. Thomas was shocked by the ghost that he summoned through its haunting melody, and he dropped the instrument, breaking it."

Father McGillycuddy looked at his watch.

"If I leave now, I can catch the ten past three and change at Manchester Piccadilly," he said.

Argana fixed him with what she hoped was a deadly stare, although she had to admit he looked more amused than frightened.

"Thomas in turn was possessed by Brink, who turned him into a poacher. He became a big game hunter, paying to take a few pop shots at endangered animals. Big, endangered animals."

She produced the photo she had taken from Janet Turpentine and drew their attention to it.

"You see this? This is Thomas Turpentine in his living room, taken shortly before he was arrested. You can see the tusks over the fireplace, and an arrangement of ivory ornaments on the mantlepiece. When he played that instrument, he was possessed by the spirit of the poacher and it drove him to his crimes against animal-kind. But you know what else you see in this photo? Right here?"

She tapped the photo for emphasis.

"The smallpipes. And you know what you notice about them?" she demanded.

"There's a spare broken bit. What's your point?" sighed the exorcist.

"Exactly. When he dropped them, he snapped the original mouthpiece off. So, it was in his workshop that a replacement was made, with this off-white material."

"Holy hephalumps," said Berkshire, as the penny dropped.

"When Mr Lovegreen was making points with his fingers, he wasn't making *horns*," she said, repeating the gesture with her index fingers against her cheeks, "he was making *tusks*. What does an ivory poacher repair his instrument with? It's not a ghost of a saint or a hanged man or a suicide that haunts these pipes. It's the ghost of an African elephant, taken before its time. *That's* who you need to exercise from Mr Lovegreen."

"Well now," said Father McGillycuddy, breaking out a smile for the first time, "I believe I can do that."

The white-coated psychiatrists exchanged shrugs and departed. Black lines left on the tarmac in the wake of their getaway spelled out their annoyance.

"That's how you do it!" yelled Argana. "Oh yeah!"

"It's always the last bloody minute with you, isn't it? I've even missed my date," grumbled Constable Berkshire.

"I'll give you a lift home, Constable. Maybe buy you chips along the way."

"Ms Zeit— ah, hell, why not. Will it be just us, or is Max coming too?"

"Don't be jealous, Fred. Max is only a dog."

She linked her arm through his and they left, navigating the revolving doors awkwardly.

The End

Argana Zeit Stares into the Abyss

"What good is a Paranormal Investigator going to be in a missing person case anyway?" demanded Sergeant Luciana Cianciolo, scowling across the station desk.

This wasn't the way Argana Zeit had expected the meeting to go when she had come down to the East Street station. For one thing, she had been hoping to speak to the altogether more approachable Constable Fred Berkshire.

"I got a tip-off. Psychically," insisted Argana.

"Fred, your nutter is here!" Cianciolo called to the back office. "I've got paperwork to do anyway."

She traded places with Constable Fred Berkshire, a good-looking young man with a long face and brown eyes.

"Hello, Ms Zeit," he said with a genuine smile. "We didn't call for you, what's up?"

"There's this patient, Ewan Enoch, missing from the funny farm," said Argana.

"*Psychiatric hospital*," corrected Berkshire. "Yes, we've got him on file. It's a low security unit; he escaped four days ago. We did a couple of searches, checked with Shelter and the soup kitchens, didn't turn anything up. Like the Sarge asked, what's it got to with you?"

"I think I can help. For my usual fee, naturally. I read the Tarot. It came up with the Thin Man and the Hospital."

"Come on now. There's no hospital card in the Tarot," he said wearily.

"What would you know? You're a cop!"

"And before I was a cop, I was a teenager. And every teenager at some point holds a séance and reads the Tarot, and if they're lucky they fail at both at the same time. There's no hospital in the Tarot."

"Ha! I admit, it wasn't the Tarot. I've never got the stupid thing to work, anyway! The tip-off came from a website that uses AI to monitor hospital admissions and death certificates for fortean circumstances."

"And they like Mr Enoch because…?"

"Who knows? Neural nets rarely show their working to us mortals. I checked up on the guy though. He's Welsh, out of Anglesey originally, moved to the Peaks about a decade ago. Worked in a garden centre until abruptly quitting back in the spring. He gets a name check in the Derby Telegraph as one of the volunteers on the dig."

"The dig?" asked Berkshire.

"Yeah, the one that's half closed The Arkwright Arms the last six months."

"You've certainly been digging, anyway," said Berkshire. "OK, we'll take you on for this one."

"Hey!" interrupted Cianciolo from the back office, who had been listening with one ear whilst typing. "You're *results only*, you hear me? If you don't find him, we don't pay you."

Argana rolled her eyes. "Done," she said sharply.

"So here's what we have on Mr Enoch," said Berkshire. "He's in our records too; two consecutive years disturbing the peace and indecent exposure at the solstice. Once at Arbor Low, once Barbrook, both stone circles."

Argana laughed. "Indecent exposure? That's a euphemism for dancing the sun up naked, right?"

"Is that what you do?"

"Wouldn't you like to know?" she said slyly.

"Where are you going to start?" he asked, before hastily clarifying, "…Investigating, I mean, not dancing. Sounds like the hospital and the dig are both good options."

"I was hoping you could drive me out to the dig. Back around Christmas they were doing renovations at The Arkwright Arms, found a bunch of Roman artifacts. There's a been a team of students dredging it ever since. Maybe they remember him."

Berkshire shrugged. "Can't you go by yourself?"

"It'll be easier to go poking around with a real cop," she said, "and besides, it's out at Cromford and my car's in the garage. It, er, got dinged."

"Your car does seem to be remarkably unlucky," observed Berkshire dryly.

"That's a yes? Shotgun! I'm going to put the lights on."

Berkshire, who had been leaning on the reception desk, stood up and went to the key cabinet, punching in his personal code.

"You're going to sit in the back where you can't reach anything," he warned.

"That makes you my chauffeur," she beamed.

She left through the revolving doors before he had a chance to second-guess himself, while he was still finding the car keys and justifying his absence to the sergeant. As she emerged, her dog Max stood up and wagged his tail. The station had a strict 'no dogs' policy, which she had tested in the past and found rigorously enforced. Still, Max was a surprisingly well-behaved animal and was happy to sit on his lead pretending to be tethered to a signpost whenever she couldn't be bothered to actually tie him.

* * *

The Arkwright Arms was a traditional Peak District pub, all rough stone facing and heavy grey tiles, an assortment of roofs ramshackling their way across a myriad of small, sloped extensions. Everything jostled for space; cyclists jostled with ramblers, wooden tables jostled with stone walls and the gravel car park jostled with the wooded hillside.

"Thanks, Driver," said Argana, and hopped briskly out of the car. Or would have if the child locks hadn't been on.

"Sorry, habit," said Berkshire as he freed her, although his amused grin didn't look sorry. Max was along for the ride too, and the constable let him out of the boot.

A row of boards marred the idyllic scene, one whole end of The Arkwright Arms sealed off with a protrusion of scaffolding and chipboard. There was a roughly made door in the centre of the boards, flanked with the signs 'dig in progress' and 'hard hats to be worn beyond this point'.

There was some small print too, and while Constable Berkshire read it meticulously, Argana banged on the hatch. Nothing happened.

"It's only manned on Tuesdays and Thursdays. Cutbacks in the Archaeology Department," said Berkshire.

"Hey!" Argana accosted a teenage girl adorned by heavy makeup and a pub logo, who was carrying a tray back from a delivery of drinks. The girl raised an eyebrow.

"Yes?" she said dully. "Find yourself a table and order from the bar. They'll give you a spoon with your order number."

Berkshire stepped past Argana, and the bargirl was first excited and then nervous on spotting his uniform.

"Hello ma'am," said Berkshire. "What my, er, colleague here meant to say is, would you be so kind as to tell the gaffer that a policeman is here, and he'd like a word? No one's in trouble."

The girl scurried inside, wide-eyed.

"Hey, is there a body in there?" yelled a patron as they waited for the bargirl to return from her errand. Berkshire shook his head but said nothing.

A decidedly stocky woman emerged, bearing the same logo as her employee. Middle-aged and sturdy with it, arms bulked out by decades of hauling barrels.

"Ay-up, Officer…?" she said.

"Constable Berkshire," said he, holding out his hand, "and this is civilian consultant Argana Zeit."

The landlady was holding a workman's helmet in each hand, with another rammed over her buoyant pepper locks. She tucked one of the spares under her arm and shook Berkshire's hand.

"I'm Patricia Bramhall; most folks just call me Pat. Hello duck, you could do wi' a meal, love. See that you stay after and have some pies."

"There's a body in the dig!" yelled the same patron as before.

"Thas' enough of that, Tony," insisted Patricia, before asking them, "What's all this about, then?"

"We're getting background information on one of the dig volunteers. He's gone missing," said Berkshire.

"Well, I am sorry to hear that. Come along then, Constable Berkshire, Agatha."

"Argana."

"Takes all sorts."

The landlady passed them a helmet each, although Berkshire kept his conical police hat on. When he insisted it was just as fit for purpose, she just shrugged and extracted a wad of keys from her pocket on one of those springy chains. On the third try she found the one to the padlock.

"I coulda' just picked that," Argana whispered indignantly, but Berkshire ignored her.

Beyond the door was the dig. The barnlike room had obviously been a storeroom rather than a room of the pub proper, its walls unplastered and its beams visible. It smelt of mud and dust in equal measure, and the ever-present essence-of-mould of an honest stone cellar. It was the floor that was striking though, or rather the lack of it. The flagstones had been pulled up and a pit as deep as Argana was tall had been dug in it.

"Behold the glory of Lutudorum!" said Patricia, and illuminated the lights strung across the dig by orange cables. They revealed metal support struts, wooden surveying squares, ladders and of course the ancient remnants of a tiled mosaic floor.

"Wow," gasped Argana.

"Impressive, Mrs Bramhall," said Berkshire. "Is it Roman?"

"Well it's not the bloody beaker people, is it? And it's Pat, or at least *Miss* Bramhall. It's all – don't touch that!"

Argana slowly put down the fragment of copper that she had been looking at.

"Can we go down?" she asked.

The landlady nodded, and first Argana and then Berkshire descended the wooden ladder lashed in place by blue plastic rope. Max took one look over the edge and, deciding that discretion was the better part of valour, padded away to see if he could shake down drunk Tony for crisps.

"Professor Fairfield could tell you more, I'm sure; she's a very clever woman. But I'll do what I can," said the landlady, who had maintained her position up at floor level. "This was an animal store once, but we've been using it for beer barrels since I were a nipper. The pub's been doing well, I'm proud to say, and we wanted to expand. Before we decorated, we were going to run pipes through for a second bar in here. Which is when a keen-eyed contractor found bits of Roman pottery."

"That's great, we'll take a loo—"

"It goes without saying I wanted to chuck it back, but he went and called the university. I'm all for history though, and now they've dug the thing up I figure we'll put a glass floor in and make a feature of it."

"Very nice, I'm sure that—"

"They think it's part of a Roman settlement, Lutudorum, that they never located exactly, although it's in the Roman records. Perhaps a temple, a private temple. It's very exciting, wouldn't you agree?"

Patricia finally paused for breath long enough for Argana to get a word in edgeways.

"Ewan Enoch! Did you know him, he was one of the volunteers—"

"Oh yes! Odd 'un that, didn't really fit with the students. I can't complain, he bought proper meals, none of this *oh, bring us another plate and we'll share it* nonsense. Sometimes stayed late and drank stout with Professor Fairfield. She were the one that did all the talking, mind."

"This Professor Fairfield, have you got her contact details?" asked Argana.

"Yes love. I'll fetch it before you go," said Patricia before taking one of the deep breaths that proceeded her monologues.

"Thanks, we'll take it from here. You've been very helpful," intercepted Berkshire.

"Yes, well, I do have customers to deal with," Patricia dusted her hands one against the other. "You know where I am if you need anything."

She threw the key to Berkshire.

"Lock up when you're done."

Argana and Berkshire circled the floor. There was a five-sided star marked out within an octagon, and various creatures and figures depicted in tiny shards of different coloured stone.

"What do you make of it?" asked Berkshire.

"I think the images are easier to see if you squint. These ones here, they're what you might expect in a Roman bath house. Those at the edge depict Roman gods, that's probably Bacchus. But these…"

She knelt to get a closer look. A patch of the mosaic was slightly raised, added by a more inept hand. It cut right across some of the older images.

"Someone modified it. I mean, not recently, but back when it was still a Roman building. These are druid magical symbols." She gestured to sections of floor apparently representing different trees.

"What does it mean?"

"I don't know. Maybe it was abandoned and druids took it over. More likely they brought druid prisoners here, tried to get them to syncretise their temples."

"You seen these?" Berkshire bent down to investigate. "Some sort of staining on the stones."

"That's just the digging process, don't worry about it."

"I don't think so. Look, this green discolouration."

There were broken lines of some stain surrounding the pentagon in the floor, an area just over eight feet across. It was green, a pale, wan colour clearest against the white tiles. Although the tiles were smooth, the marks were rough. Berkshire pressed a penknife to it and scratched at it.

"What is it?" she asked.

"Copper. That's copper rust."

Argana stood and tried to imagine the scene, seventeen hundred years earlier.

"Some structure was here, made of copper, five-sided," she said.

"Could be," he produced a digital camera and took a few photos.

Argana climbed back out of the pit and dusted her three-quarter jeans down.

"I think we're done here. Last one to the bar buys lunch!"

"That's hardly fair," he said from the bottom of the dig, but she had already gone.

* * *

After they had eaten – and the pies really were all that – Berkshire dropped Argana back at the station, and Max hopped out of the boot. He was as full of crisps as they were of pies.

It was a sunny September day in Trotterwell, the leaves still out and the sky blue. Argana walked off past the stone terraces of East Street, three-storey structures with small flower-strewn front yards and pointy dormer windows.

The tourists were just arriving, but all the same she found a vacant bench in Joseph Wright Park, a triangular green space with a view over the town into the green hills beyond. It was a good thinking place, and a good place to make her phone calls.

"Let's deal with the professor first," she said to Max. Max looked at the phone, concluded that a further walk was now a distant possibility, and took to scratching in the flowerbeds.

"Professor Fairfield," answered the voice on the phone. The professor sounded artificially posh, a thin veneer of Queen's English whitewashed over her original provincial accent.

"Hello Professor, I'm Argana Zeit, Paranormal Investigator. I'm working on the case of a Ewan Enoch, who I believe volunteered for you?"

"Out at the dig? That's right."

"I'm just back from The Arkwright Arms. It's impressive work you're doing out there."

"It's important, too. If we can prove the location of Lutudorum, that's a big deal. Most of my volunteers are students looking for extra credit, but Ewan had a day job, out at the gardening centre. Handy to have a man who knew how to dig properly, that's for sure. Hard worker; I was sad when he was sectioned."

"Did he say why he volunteered?"

"Oh, he had some theory of his own, but I won't trouble you with it, Ms Zeit. It was crackpot."

"Humour me. It may explain why he went over the edge."

"He talked about druids, from Anglesey – he was convinced the Romans brought them as prisoners to Lutudorum, fed them to some monster. Like they did Christians to Lions, but with something more sinister."

"Did you know him well?"

"Not well, no. I never saw him after they took him away. I hope he's OK; he was awfully thin. Listen, Ms Zeit, it's my day off and I need to feed the geese. Give me a heads up if you find him."

"Thanks," said Argana. "Bye. Max, get your nose out of that!"

Max retracted himself from whatever he was shnuffling and came back over, curling up hopefully at her feet.

"Let's move on to the hospital," she said. "I'll ring ahead and see if we can't speak to a doctor, maybe in person."

While she made the call, Max pootled off to herd ducks. The ducks took it with good grace – it was a more or less weekly occurrence.

* * *

It was midafternoon by the time Argana got the bus to the outskirts, where Phoenix House Hospital sat in its own leafy grounds; a modern building, painted with bright colours that only partially described its squat, square, purely functional form. Somewhere in shape between a prison and a motorway hotel.

The lawn that she and Max crossed was well-cropped, its trees prim and it flowerbeds flawless. All intended to exude serenity, like a reunion meal where no one talks about the elephant in the room. Argana knew what that like. Most often it was her elephant.

The reception was bright and airy too, with rubber plants and posters of seas and sunsets, the lights up just a touch too much and every wall white. Even the receptionist's artificial smile was luminous.

"Good morning," said Argana, surprised by her own formality. "I rang earlier. I'm here to see Dr Hussani, about Ewan Enoch?"

The receptionist looked her over, not entirely convinced by her ragged bleached hair or her casual attire. Max looked more presentable than she did, although he was not doing himself any favours by licking the doormat.

"You're not a journalist, are you? You didn't say you were. We have a *no journalists* policy."

"No, I'm – I'm an advisor. With the police."

"Very well. Have a boiled sweet."

The receptionist unlocked a corridor and ushered Argana through it, who took a handful of sweets from a bowl on the desk as she passed and shoved them in her pocket.

* * *

Dr Hussani proved to be a man in late middle age, with dramatic thundercloud eyebrows let down by a combover, the un-exorcised ghost of the haircut he had had in the 90s. His desk was cluttered with action figures from every conceivable franchise, and his door was open. She knocked anyway.

"Hello, Ms Zeit. Have a seat, tell me what the problem is," he said, without looking up. "And bring your emotional support animal in too."

"He's not an emotional support animal, he's... he's my *sidekick*."

The doctor chuckled knowingly. Argana perched on the wipe-free sofa – the room smelt of disinfectant, as had the reception – and absent-mindedly picked up one of the toys. She fiddled with it with both hands; it was some kind of penguin that transformed into an unconvincing truck.

"Anyway, it's your problem I'm here to deal with," she said.

"Of course, of course. Go on."

"Ewan Enoch escaped four days ago, right?"

"He did not *escape*, Ms Zeit, he made an *unauthorised abscondment*. Words are important; they have power."

Which is something Argana agreed with wholeheartedly, but for entirely different reasons. True names had power, and incantations were very susceptible to mispronunciation.

"Ok, he *absconderated*. I'm helping the police investigate why. I need to know more about him, why he was here, who he knew, what he said, what his possessions were."

Dr Hussani's head bobbed up and down in a subconscious nod.

"Yes, yes," he said. "He was brought in by his neighbours. He had become delusional, kept ranting about a monster from a higher dimension. By the time he was here he was essentially nonverbal; he would say things, in English, but they made no sense and definitely weren't conversation."

"Have you got any photos?" She put the penguin down, picked up a woman warrior with a sword and a shield. The shield had a tiny mirror set into it.

"The usual mugshots from arrival. Also these two, one from a group photo when they did a mural out the back, another more recently after we started getting concerned."

"Why were you…" she trailed off, looking at the photos on Hussani's screen; the reason for the concern was obvious.

Ewan Enoch was short and broad-faced, younger than she had imagined, with a furrow line that Argana associated with the single-minded. He had a broad, paint-spattered grin and gripped a paintbrush in his right hand. The rolled-up sleeves of his Oxfam chic shirt revealed tattooed forearms, runes with long lines crossed by shorter ones at right angles. In the second photo he seemed to be playing draughts. What was startling between the two photos was his figure.

"He's skeletal!" she gasped.

"He lost nearly half his body weight," said Dr Hussani, shaking his head sadly, "We have quality nutritionists here, as I'm sure you can imagine, Ms Zeit, especially for those patients least able to look after themselves. We thought he might be throwing up in secret, but we checked and he wasn't. We had some hotshots from the Northern General come over and have a poke around."

"And?"

"It turns out our man Enoch couldn't metabolise sugars properly, not right-handed ones. How he got to his early thirties with a condition like that, I've no idea. He's not short on medical anomalies either, apparently; he suffered from dextrocardia, although without symptoms. That's when the heart is on the wrong side."

"What?" said Argana. The shield fell off the toy she was fiddling with.

"The heart—"

"Yes, I got that. I don't know what you said about sugars."

"Sugar comes in two molecular forms, left or right-handed. Almost all life on earth either produces or consumes the right-hand form. The left hand is an identical mirror image, but we can't metabolise it. As it does not occur in nature, however, that's not a problem. It's not really my area, though."

Hussani reached beyond his desk and handed over a clear plastic bag with some items in it.

"He had these in his pockets when he came in," he said.

Argana put down the toy warrior and rummaged through the collection.

"Thanks, can I keep these?"

The bag contained a book, a pair of odd scissors, a receipt and a badly printed map.

"You can keep them as evidence. Be sure you log them with the receptionist on the way out. Is that everything?"

"Yes, thanks." Argana hopped to her feet.

Dr Hussani picked up the action figure. The mirror in the shield had cracked on landing, but he didn't seem to mind.

"Turbo-Boudica™, bold choice," he said. "Thanks for coming by. Be sure and log that bag, OK?"

"Absolutely."

On the way out through the reception, she was sure she meant to do something important, so she took another handful of sweets. Max looked at her reproachfully.

* * *

Back at her flat, Argana swept the clutter from her kitchen-table-cum-desk and turfed the book from its bag. On its cover a photograph, the fidelity of which was as low as the contrast was high. A man with a sweeping forehead and a moustache that must, while magnificent, have been only fleetingly fashionable, even in the eighteen-hundreds. She had seen smaller wings on a duck.

"*Nietzsche*," she said. "Just great. Nobody sane reads him to begin with."

The receipt was for mirrors from a DIY store, the map was an archival one of Trotterwell in the early 2000s. The scissors were, well, scissors.

She started with the book. It was *Beyond Good and Evil*, considered one of the philosopher's more accessible works. When she turned it over it opened easily to the most thumbed page, a single line picked out in pink highlighter.

"If you gaze long into the abyss, the abyss also gazes into you," she read.

Max looked wearily up from the sofa and put a paw over his nose.

"What? Its everyone's favourite. Apart from *The Gay Science*, and that only because it gives your bookshelf the giggle factor."

As she rebuked the dog, something brushed past her fingers. A piece of paper falling out of the book, cut from one of its pages. It wasn't a specific passage, nor could it be, for the piece of paper was hexagon shaped.

Puzzled, she turned the book spine-up and shook it. No more confetti was forthcoming. Flicking forward a few pages from the ominous quote did at least confirm the source of the scrap. Scores of pages were marred, holes in them telling where shapes had been cut out. Triangles, squares, pentagons, hexagons, the negative space left by each regular in size and angle. Seven of each, by Argana's count.

Beyond those were hasty biro sketches, made in the book itself. The diagrams showed the shapes pushed together, tessellating in kind. They all fitted together except for the five-sided ones, which were repeatedly drawn in unsuccessful arrangements and then scribbled out.

"What the sherbet is this?"

Max did not actually shrug, but he did make an elaborate show of cleaning his flank with his muzzle.

"Fat use you are."

Argana hauled out a box from under the bed – the one where she supposedly kept her craft things, although she rarely remembered to put them back. But there were at least several blocks of coloured paper. Scissors there were none though, so she raided her sewing supplies instead. Her mother wouldn't approve – for that matter, neither would any of her dressmaking friends – but some heresies were worth the risk.

Enoch's bag contained scissors too of course, but as a southpaw Argana generally found other people's scissors a pain to operate. Except that when she checked, Enoch's scissors were left-handed too.

Which was odd; she could have sworn the man in the photos had been right-handed.

Back at the table, with the book open, she arrayed the coloured card and started measuring out the shapes.

* * *

An hour or so later, Argana was back down to the East Street station. She was saved having to deal with Cianciolo by the fact that Constable Berkshire was out front and took her straight through to his crowded office.

"Fred!" she said enthusiastically. "I've got it all together."

"Ms Zeit, in my experience, you could rarely be described as having it together," Berkshire replied evenly.

"Enoch was obsessed with angles, right? With creatures from a higher dimension. In other words, from a non-Euclidean space. He had all these shapes cut out. Squares, pentagons, hexagons."

"So?"

She pushed a pile of paper off one of the two chairs and sat down, using a filing cabinet as a table. Berkshire's office wasn't well equipped for visitors. It was barely equipped for anything, really; his computer looked distinctly as if Edison had passed it by and it was hand-cranked.

"Here's the thing – squares fit together perfectly, like in a grid. So do hexagons."

She demonstrated, tipping her coloured cutouts onto the surface.

She took a hexagon, about the width of her palm, and laid it down. She proceeded to lay one new hexagon on each edge, six of them all the way around. The edges of each new hexagon matched up with its own neighbours.

"But the pentagon – that doesn't work out. Look."

In the same way she laid out the five-sided shapes, one in the middle, five around the outside. She pointed to the meeting point between two of the outer pentagons. They overlapped, the angle between them too great to allow them to fit properly.

"These are regular pentagons. You can only make them tessellate in a non-Euclidean space."

"Good thing we don't have any of those on earth," said Berkshire.

"We don't," smiled Argana, "but we *can* see into them. Those copper marks on the floor in the dig, I'll bet anything they mark out the positions of mirrors. Copper ones. If you put mirrors here, here and here," she pointed out the edges of the central pentagon, "and stood in the middle of the pentagon, you'd be able to see the floor as tessellating pentagons in all directions."

Berkshire whistled through his teeth.

"Enoch talked about staring into the abyss, about the creature that stares back. This space," she jabbed the overlap again, "this is the non-Euclidean part, where what you see depends on the angle that you look in from. I'd call that an abyss."

"If you were between the mirrors," said Berkshire, concentrating hard, "you'd see into this tessellating realm. But you'd only see one of these possibilities at a time, so it would be a Euclidean projection."

"You're forgetting we have two eyes, separated by inches. If you stood in exactly the right place, you'd see both the overlaps here, and you'd see anything that was hiding in there."

"What the blazes has this got to with Mr Enoch's disappearance?"

"He volunteered for the dig, read the druid runes there and endeavoured to repeat it. He found the entity he was looking for, the thing which lives in the abyss, but he couldn't control it. It drove him mad."

"That's a hell of a stretch," observed Berkshire.

She slammed the receipt down on the desk.

"Five mirrors, each two metres tall," she said triumphantly. "But wait, there's more!" She added the map. "Here's the map from his pocket. Notice anything? This is the cinema that shut down a decade ago. He needed somewhere to build his – I'm going to call it a mirrordrobe – somewhere unnoticed. I think he broke in and made it there, four months ago."

Berkshire picked up the map.

"I can call the security company responsible for the place, although I don't think they make manned patrols often. It's a mothball contract. Hmm, mirrordrobe? A portmanteau, and wardrobe because…?"

"It goes to Narnia, doesn't it?" laughed Argana. "If Aslan was a dark and terrible semi-god, hell-bent on madness and destruction, anyway."

"How does this help us find him?"

"Love of gods, Berk, it doesn't! This is bigger than that. That man's going to *die*, and he's left a portal to another world just hanging open, and you want to clear up your missing person paperwork? You're as bad as Sergeant Cianciolo!"

"I heard that!" screeched the sergeant from the next room in what was, after all, an extremely small police station.

"Steady on, what do you mean he's going to die?" asked Berkshire in a serious tone.

"Keep up, Berk. He can't metabolize sugar, his heart's on the wrong side, he's right-handed rather than left-handed. Isn't it obvious that he got swapped for his mirror-self in the accident?"

"Well you didn't tell me those things," said Berkshire defensively.

"I don't care if you help me or not. I'm going to build a trap, and I'm going to capture this lives-in-the-angles horror," she said defiantly.

As she passed the front desk sergeant called out, "Hey, nutter, we're only paying you if you find our missing person. You can save the world out your own pocket!"

But Argana wasn't listening. She had a plan.

* * *

Argana rummaged through the bric-a-brac on the back wall of the everything's-a-pound store. The ambitiously named 'beauty' section was a veritable treasure trove – well, trove anyway – of pink things, glittery things, elastic things. But the things she wanted were square, little square mirrors. There was a selection of folding make up mirrors, their colourful outsides daubed with cartoon characters. She checked them for cracks and scratches and took the lot.

She wondered what she might say if anyone challenged her on it, why she might conceivably need so many, but that was the beauty of everything's-a-pound. Nobody cared. Still, she went to the electronic checkout just in case, Max trotting along at her heel.

She *beep* scanned each of the *beep* little mirrors though the *beep* machine. Out of the corner of her eye she caught a middle-aged *beep* man glaring at her. From the next till, as he put his ready meals though, his glower threatened to overpower the chin that hung over all the way around his collar. What did you call back-of-the-neck jowls? Argana did not *beep* know.

"You can't bring him in here," said Grumpy, pointing at Max.

"Of course I can. He's like a guide dog, only he's a business dog."

Beep.

"A business dog?"

"A mind-your-own-*beep*ing-business dog."

Last *beep*. She did the thing with the card, and while she waited for the transaction to verify, she entertained herself with a daydream of Max rending the abundant flesh from Grumpy's throat. Max harboured no such intentions, instead making moon eyes at the jerk and wagging his tail.

"Come on, traitor," she said, and they left the shop.

They went next to the stationer's for some purple card and double-sided tape. Then on to the butcher's for Max's thirty pieces of silver, which took the form of lamb's thigh bone.

* * *

Yasmin Nuri's apartment was in many ways the opposite of Argana's. Where Argana's was messy, Yasmin's was tidy but dirty. It smelt bad even coming up the stairs, an odour of unwashed clothes and cat litter, all thoroughly undisguised by incense. The incense amused her a great deal; she associated it with pagans and vegans, but Yasmin was one of the most profound atheists Argana knew.

Argana pressed the buzzer. She was answered by a yell from somewhere beyond the door.

"That you, Argie? I'll be there in a minute, I just got to …"

There were earth-gurgling screams punctuated by rattling bursts of gunfire that Argana could feel reverberating through her feet. It was fortunate that the downstairs neighbour was deaf, she reflected. She shifted her weight randomly from foot to foot as she waited, missing Max, who she had left at home on account of Yasmin's cat. Under her arm she clutched the half-built monster trap.

The gunfire stopped and the door opened, revealing Yasmin in her "It worked on my computer" t-shirt, plain blue jeans and odd socks.

"Hey," she said, a smile materialising for only an instant on her shallow face. Her expressions were always like that, like cats scared of their shadows, disappearing the moment they were aware of their own existence. She held the door open.

"Hey," said Argana, and came in.

An oversized curve-screen TV took the prime spot above the electric blue fireplace, mounted at not quite the right angle and a tangle of cables growing from it, roots and branches that sported a myriad of consoles as fruit. A dinosaur hovered on the screen, with assault cannons bionically mounted to its neck.

"Nice T-Rex." Argana nodded at the paused game.

"Dino Rampage 3," said Yasmin, "and that's an Allosaur. You can tell 'cos, well, it doesn't… what did you come over for?"

Argana moved a wide puddle-of-fur cat off of the sofa and squeezed in next to a soft toy Predator the size of a child.

"I'm hunting demons. Or, I think demons. A creature that hides in mirrors."

"Uh huh. You know I don't believe in any of that stuff? You know, it's just so, well, y'know."

The cat turned in a lazy circle on the floor and started hauling itself up the side of the sofa, claw over ponderous claw.

"That's OK. I need you for the science part. I've built half a trap; I'll need you to make the clever part."

The cat tumbled over the sofa arm and onto her lap. She tried ineffectually to move it, but it kept blinking happily at her, its body somehow becoming a formless blob that redistributed effortlessly around her hands. Argana looked up for help, but Yasmin was in the kitchen, poking something in a bowl into her disgusting microwave.

"What?" yelled Yasmin, over the sound of the machine's mechanical whirring.

"I'm going to capture it – the demon – in a tiny mirrored chamber of my own. I've built the thing, but I want you to make a trapdoor for it that will shut when the light enters."

"That certainly sounds… You're going to have to show it to me. Come over here."

"I can't, the flump's got me."

"Ramoth? Don't mind him, just dump him off."

Argana tried again, but Ramoth just blinked lazily once more. Finally, she settled for simply standing up – fast enough for him to get the message, slow enough that he wouldn't claw her. She brushed at her legs, now be-cat-furred, and wondered what Max would think.

The microwave announced a stench of sardines-and-noodles with its soulless beeping as she entered the kitchen. There was a breakfast bar halfway down with two stools, and Yasmin perched on one, bowl in hand. She made slurping noises as she ate. The bar itself was clear but for a box of half-assembled anime models, with plenty of room for Argana to demonstrate her work so far.

"Here's the thing, the entity can only be held by mirrors, and it has to be a prime number. More than three, at that."

"So, the internal reflections are non-Euclidean," nodded Yasmin, requiring no explanation.

Argana placed the trap on the table to demonstrate. It was a miniature of what she conceived the mirrordrobe to be like. A cardboard form around six inches high, cut from cereal boxes, an excited cartoon tiger neatly beheaded by her clumsy scissor-work. It had five sides and a flat top and bottom, and she had plated the interior with the square mirrors acquired from the budget store. She had left a square in one side open.

"But I have to leave a little gap, just here," she pointed to it, "so the light can get in. I want a little hatch that snaps shut on that when something goes in."

"*Something* goes in? I can't rustle you up a Tindalos detector; the RS catalogue doesn't carry those."

"A Tinda – what, I thought you didn't believe in—"

Yasmin laughed.

"I don't. But I do have the tabletop RPG, don't I?"

"How about a light detector? Use that. A creature that lives through reflections has to travel as light, doesn't it?"

"I'll make you your trap," said Yasmin, already setting up her soldering equipment. "I still don't believe a word of it. I'll make a little mechanism that counts photons, spring loaded trap door. Hmm, a linear pot on the top for you to make manual adjustments."

"How much?"

"Owe me."

"A favour?"

"A big favour," giggled Yasmin.

"Done."

"Say, you want some noodles?"

"No, thanks, I ate before I came out," lied Argana. The smell of Yasmin's food made her stomach do little somersaults.

All the same, she stayed for three rounds of Dino Rampage 3 and a can of dandelion and burdock while Yasmin did her work.

* * *

On the way back to her flat, Argana rang Berkshire's mobile, but he didn't pick up, so she rang the station number instead.

"East Street station, Sergeant Cianciolo. Can I help?"

"Hey, it's Argie," said Argana, with exaggerated cheer. "I need an address for Professor Fairfield, her home address. She's not listed publicly."

"The archaeology lecturer? You know I can't give that information out," Sergeant Cianciolo sounded short on patience.

"Wait! You said you'd pay me if I found Ewan, and I think the good professor is harbouring him. I'm going to go get him."

"What makes you think the Professor has him?"

"Something she said. She said Ewan was awfully thin, and I saw that for myself in Dr Hussani's photographs, but he didn't get emaciated until after he got to the nuthouse. So she was flat-out lying about not seeing him. Why would she do that?"

There was a silence at the other end of the phone. Argana hoped it was the thoughtful variety.

"It could be, Ms Zeit," said Cianciolo reluctantly. "Here we go – 178 Bonnie Prince Heights, here in Trotterwell. You could be right. Go and check it out, and if your hunch pays off, call us. Do not – I repeat, do not – try and move Mr Enoch yourself. If *we* take him back to Phoenix House, that's in *our* line of duty. If *you* do, then it's kidnapping."

"Sure. Cheers, Luce."

"*Kidnapping*, Ms Zeit," stressed Cianciolo. "And don't call me Lu—"

Argana hung up and summoned a taxi. She had just time to grab Max from her flat before it arrived.

* * *

The taxi driver charged her extra for Bonnie Prince Heights, not because she was awkward (and Max was *very* well-behaved) but because he assumed anyone going to the most expensive street in Trotterwell must have cash to spare. When he pulled up on the roadside, he had even more cause to rejoice.

"Stay here," said Argana. "We're going to need you in five minutes."

"Meter's still running, duck."

"Bill it to the police," she said, waving her ID at him.

He nodded without reading it. Nobody ever did, which was fortunate. Student, Parapsychology Diploma, Astral University of Tibet was not a title that exactly begged compliance.

The professor had done well for herself; her four-bedroom newbuild with double garage and pointlessly oversized BMW attested to that. The lawn would probably have been immaculate had it not been for the ministrations of a score of geese. Argana vaulted over the gate without opening it, and Max took it with a single bound.

"Stay," she said, as the herd of geese on the lawn gave them the side-eye. Well, everyone needed their hobby. Max looked longingly at them, but he did as he was told and settled down by the gate.

There were French doors at the front of the house, and she got a glimpse inside as she went up to the main porch. It was all glass tables and masks-from-Africa, pretentious lampshades on pillars of driftwood. Sitting at the table in front of a bowl of porridge was a man thinner than she had ever seen. Ewan Enoch.

She rang the bell.

Professor Fairfield opened the door just a tiny gap, the chain on the other side. She had long dark hair and an angora cardigan, a broach at her neck of a sphinx. Everything about her was prim apart from her fingernails, broad and short with dirt under them.

"Hello?"

"I'm Argana Zeit; we spoke on the phone. I'm looking for Ewan Enoch."

"He's not here," snapped Fairfield, and slammed the door.

Argana whistled three times.

Max was in action immediately, running flat out in a curve behind the geese. Honking filled the air, unlike the geese, whose wings had been clipped.

Argana banged on the door with her fist.

"Hey! There's a dog in your garden! It's chasing your geese!" she yelled.

The professor flung the door wide and ran out onto the lawn, trying to catch Max. Max had rarely had such excitement and channelled a hundred generations of sheepdog into simultaneously rounding the geese while playing hide and seek with the new human, who obviously only wanted to be entertained.

The taxi driver had got out his cab and was watching over the wall with amusement.

Argana ran into the house, turned left, found the room with the thin man. He looked right at her, but there was nobody in.

"Ewan!" she insisted. "It's time to go. We're going to fix you; everything is going to be OK."

Ewan smiled broadly.

"Vector impenetrable. Side angle," he said.

Argana glanced out of the French windows. The professor-collie-geese dance was still in full flow, but it could only be seconds before Fairfield saw what was happening.

She pulled *Beyond Good and Evil* from her bag and waved the book at him. For the first time his eyes focussed. He stumbled forward, and she led him to the door with it.

"Ordovician timeline," he garbled, and reached out.

She threw the book as far as she could, and it landed just beyond the gate. He ran after it, or at least tried to; his legs were broomsticks that barely held him. What he managed was more of a waddle.

He had almost made it when Fairfield spotted him. And Argana.

"Stop! Stop that man!" shrieked the professor.

Argana legged it to the gate and opened it, letting Ewan through.

The taxi driver stopped laughing abruptly, realising that he was going to be needed sooner than he thought and that possibly, just possibly, not everything was above board. Argana pushed Ewan through one door of the Octavia and whistled for Max who came bounding up. They piled into the other side of the car.

"The old cinema, make it fast!" gasped Argana.

"Fear the acute, fear the acute."

"Is this, er, is this whole endeavour legit?" asked the taxi driver.

Fairfield was running down her driveway toward them, fists raised, the geese scattering before her.

"Absolutely," said Argana. "he's a Romanian immigrant."

The taxi driver nodded as if this made complete sense and put his foot down.

The revving engine hid Fairfield's shouting, as she reached the gate.

"I'm calling the police!" she screamed.

* * *

On the way to the abandoned cinema complex, Argana had a dozen missed calls from Constable Berkshire. Naturally, she turned her phone off, unwilling to face the music. The driver pulled up at the end of the road without driving into the complex itself, depositing his unruly passengers and driving away.

It was midevening, and Argana, Ewan and Max stood in what remained of the parking lot. Plants poked through the concrete, some of it just grass, others new-sprung ash trees reaching eagerly for the sky. The complex hadn't fared any better, sections of roof missing or replaced with greenery, its sign hanging half-off and a dozen windows smashed or boarded up. A banner celebrating one of 2010's most popular films was badly torn, and all that remained were the words *and the Deathly Hall*.

"How do we get in?" asked Argana.

"Shadows. The shadows are coming."

Concluding not unreasonably that Ewan was going to be no use whatsoever, Argana started searching. Max searched too, using his flawed but favourite tactic of running ahead, running back and running ahead again, incidentally disproving Zeno's paradox.

When she caught him up, Argana found that a couple of first floor windows were out. She didn't fancy the climb, especially accompanied by the clueless Ewan. Lower ones were boarded up. A side entrance proved to still be there, possibly through to what had once been the kitchens, but a heavy chain and lock hung across it. The lock was barely rusted, less than a year old.

"Angles. Angles in my attic," muttered Ewan.

"Keep lookout, will you?" Argana asked, pointlessly, before crouching in front of the lock.

She took a pouch from her bag and unfolded it, revealing a neat set of lockpicks. She put the first into the lock and turned it tentatively, shook her head, then drew the next one.

Ewan lurched suddenly and started unevenly toward the car park. Argana exchanged glances with Max, who reluctantly stood up, shook out his mane, and went to round up the errant madman. Having a Border collie along for the ride had definite advantages.

Click. The lock gave out and she pulled it open, then jumped back reflexively as the heavy chains fell at her feet. Their ground-pounding *thunk* wasn't the only sound she heard. The wind carried distant sirens to her, lending her urgency.

"Ewan! Max!" she called as she pushed the doors open.

The corridor beyond was dark, both painted black and lightless, and it smelt of mouldering carpet. She swapped her lockpick set for a torch. It illuminated nothing beyond a couple of exit signs pointing her way. She took a deep breath and pressed on.

Behind her, Ewan swayed unsteadily at the entrance, big tears welling up in his eyes, horror further stretching his already gaunt face. Even Max looked trepidatious, hugging his body low to the ground, his tail between his legs.

"Max!" she implored, but the dog couldn't persuade Ewan to move inside. "Come on, we're going to take you home. You'll be *safe.*"

She grabbed his skinny wrist and pulled, horrified by how easily she could move him. He was all bones, more of a corpse than a human.

"Crawling vertex, up and then up!" he insisted, but hadn't the strength to resist her.

They passed a broken side door, which revealed an abandoned kitchen when she shone her light in. Stainless steel surfaces had remained stainless, but a heaving mass of rot cascaded from the open cupboards. Cracked tiles covered the floor. Ewan shook uncontrollably, so she pressed him onward toward the door at the end of the corridor.

Outside, the sirens grew louder. In this forsaken place, the sergeant's accusations of kidnapping had a reality they hadn't had before. What lay in wait for them in the cinema was dangerous, and taking an incoherent man into it was risky. Berkshire she could maybe talk around, but Cianciolo? No chance. Her only hope was to make it fast.

The door at the end was shut and Max growled at it. Large double doors on springs. The tatters of a sign read 'Interval entrance'. Argana regretted not carrying a weapon – not that she would know how to use one – but as least she had Max.

"On three," she said, and barged the door open without counting.

* * **

Argana stepped out into the largest screening room in the complex. It wasn't entirely black, although nearly so. The last rays of dusk came through cracks in the ceiling, casting the upper rows of chairs in an amber light that only served to make the rest of the darkness seem more impenetrable. She swung her torch like a searchlight but couldn't pick out any other walls but the nearest, only the endless rows of chairs, some broken, some missing, some sprouting vegetation.

An aisle led between them, to the steps that would take them down to... what? The screen? A stage? Ewan had a new expression on his face, a near beatific wonder, and finally moved of his own volition. He walked ahead of her, his steps confident, still muttering as he went.

She followed.

"I don't like this," she said to herself.

Max, slinking alongside her, let out the lowest of whimpers.

At the top of the stairs, she pointed the torch down toward the screen, some eighty feet further on. It picked out Ewan's lanky shape and the tattered rags that the projection screen had become. And something else, something that caught her light and threw it back full force, something five-sided standing in the gap between the first row and the screen. Five mirrors, each the height of a man, all facing inward. She swallowed.

Ewan strode ahead of her, reaching the bottom of the stairs. She started to run after him, her trainers pounding the steps, Max hurtling behind her.

The thin man stopped at the mirrors, his back to her, put out a hand and ran it along their edges searching for something, and found it. The torchlight bounced unevenly as she ran, revealing his movements in the jerkiness of a strobe. He undid a clasp, opening the upper section of a mirror toward him like the top half of a stable door. There was a step just in front of it, and he levered himself up onto it, his skeletal body shaking with the effort.

"No, wait!" Argana screamed, only seconds from him and running flat out.

She fell. The bottle she tripped on went skittering away. So did her torch.

Ewan climbed over the doorway. The mirrors, facing inward, exuded their own light now. Something *inside* the reflections was building in brightness.

Max was at her side, tugging urgently at her body warmer with his teeth.

She struggled up. The dog's hair was standing on end. So was hers. The air smelt of burning batteries. Max growled at the mirrors.

But it was the screams that set her teeth on edge, had her spine crawling.

"We've – we've got to go in."

She took the last few steps up to the mirrors. Max refused to come with her, digging his claws into the black carpet. The only light came from the mirrors, out of the cracks between them or reflected from the ceiling above, a flickering light, now fey green, now man o'war purple.

When she checked, her pack still contained her own miniature version of the mirrordrobe, fortunately unbroken by the fall. She put her nose up against the gap between two mirrors, and they were deadly cold against her cheek.

Through the hairline crack she saw another world beyond. Mirrors beyond mirrors beyond mirrors, repeated into infinity, the strange light crawling through them. The angles bent and tore. The gap between the first layer of mirrors, the space in her own world, was the same as it had been at the dig, a dozen feet.

But Ewan wasn't within it. Somehow, he was beyond, running deep within the reflections, caught up in the non-Euclidean madness. Far within the mirrors, where he should have had reflections of reflections of reflections, there was only one of him. No, two Ewans, two Ewans meeting. On the periphery of her vision, in the abyss between the reflections, the place where she could see around corners, a living shadow lurked. A thing ancient and evil, a formless monstrosity that slid along the angles.

Still rooted to the spot, Max was barking.

Above him, at the back of the cinema, torchlights were visible, reflecting off a corridor wall as people approached. The police. The last rays of the sun went out.

"It's now or never," Argana insisted to herself.

Argana swung wide the upper door in the first mirror. Inside she saw myriad versions of herself, myriad versions of that door hinging. Saw her own fearful face, saw the mirrordrobe trap rising in her hands. The living shadow sensed her at once, swarmed along the edges of her vision. It ran up the outside of one of her own reflections, shattering it, consuming in. Her reflection screamed and faded.

"Not me," she insisted. "Come and get me, the *real* me, I'm right here."

She held up the box, pinching the balance controller between thumb and forefinger. The torches above her had entered the building, had Max in their sights. Had her in their sights.

"Step away from the – step away from whatever that is. Put the box down," commanded Sergeant Cianciolo.

"Come on, Ms Zeit. You've gone too far," begged Berkshire.

It would have been a stab in the heart for to hear him say that if she had been less concerned for her imminent survival.

The shadow came for her.

Up close, it had teeth, thousands of them, in one long moebius row that kept on unfolding out of itself. She threw herself backward and the creature rushed over the top of her. The trap hadn't triggered, had failed.

Max ran barking into the darkness. The torches continued to sweep from the top of the stairs.

"What's going on down there!"

She didn't answer. The shadow couldn't exist in the space within the cinema, too three-dimensional. It had plastered itself to the flat surface of the wall, a patch of infinite darkness amid the merely pitch black.

Max barked madly at it.

The mirrors went dark, leaving the torches of the police as the only light source. Yet still she could see the shadow, the afterimage of its light-swallowing form indelible in her eye. It swarmed toward the light sources.

"Put the box down! Now!" screamed Cianciolo again.

But Cianciolo was going to die. The shadow beast was going to eat her, drag her into another world.

"Fetch!" demanded Argana, and then to the police "Trust me, Berkshire, kill the lights!"

"You've gone too far this time, Ms Zeit!" he called back.

Argana rocked as a collision at knee level nearly knocked her down. To her relief though her assailant was warm and furry. Max wagged his tail vigorously, her lost torch in his jaws. She took it.

Cianciolo screamed in pure terror, the shadow upon her. At the last second, Berkshire got the message and shut down both his own and his colleague's torches.

Argana lit hers up.

"Down here, monster!" she screamed. It flowed down over the chairs from the back to the front of the cinema, moving with the chitinous relentlessness of an army of insects. Argana flipped open the hatch on her hand mirror trap. In the instant separating her from her doom she tweaked the calibrator. Then the creature was on her. She turned the torch into her box of mirrors. In the moment that it followed the light inside, the crawling horror was simultaneously as big as a cathedral and as tiny as a tarantula. In a nanosecond the trap sprang shut, sealing the reflections inside.

There was an explosion behind her as, unseen, the full-size mirrors exploded into fragments. She felt shards of glass slice her skin, become caught in her hair. Clutching the trap tight, she sank onto the floor, breaking into sobs of released fear and tension.

Fred Berkshire was there, come down from the back. Cianciolo was leaning against him, wide-eyed.

"Ms Zeit," he said, "it gives me no pleasure, but we're going to have to bring you in on kidnap charges."

"Buh," said Cianciolo.

Berkshire raised his torch back to the stage, suddenly concerned.

There, a human figure stood carefully up amid the shattered fragments of mirror.

"My name is Ewan Enoch," the figure said. "I am back, I am well, I am of sound mind."

He walked forward and put his *left* hand on Argana's shoulder, who was still crouched.

"I owe this woman my life. I don't believe I will be pressing charges."

Berkshire breathed a long, relieved sigh. He put his handcuffs back on his belt.

* * *

The fresh air of the car park was never so welcome. The stars crowded, night having fallen during the struggle, but the outdoor space was floodlit with streetlamps.

Berkshire guided Sergeant Cianciolo to the passenger seat of the squad car. She was still unsteady on her feet, her uniform torn and her face bloodied. He said something to her in a reassuring tone before turning back to Argana.

"Sure I can't give you guys a ride?"

Argana flashed him a look that could freeze brine.

"I don't think so, Constable. You were going to arrest me!"

Berkshire shook his head and got in the car. He put the lights on and left in the direction of the hospital.

Ewan and Argana were alone. Max trundled in circles around them, sniffing at old hubcaps, for all the world as if he hadn't just been in a face-off with an eldritch horror.

This new Ewan was fuller than the last one, a more normal weight. His skin was filled out with muscle and fat, his face ungaunt. He had thicker hair and his eyes were clear.

"It's really you, isn't it?" Argana asked. "You're left-handed; I saw your scissors. The other you wasn't."

"Yes, it's really me. For me though, very little time has passed, or that hellscape would have driven me mad," he said, before adding thoughtfully, "That box, what are you going to do with that?"

Argana lifted the mirror trap to eye level, shook it, and put her ear to it. It was filled with a mournful, ethereal buzzing.

"I haven't a clue, mate," she admitted.

"I'll take it off you, then. As you can't dispose of it, consider it my repayment of my debt." His voice was calm, resonant. Convincing. She handed it over.

"What will you do with it?"

"You don't need to know. Goodbye, Argana Zeit."

To her surprise, he bowed. And then walked away. Watching him until he turned a corner out of sight, she was filled with a certainty that were she to follow him around said corner, she would find him vanished already.

"Bloody druids," she grumbled, to no one in particular. Max wagged his tail sympathetically.

"It's just you and me, hound. Looks like we're hitching home."

"*Wuff.*"

The End

Argana Zeit Ruins Halloween

Argana Zeit, the town's only (thoroughly unlicensed) Paranormal Investigator, detested Halloween. It was like being a rat catcher on a national holiday when everyone dressed as rats. Trudging home in the dark, all she wanted to do was forget the whole thing and watch reruns of *Columbo*.

There was a littered beer can in the gutter with a pumpkin and a hobgoblin emblazoned on it, leering at her. When she naturally booted it down the road, her dog Max, who had been following at a respectful distance, careened after it. Tin can and dog alike stopped outside a haberdashery called *Sew Good*, which sported a mannequin in the window dressed as Medusa, complete with knitted snakes.

Instead of fetching the tin back, Max stared at a grate at the side of the road. The first thin rivulets had formed from the October rain and were swirling down the drain hole. But that wasn't what had his attention; there was a light reflecting from his pointy face. It was coming from the grate, brighter even than that of the full moon above. His fur stood on end.

"What is it, buddy?" Argana asked.

She knelt beside the grate and peered in. There was a chamber below the ground, part of the system of storm drains to carry away the torrents that could come off the hills.

And in that chamber stood a boy, maybe nine years old, amid the dark tangle of detritus washed through the system over the years. Despite her general disinterest in the infants of her species, three things struck her as increasingly odd about the child. Firstly, he was wearing a 17th century Quakers' outfit, not usually considered a Halloween trope. Secondly, he was quite clearly glowing with an interior light that pulsed through his translucent skin. Thirdly, and most unusually, there was a good inch of air between the soles of his clogs and the brackish water beneath them. He was hovering.

The boy didn't notice her shocked gasp. He was too busy chewing on a rat that he gripped firmly, holding it to his face like a grizzly with a salmon. It was still wriggling.

Argana retreated to a nearby bench and hid behind a litter bin, leaning against it. Max, who had remained silent, tucked in close to her, abandoning his usual bombast in favour of a more a stealthy attitude.

"That's a ghost," hissed Argana, her voice quiet and insistent. "I thought I trained you to sniff those bloody things out."

Max's eyebrows came up and in at the same time, giving him the appearance of wounded pride.

"Why's every bloody ghost in this town my problem? Let's leave the thing there, eating its rats; it will probably be gone in the morning when it gets bored. This evening is far too eventful for my liking – I just want to put my feet up and watch a man in a scruffy coat outwit rich idiots."

* * *

Of course, she had to stop by Becky Makepeace's house to pick up her Blu-rays, and she kicked herself for not doing it earlier in the week. There was bound to be a party, and they would demand her party trick.

When Becky opened the door, she lived down to Argana's expectations, a twenty-something woman in a Frankensteinette costume.

"Oh hai!" said the monster, all faux frivolity. "You simply *must* come in, the gang's here."

"No thanks, Becky, I just came for these," Argana said, leaning in just far enough to grab the stack of *Columbos* that were just inside the door. She could hear music down the hallway.

She started to walk away, but Becky stepped out into the street after her.

"Oh come on, pleeeeease? You're the only person we know who can operate a Ouija board properly."

"You don't want to operate it properly on Halloween. That's the best time to just fake it, trust me," Argana said, whirling on her friend. "You don't want the real thing."

Becky let go of her smile.

"Jason's coming," she ventured without conviction in her voice.

"Oh my heavens," Argana said, rolling her eyes. "We're not at sixth form anymore."

All the same, Jason was cute, whenever he wasn't talking about motorbikes. A small town like Trotterwell didn't exactly have a surplus of eligible bachelors.

"You can bring the dog in," said Becky.

And that was the clincher. Argana and her collie both went on in. Becky, who worked some legal job Argana didn't remotely understand, had done reasonably well for herself and was already on the property ladder. Her three-storey town house impressed Argana despite herself.

"Go on through," said Becky.

The party seemed to be in the front room – a sure sign, thought Argana, that it was a bit naff, as all the best parties happened in kitchens. Still, she knew her way around and left Max in the utility room at the back. He was happy enough there, and Becky's lodger kept ferrets. A big bag of ferrets. Technically there was a hutch involved, but Argana was sure the plural noun was a bag. The feisty creatures fascinated Max as much as he fascinated them, so she left them all to it. She put a bowl of water out just in case he got thirsty, then went back through to the sitting room, where everyone was waiting.

* * *

"Hey, Argie's here! We can do the thing!" said Becky extravagantly.

Argana pushed into the front room, and suddenly all eyes were on her. There were occupants on two large sofas, a couple of kitchen chairs had been dragged through and a scattering of people on cushions. All were already drunk despite it being only early in the evening. To her disappointment, Jason wasn't among them. She looked accusingly at Becky, who smiled sheepishly.

The tension was interrupted by a well turned-out vampire with ill-fitting plastic teeth.

"Thith ith going to be gweat," he said. "Haff woo got it wiv woo?"

"You think I carry a Ouija board with me? Do you know how *big* those things are? Here, let me just pull one of out of my jeans!" Argana snarked, and mimed the action of tugging something the size of *Monopoly* from her back pocket.

"Woo *arr* a pawanormal inethtigator."

"Take the fangs out, Nate, it's not sexy."

There was a chorus of giggles from the sofa behind the vampire as he took his teeth out. Taking fakes out wasn't a sexy look either, and he waved the gob-spattered dentures around looking for something to store them in. Now he was just a slobber-faced young man with a black hairpiece and a crucifix hung around his neck. The cross was incongruous rather than ironic, Argana recalling from their school days that Nate was genuinely religious, possibly Catholic.

"So what *can* we use?" asked a girl by the door, apparently dressed as an Italian plumber with a fake moustache and a penchant for mushrooms.

"Just make one. Hurry it up, I'm not in the mood for this and I want to go home and watch reruns of *Columbo*. Becky, you got any cardboard?"

"Uh, sure."

"And permanent marker?"

"Why would I have that?" said Becky, screwing up her face.

"OK, lipstick then," Argana said and, it being Halloween, eight unconvincing monsters produced a black lipstick each.

"Grand."

"You're, like, not dressed," said a werewolf on the end sofa, "in a costume, I mean."

Argana shrugged. She was quite happy in her jeans and t-shirt, body warmer and scarf. The scarf didn't even have skulls on it. She had not intended to be out, and anyway, she knew more about the occult than any of this rabble did and didn't have to advertise it.

"Should have done a werewolf, like me," continued the werewolf, who without his mask on looked more like he was wearing a Wookie onesie. "It's not just a full moon, it's a *blue* moon. Double the moons, double the wolves!" He howled unconvincingly.

Becky came back with the corrugated box she had flattened, and a posh crystal glass. Argana took the cardboard and volunteered a woman in a pumpkin costume whose makeup was particularly immaculate.

"You look like you've got a steady hand, love. Put the all the letters and numbers on the cardboard, would you?

The pumpkin nodded, and when she had done as she was told Argana gathered everyone into a circle on the floor.

"So, how this works is—"

"I know how it works," Becky cut her off. "Everybody, put your hands on the glass and it'll spell out the letters. Oh, and hold hands too."

"You can't hold hands if you've got a finger on the glass, duffer," said the vampire.

"Our knees are touching, will that do?" asked the pumpkin.

Argana ignored them all, with their confused instructions. It reminded her too much of New Year's Eve, trying to work out whose hand went over or under for *Auld Lang Syne*. Usual Ouija etiquette is to be clear if you are faking it, even if no one believes you, but Argana was never big on etiquette and ploughed straight in. And she was determined this would be a fake, because doing the real thing on Halloween was just asking for trouble.

"Spirits of the dead, we beseech you," she said, in her best look-at-me-I'm-spooky voice… *not to come at all*, she added in her inner monologue.

The revellers began humming or swaying and shut their eyes, although Argana kept hers open.

"We call to you in your place of light," *and hope that you will stay there.*

"If you are out there," she continued, "knock three times."

Nothing happened.

"I *said*, KNOCK THREE TIMES."

There were three loud knocks. Everyone except Argana jumped with fright, and vampire-boy's wig fell off. The sounds reverberated through the house as if they came from another world. Or from another room.

Argana went wide-eyed, but it was all for show. The sound *was* from another room, as well she knew, having trained her dog to respond to 'knock three times' by stamping.

"The glass! It's moving!" exclaimed the owner of the pumpkin dress.

"*The garden of the wise,*" she read out.

"Lame," said Becky. "Hey – watch out, dog!"

Max had raced in and was trying to bundle his way over the ring of people to reach the board, but was prevented by his sense of impropriety at trampling humans. He settled for barking, his teeth and eye-whites showing.

"Er, Max and I'd better get going."

Argana stood up.

The glass shattered.

There were screams, and in an instant the partgoers were up on the sofa, behind the sofa or legging it into the next room. Becky, aghast and with a cut on her forehead, complained, "That was my grandmother's! My grandmother's best glass! What have you done, you idiot? Argana, you've *ruined* Halloween!"

"It was already rubbish," snapped Argana.

She and Max left them to clear up, heading out into the street.

"I told them I didn't want to do the stupid thing," she muttered.

* * *

She had to pass The Green Dragon pub on the way home, a timber framed boozer with wonky walls and warped glass in its compound windows. The autumn rain had driven everyone inside from the beer garden benches. There were abandoned chips and lumps of uneaten sandwich on the floor, so she paused while Max investigated each morsel in turn.

As she waited for him, she recognised a voice carried to her by the window vents that had been opened to let the condensation out. A deep, authoritarian voice with a scouse undercurrent to it.

She peered into the window to confirm the voice's owner. He was of retirement age, but with a face that time had hardened rather than softened, a full head of white curls above his dark and dangerous eyes. Around his neck was a dog collar, and a heavy black dress completed his uniform. Father MacGillycuddy, a Catholic priest who specialised in exorcisms. He was talking animatedly to someone just out of view.

Her desire to avoid him – he had little love for her since Salford – wrestled with her curiosity. The winner was inevitable.

"What's he doing here?" she asked Max. "I'm going to find out."

She pulled the dog over to the side of the entrance and put his lead on.

"Hold this," she put the other end under his paw.

Max whined a little, objecting to having to stay outside the building. It wasn't that he would be unwelcome, rather the opposite was true. He was a handsome, engaging creature and whenever Argana took him into a bar he instantly had a dozen new friends. They would try to pet him, ask his name or surreptitiously feed him crisps, and he would lap it all up. He would have to stay outside because he would otherwise draw too much attention.

Argana went into the pub, bought a cider and sidled closer to the table for a better grasp of what was going on. She pretended to play on her phone, but only succeeded in making herself sad seeing old conversations with Fred Berkshire, with whom she had recently fallen out.

The two women MacGillycuddy was talking to were identical. Not in the cosy, recognisable way of identical twins, so beloved of the horror stories Argana read, but rather in their bearing and mannerisms, their clothes, their facial tics. And she found that so much more disturbing. Both sported grey cardigans, buttoned their blouses to their necks and wore stern-but-uninterested expressions. Despite the gloom indoors, both wore mirrored shades. Neither reacted to Argana and, as for the priest, he had his back to her. So far so good.

"What do you know about angels?" the first woman was asking.

"You see, we're expecting a visitation tomorrow," said the second.

"A visitation? Yes, I had heard. I intend to be here for it. Will it be us, or the C-of-E?" MacGillycuddy asked in return.

"The Church of All Saints. Father Jacobus' flock."

With his back to Argana, MacGillycuddy nodded.

"Good. Ah'll be here to record the miracle on behalf of the mother church."

"We will watch from afar, and record for the Order."

MacGillycuddy bobbed around a bit in his seat, apparently staring at something on the first woman's face. Argana couldn't make out what it was; apart from her fairly sinister vibe and rather wooden vocal delivery, the woman didn't seem particularly unusual. There was a reflection in her dark glasses, the reflection of MacGillycuddy, and all too late Argana realised why he was angling his head.

The priest whirled around, pointing an accusing finger at her.

"Wha' do ya want, Miss Zeit?"

"I came in for a pint of cider. I didn't know you were—"

"Don' take me for a fool. You were eavesdroppin'."

Argana didn't care much for his aggressive tone, so she said brightly and cheerfully, "Hey everyone, look who it is, Father MacGillycuddy! All the way from Liverpool, and he's great."

A lot of heads turned, some laughed, some looked puzzled, all went back to their drinks.

"I gerrit," said the priest. "I don' wanna scene, like, so I'll answer ya one question, and answer it properly, and then you'll leave the rest of yer drink and stop bothering us. Deal?"

"Deal. You're the *best*," she said, as she came around to their table and pulled up a barstool. "You were talking about angels. I want to know about them too. The truth."

"'Av ya read the bible, Argana? I mean, actually *read* it?"

"Bits of it," she hedged.

MacGillycuddy's stare cut through her lies, but he carried on anyway.

"Angels are ancient beings, from before the earliest days of the Abrahamic faiths. Oh sure, the Lord recruited a few – Gabriel, Michael, n' sure, he rubbed up against a few as well – Azazel, Lucifer. 'Ee likes to imagine that they *all* took sides, but read between the lines in the Old Testament and they're independent spiritual entities, some of them of great power."

"Like the fae?"

"Not even slightly. Ya unnerstand angels are *celestial* beings? If we see them as men with swan wings, that is their chosen form. Their actual form is far, far vaster. Occasionally one gets commissioned for some task or another, and even more occasionally, they get bored and act the tourist. It's a tourist that's coming to the church tomorra, because it's All Saints' Day. Angels are connoisseurs of spiritual power, and I have heard that it is on the high and holy days that the spiritual power tastes proper boss."

"That doesn't sound like official church doctrine."

"It isn't. I shan't bother swearing you to secrecy, Argana; you don't have a lot of credibility in this town, and no one will believe ya. Now, we hava deal, leave us alone."

Argana didn't move.

"What about ghosts? Do you know anything about small, Quaker ghosts?" she asked.

MacGillycuddy let out an exasperated sigh, and the two older women muttered something between themselves.

"Listen to me, Miss Zeit," he said. "We've got things to do tomorrow, and we don't want you in the way. Wha'ever it is that you're messing around with, let it go. There's a party somewhere with your name on, so go and get bevvied with the rest of the youth."

Argana stuck out her jaw, "I've got the right, I'm a Paranormal Investigator," she said, flashing him her ID.

MacGillycuddy's sharp eyes missed nothing.

"Parapsychology Diploma, Astral University of Tibet?" he asked, his voice trowelled with disdain. "But you've never been there, 'ave ya?"

Argana was taken aback, no one ever having taken the time to read the pesky thing before.

"It's online," she blustered. "You wouldn't know what that is, would you, grandad?"

"It's run by two lads in Barnsley, is what it is. They use a barrel VPN to jarg the location. Now who doesn't know what they're talkin' about?"

"Who wants to talk to you fuddy-duddies anyway?" said Argana, deciding that discretion was now very much the better part of valour.

She made a show of downing the rest of her cider in one go – although, disappointingly, neither of the strange women seemed to notice and Father MacGillycuddy looked amused rather than impressed. She left the empty glass on the table, tucked her coat under her arm and pushed her way back to the exit.

When she came out of the pub, she found Max being patted by ghosts. Small ghosts with the texture of sheeting, shrill giggles of children and trainers sticking out under their hems.

"Shoo," she said, waving her arms.

"Trick or treat!" squeaked the lead ghost hopefully.

"Go on, hop it."

The ghosts were rounded up by an adult who had been waiting in the wings and left empty-handed.

***

Argana finally got back to her flat on the top floor of a Victorian terrace, shoved the clutter off the sofa and made herself a cup of hot chocolate to soothe her nerves. The front window would never quite shut; she could hear party people passing in the street below, and someone letting fireworks off in the graveyard up the hill.

Max had curled up in his dog bed, put a paw over his nose in his usual fashion and was dozing happily. Mug in hand, she sank back into the sofa.

"You've got a point, kid," she said. "Maybe we *should* leave this to someone else."

Twenty minutes into a box set of her favourite detective, she found herself getting twitchy. It was comfort telly that she had watched with her parents as a child. But not comforting enough to shake the sensation that she should be doing something. It wasn't fair; the stupid trapped ghost wasn't her problem. It wasn't like she was the prophesied one, or the secret descendant of a powerful warlock, or even the seventh daughter of a seventh daughter, although she had daydreamed about being all of those things at one time or another.

She got up and paced the room, hoping for another distraction. Things to straighten, or dust. Or the calendar that she had not turned over since August. It was a 2020 dragons calendar, given to her by her uncle when he finally figured out what happened to the ornamental dragons he used to give her and marginally changed tack.

"What's wrong with them?" he had asked, and she had answered, "They're just not useful," when what she should have said was, "They're tacky and stupid and don't suit my house at all and I have no interest in dragons because they don't bloody exist."

So here she was, with a calendar full of beautifully painted dragons. Famous dragons; Smaug, Pete, Puff, Toothless.

Toothless.

The calendar has no teeth.

She pulled the calendar from the wall, ripping the picture hook out in the process, and flicked through to the picture of the dragon in question. It was grinning all over February.

"Max…" she said, reluctantly spelling out the obvious. "Look lively, the Ouija board gave us a message. Not only is there something out there, but it knows about my sodding calendar!"

She stood up and paced up and down in front of the dog.

"All that nonsense wasn't nonsense, which explains why it wasn't about how much Nate's feet smell, or the usual banter. *The calendar has no teeth*, the spirit said. What else? *The voodoo doll's ailment*, and *the garden of the wise*. We ought to figure out who our ghost Marie Donovan was. Er, is. It doesn't do well to ignore a message from the dead. Not on Halloween."

She picked up Max's lead from its place beside the door.

"Walkies," she said.

* * *

Back outside it was getting late in the evening, the sun well and truly down and the wind beginning to get up. The streets were empty. Child monsters had gone home to count their candy and work on their sugar rushes, while older monsters had long since reached their destination pub or house party.

Argana and Max walked to the town centre, which honestly wasn't that far from her house anyway, taking a shortcut through the park where Max was disappointed to find the ducks asleep and not willing to play the herding game. They were headed toward the museum, which she figured must be the closest thing Trotterwell had to a 'house of the wise'.

The museum garden, when they reached it, was laid out as a grid of gravel paths all leading to a fountain in the middle, with rose beds in the gaps between the paths. Ornamental trees fronted it, although they were in the final stages of moulting their leaves. There was a chained gate at the front, but as there was no wall either side of it, Argana and Max pushed easily through the trees.

It being Autumn, the fountain was unsurprisingly turned off. A circle of stone contained old water, pond weed and a smattering of coins. In its centre was a half-height statue of a man in 18th century garb holding a set of intersecting metal rings over his head. She had learned on a school trip that this was a riff on Joseph Wright's painting 'The Orrery'. She wasn't sure what an orrery was meant to be when it was at home, but this one was represented as a ring within a ring within a ring, all of them perpendicular.

"It looks like a gyroscope," she said.

Max put his front paws on the edge of the fountain, looking for all the world like he was trying to get a better look. Then he spoilt the illusion by putting his head in the water and lapping loudly.

"Well, it's some kind of clue to the ghost's message," she grumbled, "but I can't make sense of it. What's left eh, animal? *The voodoo doll's ailment* ... I don't know any voodoo practitioners around here – not real ones anyway – so we can't go look them up. But our

The next bit was always the best, in Argana's view. She was the only one without her hand on the glass but could rely on the subconscious of her audience to spell out something entertaining. Nate blows goats, or Becky has no knickers, something like that.

"What is your name, oh spirit?" she asked.

As the participants pushed the glass to and fro, Argana read each letter in turn until it came to rest.

"*Marie Donovan*," she read. Seeing as the name came from the subconscious of the group, she had been rather expecting Oujee McOujeeface.

"Dearest ghost, we beseech thee, tell us now your secrets three!" she commanded.

The attendees giggled, and between them moved the glass over more letters.

"*The calendar has no teeth?*" she read. "You guys suck. Come on now, make sense. Tell me something about Jason!"

"It's not us, it's the spirits!"

The glass was moving again. Argana felt a tingling at the back of her neck that she tried hard to shut out. There was a commotion in the kitchen too, although she did her best to likewise ignore that. Again the Ouija board spelt out its message.

"*The voodoo doll's ailment?* Nate, you got any pins in you?"

"This is stupid," said Becky. "Make it do something proper."

"And now for the third and final and best secret!" said Argana in her most authoritative voice.

ghost Marie Donovan was probably no specialist, so I'm going to assume that she was referencing the stereotype. Dead end, isn't it?"

She threw a tuppence into the fountain, spinning it so that it skimmed across the surface and clinked against the other side before sinking.

"Hmm, *Dead* end," she repeated. "Well, we can always go try find Marie's gave, can't we? Sounds like a Catholic name to me; we'll start up at All Saints."

* * *

The church was stone-built with faced corners and flint infills, an ancient structure still commanding its own grounds, or more accurately, its own cramped graveyard. There were lights on inside, oddly coloured through the stained-glass windows, and cars beginning to pull up outside. Perhaps they were gearing up for a service. A perfunctory modern extension had been tacked on the side without any respect for architectural dignity.

The moon was full enough not to need a torch to search the graveyard for their ghost's resting place. Twice she and Max had to hide in the shadows as more people arrived, although they always went straight into the church. One of these arrivals was a surprise – Nate, the vampire from Becky's party. He was still mostly in costume, although he had changed his shirt for something less frilly. Now he just appeared oddly formal to anyone who didn't look too closely. He went on in without seeing her.

Finally, they found the gravestone they were looking for, near the back where the nettles grew. Marie Donovan, 1831-1889. Max, who had a flair for the dramatic when he wanted it, flumped full-length down on the grave. Argana knelt next to him, running her fingertips over the stone, feeling its weathered surface and textured lichens.

"Why is it you, Marie?" she asked. "What do you know? I never asked you to come at the séance; you just spoke of your own accord. Something about this place, maybe the angel visit tomorrow. But whatever has that got to do with a ghost boy in the town? There's nothing for it – we're going to have to go in and ask. I hope your god doesn't mind, Marie; he and I are rarely on speaking terms."

* * *

As she approached the heavy oak door of the church, Argana liked to imagine that she had a plan, which was only true if 'totally winging it' counted. She had not heard anything yet to suggest that a service had started: no bells, no singing. She hoped the congregation were just milling about and she could nose around unseen, so long as she avoided being spotted by MacGillycuddy.

She was in luck. Nate was at the door, welcoming visitors, and he smiled when he saw her, still swaying unsteadily from his earlier drinking.

"Argie!" he said cheerfully.

She put a finger to her lips.

"Shhh, Nate, what's going on?"

He leaned forward and put a steadying hand on her shoulder.

"We, my dear, are going to start our rainbow service."

"For Trotterwell's gay community? They're all out partying."

He giggled as if she had made the funniest joke in the world.

"Good one, good one. The rainbow is a symbol of hope. Our service will be a light in the darkness for people of peace to come together on Halloween. Some people," he wagged a finger, "find the whole *trick or treat* thing tiresome, and this gives them something positive to do instead."

She felt exposed in the porch, and peered past him. Saints stared down from plinths between the pillars that held up the vaulted ceiling. People in sombre clothes sat on wooden pews or chatted in corners. There was incense burning already, and an ancient woman was warming up the even more ancient church organ. At the back there were tables set with coffee and biscuits. MacGillycuddy couldn't be seen – hopefully he was in some antechamber talking to the vicar.

"Let's get a coffee, eh, Nate?" she said, gently.

"Yesh," he nodded. "I'm totally wazzocked; wouldn't do for the vic to notice."

She guided him by the elbow to the tables at the back, relaxing a little now that they were no longer in the entrance way. She still couldn't see MacGillycuddy.

After she had poured them both caffeinated drinks, and tucked an apple into her pocket, she started her interrogation.

"You ever heard of a Marie Donovan?"

He shook his head. Another tack, then.

"What about angels? There's got to be stuff here about angels."

Nate swung his arms wide, an effect which threw most of his coffee over several centuries-old tapestries.

"UFOs!" he shouted. "You're thinking of UFOs!"

Over Nate's shoulder, at the front of the church, she saw MacGillycuddy rise from the pew he was praying at, black-clad and vengeful, looking over his shoulder for the source of the commotion.

"Show me some books, preferably heretical ones," said Argana insistently, and steered Nate toward the side door of the church.

"Of course, of course," he stumbled with her, pushing the door open.

"There's the lending library down the hall here. I don't know about heretical, but there's books on angels, and books on witchcraft. Know your enemy and all that."

They were in a corridor in a modern extension to the ancient building, cheaply built, with doors of the cardboard-and-ply variety. The 'lending area' was a place where the corridor widened enough to put in some extra bookcases. Other than that there was a kitchenette, two sets of toilets with the half doors beloved of schools and hated by everyone else and a locked door to a church hall.

"UFOs?" she prompted.

"Yeah, yeah," said Nate. "In the book of Ezekiel, the angels are totally UFOs. God has this kind of space chariot, where the angels are the wheels, each of them made of these, of these," he hiccupped, "rotating wheels of, you know, glowing eyes. Lots of wheels inside each other, at funny angles."

That made her think of the orrery, with its circles within circles, that she had seen in what she hoped was *the garden of the wise*.

"Marie Donovan," she said, "wanted to tell me about an *angel*."

"What?" asked Nate, struggling to get both eyes looking the same way.

"Hey! Youz stop there!" There was a yell from the end of the corridor, where MacGillycuddy was entering alongside the henchest deacon Argana had ever seen.

"I din't do a séance," said Nate, defensively jumping to the wrong conclusion.

"Sorry, love," said Argana, and shook him.

Nate was sick. Gratuitous, ballistic, beer-and-cocktails sick. In the commotion, Argana grabbed a book entitled "Host of Evil: A List of Fallen Angels", shoved open the door to the toilet and scrambled out through an unsecured window.

* * *

Argana was already out of breath by the time she reached the grate in the road by the haberdasher's, coffee cup in one hand and book in the other. Max had met her outside the church and they had hot-footed it over. The ringing of bells behind them told of the start of the rainbow service, which would hopefully tie up MacGillycuddy from pursuing them.

She looked in the grate.

"Damn it all!"

The grate was empty.

She threw the coffee cup to the floor in anger, smashing it.

"Well?" she said, looking hopefully at Max.

Max thoughtfully batted at his ear a bit with his back leg, then shnuffled at the drain cover, trotted in a couple of circles and finally loped downhill to the next drain cover and sniffed at that. And then on to the next one.

Argana, who had taken the opportunity to flick through the book, put it away and jogged after him.

* * *

She guessed where they were going before they got there. The grates led to a storm drain under the town and exited into the river. The Derwent, a fat, mostly lazy river that had bedded itself in deep loops through the green lands of the valley floor. There were warning signs and high fences clear in the moonlight, protecting the cement-built outflow itself, so instead she levered up an access cover a couple of hundred feet back.

There was a ladder below it, and beneath that a darkness that had ripples in it, the sound of running water. She hoped it wasn't too deep. Max whined when she commanded him to stay, but his paws were not built for rung work and she wasn't strong enough to carry him down, so he had to stay behind.

She dropped the last few feet into the water, and an instant of expectant dread passed when she found a solid floor beneath it. All the same it surged, bitter cold, over her trainers and midway up her calves. Aboveground the moon had illuminated everything in its silvery light, but down here all was darkness. The only light was the opening to the river, some distance ahead of her, its oozing waters reflecting the sky.

And in that opening stood a boy with his back to her, glowing gently.

* * *

Argana's feet were so cold she could barely feel them by the time she had got as close as she wanted. From three metres back, he was clearly the boy from the grate by the haberdasher's, standing in the space where the storm drain met the river. Although the water must be knee-deep there, his clogs skimmed the surface. Well, one did. The other dragged slightly behind him. He looked out longingly toward the round moon.

"Hey!" she called, and she threw the apple from the church.

The boy put out a hand sideways and caught it without turning his head. As he looked at it, it withered in his grip, drying up and rotting until he dropped it.

"You can see in every direction, can't you?" she asked.

She took a step forward, the cold water turning her ankles numb. The boy said nothing, although the moon seemed to his strengthen his pale glow, making them appear of the same substance.

"I'm going to tell you what you are. I'm going to name you," she said, her voice steady despite her shaking body, "then I'm going to help you and then I'm going to set you free."

The boy turned around, rotating without moving his legs, and she flinched at his visage. The face was a child, but the eyes belonged to something eons old, an unfathomable and dangerous entity born of the stars and unconcerned and uncaring of so slight a thing as humanity. Dead rats bobbed in the water around it. This was no ghost.

It half-raised its hands and moved ever so slowly toward her, walking with one foot, dragging the other.

"I spoke to the dead," she said, hoping that this particular astral being wasn't au fait with the Lord's opinions on mediumship. "They said you're an angel, like in Ezekiel, and that you're hurt. You're hurt with a pin, something – something is stuck in you…"

She faltered. It had almost reached her, hand still in front of it, ready to hold on. Ready to drain the spirit from her body. She tried to walk backward to the ladder but stumbled on something unseen in the water. It was cold as she fell down, landing with a bump on her arse, the water up to her waist. The torrent swept her almost to the opening, just past the horror. She barely caught the edge fast enough to avoid tumbling in the river.

Gasping with shock at the cold, she struggled up.

"I thought – I thought to myself, what is special about *this* Halloween, that your power would be enough for you to contain yourself in so small a form?" she stammered, her teeth chattering. "It's the moons, isn't it? Not one, but *two* full moons in one month, and the second one right now."

The not-boy caught her wrist with one hand, and it burned with an indescribable pain. The pain drove her back to her knees, shocks trembling through her body. She could feel the lifeforce draining from her.

"That makes you a moon angel," she gasped, recalling what she had skimmed in the stolen book. "*Sarealle*, perhaps, but she's an archangel, and wouldn't come here to so small a place."

The pain was reaching a crescendo, dark dots swimming in front of her eyes. A rat corpse floated past her, its tiny face still contorted in the pain of its final moments.

"I name you *Aglibael*, Guardian of the Moon, once first servant to Ba'al," she pitched desperately.

The pain stopped.

The boy had a new form, shimmering at the edges, that of a buff man with two sets of wings and eyes of cold fire. It had a dark monobrow, a magnificent nose and a rectangular black beard in regular curls that reminded Argana of Sumerian statues.

Whatever he had stolen from her, she felt it rushing back and she could breathe again.

"You have named me," it said, with so many harmonics in its voice that it made Argana's ears spin, "so I will spare you. But you claim to know more about me, and if you cannot back your claims you will forfeit your soul."

Argana swallowed. There was far too little in her literature on the subject of negotiating with angels. Fae, Demons, sure, there were extensive protocols. But angels were just meant to turn up and sing something joyous.

"When you arrived, you disturbed the souls of the dead. Marie Donovan, buried up at All Saints, said a few things about you," she started.

The angel remained impassive, staring. The water flow around them seemed to slow, the midges out in the river reducing the speed of their dance. It was, she realised, eking out the time for her, so there must be little left.

"I have a calendar with a dragon on it – that's not important, but Marie wanted me to look at February. What's important about February? Not the month; you didn't arrive then and hang around for ages. No, it's about February the 29th – there is an extra day because of the leap year."

She put a hand against the concrete wall, pulling herself upright.

"You've been gone hundreds of years," she continued, "and you miscounted a day. Instead of arriving for All Saints' Day, when you would have had a great deal of power to draw on, you arrived a day early, on Halloween. And, being in the wrong time, you were also in the wrong place, in the haberdasher's instead of the church."

It nodded at her, the tiniest perceptible movement.

"In the haberdasher's, as you materialised, you were *wounded*," she continued. "It's – a dimension thing, I suppose – but you got a pin in you, I'm thinking in your foot, but because you changed form it's terrible. Marie called it the voodoo doll's ailment."

The angel stepped carefully backward from her, still dragging its foot, and the water resumed its normal speed.

Slowly, very slowly, she reached out and took its foot in one hand. It was statuesque, even feeling like stone to the touch, and, more importantly, didn't burn her. She turned it, and in the arch on the underside was a plastic bobble. The head of a pin.

She pinched it between her fingers and pulled it free.

"And now," said the angel, "you may release me."

A dozen grandiose responses flickered through her mind. She picked her favourite.

"Well piss off, then," she said.

* * *

Aglibael unfurled in front of her, sighing as it did so. It had a glowing white centre, a miniature galaxy of fireflies, and ropey circular arms that extruded, pushing their way into the world the way lava tubes do under water. The arms linked up and completed their circles, orbiting around one another in gyroscopic splendour. Their surfaces were translucent, white pulsating inside them, their skin pitted and pocked and encrusted with tiny protrusions like a starfish. Blisters formed, swelling and bursting, hundreds of them, and when they burst, what was within them blinked. Eyes blinked. Each rotating circular limb was infested with them, staring at her.

Despite herself, Argana took a step backward, her feet moving by themselves, driven by a primeval fear she would not herself acknowledge.

The angel rolled toward her without moving, blowing her mind with its sense of being in many places at once. It was right there, three metres across now, filling the sewer-mouth. It was simultaneously far further away, far larger, a being the size of a comet.

The water drained away around it, piling up over itself in a mindless dread, repelled on some elemental level by the creature's fiery nature.

Argana took another step backward. The water was climbing around her ankles as if seeking her protection. She had none to give. Her heels hung on the very edge of the precipice, the limit of the concrete, teetering above the river dark below.

"Daughter of man," said the angel, its voice the crackling embers of Krakatoa, "you have done us a service."

It reached out for her, not the many-eyed limbs, but a tendril of light that extruded from its core.

"I—" Overwhelmed with an emotion that she refused to acknowledge, she reached back, her index finger searching for the point between realms.

"Daughter of man," it said again. It pulsed with an inner light.

The water fleeing from it mounded up around Argana's knees and she slipped.

Her fingertip passed so close to its grasp that a tiny spark shot between them.

And then she was away over the edge, banging her shins bloodily against the lip of the sewer, out into the river two metres below.

She gasped at its ferocious coldness as she went under, choked on mud-flavoured waters. Broke the surface. Spewed up lungfuls, went under again. Broke the surface a second time, this time thrashing to stay afloat.

The river swept her away and already she was thirty metres distant as the angel left the storm drain. Its circles of eyes spun so fast now they were elliptical traces of light rather than flesh, and it hung above the river for a moment, a ball of caged lightning.

Did it look her way? She felt as if it did, although it looked all ways at once, before it sped into the sky, climbing away with ever greater speed until it was one among many stars.

Argana lay back and spread her arms and legs out as wide as she could, bobbing on the surface but no longer fighting the current. A black shape was silhouetted against the moonlit clouds, bounding along the bank parallel to her. A shaggy, loping shape. It barked as it came before launching itself into the water alongside her, and she was filled with a weary gratitude.

Max nudged her to a kind of pebble beach where the river had worn the bank low at a bend, and she crawled out. Her body was wracked with shivers. She coughed up water, wishing she could shake herself dry the way her hound did.

There were lights above her. Someone had driven into the field and stopped a car, and she counted three people. Two of them walked away into the darkness, their identical body language inscrutable. The third, however, was striding toward her in front of the headlights.

"Argana," called Father MacGillycuddy, pulling her to her feet and wrapping a blanket around her. "You look like you've had a mad night. Let's take y' back to town."

She let him guide her back to the car, an old black Saab sedan with a fish logo next to the numberplate, and sank into the thankfully leather passenger seat. Max, who usually rode in the back, climbed awkwardly onto her lap to keep her warm. The priest started the engine and headed back toward the town.

"Why are you helping me?" she asked.

"Yerran' idiot, but you're not a *bad* idiot," he replied. "Your mate Nathan Squire was worried about you."

They carried on in silence until he drew up just outside the town square, and Argana found she was laughing uncontrollably.

"What?" he asked.

"An angel," she said, unrolling her hand to reveal what was still clutched in it, "dancing on the head of a pin."

MacGillycuddy shook his head.

"Yerran' idiot," he repeated.

But this time he had just the tiniest hint of a smile.

The End

Argana Zeit is on the Menu

Across the road and behind a line of police tape was *The Taste of Chandigarh*, a mostly vegetarian restaurant on the outskirts of Trotterwell. It lacked its usual hustle and bustle. A policeman was talking with a couple, both in turbans, one of whom was sobbing uncontrollably.

Argana Zeit climbed out of her badly-parked Nissan Micra, letting her dog Max out of the back seat. She tugged on a body warmer and scarf as she crossed the road.

"Thanks for coming, Ms Zeit," called out the police officer, whom she recognised with disappointment as Constable Fred Berkshire. "There's been a disturbance. They're reporting a monster, so I thought it best to call you in. I'll do the dangerous stuff though."

"Do I have to work with *you*?" she said, still bitter about the time he had nearly arrested her out by the old cinema. A scowl formed on her freckled face, and she glared at him with green eyes.

"No, you don't. I'm sure we can call in a different paranormal investigator."

"You know that's not true. But Trotterwell does have other cops, any of which could have been here."

He gritted his teeth.

"This is my badminton partner, and a good friend," he insisted, gesturing to the couple.

The man in the turban nodded, holding his hand out to shake, although his sobbing companion only stared into space.

"Keeran Kapoor," he said, with a trace of Wolverhampton accent. He was in his late thirties or early forties, with an expansive moustache, smile lined face and eyes a warm shade of nearly black.

"This is my wife Khala; she's barely said anything since she escaped."

Mrs Kapoor nodded silently, distraught and fearful, before turning her damp face into her husband's shoulder.

"I'm sorry," said Argana, abruptly softening her voice after her exchange with Berkshire, and feeling the heat behind her ears. "What happened?"

"I wasn't here," said Mr Kapoor. "We always take Mondays off. We hired the restaurant out to two kids who wanted it for filming."

"What kids?" interrupted Argana.

"Couple of YouTubers, Ben and Daz the Medieval Chefs, maybe you heard of them? Uni dropouts, I think," Mr Kapoor turned back to Berkshire. "Khala was helping them out. I just came by to check on things, and she was out the back, screaming, talking about – about a monster."

"It's okay, Khala," Berkshire said to her, "we'll figure out what's going on," and then to Keeran, "You take her to the hospital, alright?"

Mr Kapoor nodded.

"I've locked the front," he said. "Whatever is in there, it's staying in there. You'll have to go around the back."

"Are there diners in there? The Medieval Chefs normally have some on their show," asked Berkshire.

"There were. I can't hear anyone now, I don't know…" trailed off the owner, shaking his head.

"Okay. Let's go," said Argana, and Max fell in at her heel.

"You – you can't take the dog," Mr Kapoor said hesitantly. "Health and safety, y'know?"

"You've got a monster in there! How's Max make any difference?"

He shook his head, tears welling up in his eyes.

"Leave him be," Berkshire said gently.

With grumpy, jerky movements Argana took Max over to the side of the road, clipped his lead on and tucked the end under his foot. His eyebrows came up and together, giving the collie an affronted look.

"Be a good boy and stay here," she said.

* * *

A steep ginnel took them between the restaurant and the next building, down to a small car park accessed by a service road. Hilliness being Trotterwell's signature feature, the back of the restaurant proved to be a full storey below the front. There was an unadorned green door almost hidden behind large wheeled bins and folded stacks of cardboard. Cigarette stubs littered the floor, and Argana idly wondered what they did to the chef's sense of smell.

It was already dark – the night came early in November, and there was a lot less lighting around the back of the building. A single security light cut everything into a collage of black and white, with little in between.

"Are you with us, Ms Zeit? Concentrate. This could be dangerous," said Berkshire in his best serious voice.

"Lead on, MacDuff-er," she said, exhausting her knowledge of classical literature. "You're the one in uniform."

He took up a position by the door, a torch in one hand and his other hand by his hip loosening the buckle on his police baton. Mimicking his professional pose, Argana put her hands together and made a pistol shape with her fingers for her own entertainment. When he looked around to check she was still there, she hastily converted the motion into scratching at the side of her face.

"With you, constable," she said. For all her mockery, he did look the part, lean and square-shouldered. Far enough into his twenties to have put on some muscle, not so much as to be ancient.

Berkshire rolled his eyes. He banged three times loudly on the door, succeeding only in flaking more paint off.

"Police! Open up!" he yelled, before barging the door open.

As he squeezed through the gap, his belt caught on something. The door frame was ill-fitting and had been bodged with a couple of nails. He jerked the belt free with a twanging noise and a mild curse, and Argana followed him, suppressing a laugh.

* * *

They didn't need their torches for long. There was a metal-clad light switch inside the door, and Berkshire flipped it. Fluorescent tubes stuttered into life and illuminated a short unpainted corridor. Nearest to them was a stock room, entrance slightly ajar, and beyond that a pair of functional doors opposite each other, each adorned with a stylized man or woman. They were in a kind of a lobby that also included a fishtank, and beyond that stone steps rose to the level of the restaurant proper.

Argana stuck her nose around the corner of the stock room, which was still unlit.

"They'll put any old junk in here," she said.

The expected boxes of plates, coffees, pastas and other long-life items were all present, but only took up one corner of the room. So too were less restaurant-oriented items; a mower, several spades, a leaf blower and piles of compost.

"It's the Kapoors'," nodded Berkshire. "Before the restaurant took off, they did landscape gardening in the mornings."

Argana hoped they were better chefs than they were gardeners; the equipment looked worn. A garden rake was half-eaten with rust, and the hardened plastic shell of a woodchipper was crisscrossed with nicks and scratches.

She shrugged. "Too bad they don't do seafood, they could have called it Surf n' Turf!"

"Keep it down," said Berkshire before gesturing at the stairs, "and we'll go up."

"Well, that made sense," muttered Argana.

The toilet doors were unlocked, and there was no one in them when they checked. Beside those was a stand with what had once been an aquarium on it, but it had been left to dry up and now it contained only dead plants and a single fat spider. The spider had collected a dozen hapless almost-corpses encased in webbing for a future snack.

Stilton boxes had been discarded empty in a loose pile, pending recycling.

"I hate blue cheese," said Argana. "It makes me want to puke."

"You make me want to…" retorted Berkshire under his breath. She let it go.

There was a fire-door at the top of the stairs, with a little window in it, although someone had helpfully put a poster up on the other side of that so she couldn't see through.

"Let's find out what we've got," said Berkshire.

He pushed the door open.

* * *

They were holding their breath, braced for something to happen. It did not. The restaurant was in a dire state. There was a score of tables, some upright, some knocked over, but none of them in their original positions unless the Kapoors had taken a *particularly* avant-garde approach to their layout. Chairs too, and a proliferation of coats and bags that had been hung on them before they fell over. Plates and uneaten meals, smashed glasses. In the far corner was a pile of garden cuttings, although why the diners would have accepted that without argument was anyone's guess.

"I don't see anyone," said Argana.

Berkshire, still in the doorway at the top of the stairs, shook his head.

"Me neither. No victims. Nor anyone who might pass for an assailant. But there was clearly a hell of a struggle here."

"Let's have a poke around," she said, already several strides in.

They skirted the room in an opposite direction, Argana habitually travelling widdershins. The room was maybe ten metres in each direction, surrounding a central bar-cum-kitchenette. Irregular pillars and buttresses paid tribute to the fact that it had once been several smaller rooms, long since knocked through.

On one of the tables she passed, one of the few still the right way up, was a menu. It only caught her eye because it was not glossy printed in the way the menus usually are, instead being two pieces of A4 paper folded in half and stapled. A one-shot for the evening, then. She stuffed it into her pocket.

There was mood lighting from frosted lightshades set high on the red walls, although some were broken. The walls themselves were more curious; there were scraped lines of freshly chipped plaster that went all the way along them, running under the high windows. She ran her fingers thoughtfully over them. At her parents' house she had helped remove ivy from the garage wall, and it had left the same branching patterns that she saw now.

"I've got something!" called Berkshire.

He was shouting from a crouched position just the other side of the central bar, peering at a metallic object the size and shape of a beach ball. She jogged over, skipping the spilled cutlery and abandoned coats and bags underfoot.

"What is it?" she asked.

"I haven't a clue. But it's not normal, I'll give you that for nothing."

The ball was half-trapped under a table, with two more visible nearby, one half under a heavy overcoat.

At first, they looked like metal footballs, metallic and glistening, but as Argana watched they wobbled slightly, moving liquid masses. Like jellies or balls of mercury. But even that was not quite right. The reflections on their surface were in layers like swirling clouds, reminding her of condensation, or of misty valleys seen from space.

It wobbled when she poked it, disturbing the swirling shapes into a flurry. Although it looked cold, it was warm to the touch, and the unnaturalness of it gave her goosebumps.

Looking around now that she had her eye in, she counted at least a dozen more of the strange orbs. And something helpful, too. Set up close by was a tripod with a cameraphone mounted to the top of it. Argana seized it with glee. Someone had been recording.

"This is awesome, this will explain *everything*!" she squealed.

But Berkshire was not listening to her. He was staring past her, an expression of alarm growing on his moustached face.

"You, er, you know that pile of leaf cuttings that my foolish buddy left?"

"Yes?"

"He didn't leave them, and they weren't leaf cuttings."

"Never mind that," she said, unscrewing the phone from its stand.

"Ms Zeit, it's *moving*!"

This time she looked around. And shrieked in terror and surprise.

* * *

The pile of leaves was unfurling. A monster was stirring inside it, having made its nest there. No, that was not what had happened – the pile *was* a monster. Trails of brambles lashed out of it, clinging onto the wall and digging in with grasping tendrils. Something that passed as a face lifted itself in the centre, a circle of petals around a spined beak.

It started moving. Not directly toward them, but sideways along the wall, with a motion that was all at once that of a crab scuttling and of a tree thrashing in the wind, although there was no wind. At the same time, it reached out, uncoiling thorn-laced vines at them with startling speed.

Berkshire's mouth dropped open, and although he instinctively pulled the baton loose from his belt, he did nothing while Argana advanced toward it. She was filled with curiosity, phone in one hand and tripod in the other.

"Get back!" he called out, but the warning came too late.

A bramble lashed out at her, and she ducked. It shredded the surface of her body warmer, drawing blood from her upper arm. The leafy mass that it had instead of a face lurched toward her, spined pseudo-jaws gaping. Still anchored to the wall behind it, it stretched out, swarming up and over an upturned table.

Argana swung from the hip. The tripod clattered into the monster's face and knocked it sideways. Before she could follow up, its next swipe tumbled her from her feet. The tripod scattered from her hand.

She scrabbled backwards away from it, moving on her back like a crab, her fingers searching desperately for another weapon. Her fingers found nothing.

It lunged.

Berkshire pulled her out of the way. There was a hatch in the floor, just to the side of the central counter, and he had yanked it open. He dropped lithely into the darkness, and she followed him.

There were used boxes down there, a safe landing, but she missed them all. Something punched her three times, once each in the coccyx, the back and the head, and it took her a moment to realise that that something was the floor. The monster gurgled above the trapdoor, looking down without comprehension, and turned away. She breathed in a ragged lungful of air, winded.

Her backside was sore, but her head was worse; her fingers went on a little expedition by themselves and found the skin on the back of her head sticky and tender. That was going to be a hell of a bruise. A well of light from the trapdoor illuminated her, the stone flagged floor and the first rows of boxes to either side.

"You okay?" Berkshire crouched in the darkness, clutching the bauble under one arm, still wrapped in the coat. His own landing was significantly more athletic than hers had been.

* * *

Berkshire slammed the trapdoor down above them, engulfing the cellar in darkness in the time that it took him to fumble his torch free. He swept it back and forward, revealing that they were in a cellar far smaller than the room above, although it had doors into what were presumably similar size chambers.

"Can it follow us down?" he asked.

"I don't think so."

As Argana shook her head it hurt, filling her vision with little specks of light.

"It seemed anchored to the wall," she said, "like ivy or something, I think it can go around the edges of the room, but not into the middle."

Berkshire let out a relieved sigh.

Argana's eyes adapted to the darkness, taking in the walls that were stone with damp crumbling mortar, the floor beneath them flagstones. Pipes and cables crawled along the ceiling, and a proliferation of mostly empty boxes obscured the walls. Everything smelt stale and earthy.

"What the devil was that?"

"A dryad," said Argana firmly, with much more certainty than she felt. "A wood spirit. Perhaps it is taking its revenge on the Kapoors. Did they do any work chopping down sacred groves?"

"It's 2020, Ms Zeit. There haven't been sacred groves for hundreds of years."

"*Thousands*. And I was kidding."

"And you've, er, you've met a dryad before?" asked Berkshire.

"Gods, no. I wasn't even sure they were real."

As she talked, Argana assessed their exits. Ill-fitting doors provided routes to at least two more cellars, and one of them had the faintest glimmer of an orange-yellow light peeking around its edges. She picked that one.

"I'm going to call for backup," said Berkshire definitively.

Argana laughed. "I hope the armed response unit have shears and secateurs in their toybox!"

"I don't have it!" Berkshire frantically patted first the belt and the pockets of his uniform. "My radio – it must have fallen off my belt when it was caught on the doorframe!"

"Can't you just shoot it?" Argana tried the door, but it would not come free.

"What with, Argana? Have you ever seen me carrying a gun?"

"Taser?"

"No. I've done the training, but only Sergeant Cianciolo actually carries one."

The door's heavy bolt was held in place with a rusted padlock. Grasping it with both hands, Argana shook it with all her weight. There was some give, and with each movement the screws holding it in place pulled out a little further.

"What do you do when you need to shoot someone?" she asked.

"I don't, do I? If there's trouble at The Green Dragon, we turn up with the blues and twos and everyone just runs off. This is Trotterwell, not Manchester. It's all about building community relations..."

"That's a highly ineffective system for dealing with interdimensional plants."

Berkshire laughed bitterly.

"That is true."

"So, all you've got is your dobby stick?"

"It's called a baton."

The lock gave and the door swung open, a dim light reaching them from beyond it.

***

The next cellar chamber was like the last one, only smaller, the same cramped headroom. It had illumination of its own though, filtered through a cracked air brick at head height that must come out of the side of the building. At one time it had perhaps been a coal chute. Argana gave it an experimental shove, but it was too solid to shift.

"Damn," she said.

"It's a dead end," said Berkshire, looking around. "If it does find a way down here, we don't want to get trapped."

"Wait – I have an idea," she said, standing up on a crate to reach the air brick more easily.

"Max!" she hissed. "Come here, boy."

Berkshire shook his head,

"What's that dog going to do for us?"

"Fetch your radio, unless he's a good doggy. He *should* sit out there on his lead until doomsday being a good doggy. They don't teach them to use their initiative at puppy training, they teach them obedience. That and not humping the lampshade."

No one had told Max about obedience. There was a padding sound from outside, followed by the anxious whine of a dog suppressing a bark. And there he was the other side of the air brick, out in the passageway, where for him it was at ground level. He poked his snout through the hole in the brick and snuffled at them.

"Good boy," she said, able to reach the end of his nose to pat him. "Good boy! Berkshire here left his radio by the bins. Can you get it?

Max blinked at her through the gap.

"Fetch!" she said.

This time the hound disappeared.

"That's all it takes?"

"He's very clever. He'll go try and find something that either of us might have left behind."

The creaking noise was growing louder. Dust was falling down between the floorboards.

"If we're by the outside wall," said Berkshire nervously, "then, er, we're right under an edge that that thing could be on, aren't we?"

Argana's smile was gone in an instant.

* * *

They ran back to the original cellar, the one under the middle of the restaurant, for a marginally safer place to await Max's potential return.

"Give me some light," said Argana. "Let's figure out what's going on here."

In the glare of his torch, she fumbled the stolen phone from her pocket, the one she had taken from the tripod upstairs. It was blue, with two dinosaur stickers attached. There were smudgy swipe marks on the screen, but when she tried to thumb it into life it displayed a keyboard, wanting an alphabetic password. '1234' she chanced, without success. 'pa55w0rd' drew a similar blank. She looked at the dinosaur sticker and smiled. Her inner six-year-old woke up with glee. "Ankylosaurus," she said. Six-year-old Argana had been a huge fan of the late cretaceous era.

"Eureka!"

It beeped into life. She scrolled through to videos and picked the most recent. Two young men appeared in the screen, both with excitable expressions, wide eyes and overproduced hair.

"I'm Ben!" exclaimed the blond, as if this were the greatest announcement in the history of announcements.

"And I'm Daz!" exclaimed the brunet, proving that it was possible to be even more enthusiastic than his buddy.

"And together we are the dread medieval chefs!" they said at once. In their background was the restaurant, still at that time pristine. Diners were at the tables, some bored, some playing on their phones, all waiting to be part of whatever it was Ben and Daz had planned.

"Every week," continued Ben, "we bring you a new meal, dredged from the halls of history!"

"That's right, true believers! Every single week we track down an ancient manuscript and recreate a recipe from the past!"

"If you missed it, click in the link for last week, when we baked four and twenty blackbirds in a pie!" Ben said, making pistols out of his fingers for post-production.

"Japes, Ben, japes! Or who can forget episode seventy-four, when we recreated the last supper after a painstaking analysis of Leonardo's painting?"

"This week, we got our hands on this!"

Ben shook a pamphlet at the camera that had been badly printed on A4 paper and folded in half, identical to the menu that Argana had pocketed earlier. It had strange, twisted shapes on it, unreal plants and flowers, the pictures mortared together with a writing that was spidery and unreadable, especially on the mobile phone screen.

"That's the Voynich manuscript!" yelled Argana.

"The wha—" started Berkshire.

"The Voynich manuscript!" said the kid on the phone. Not Ben, the other one.

"For years—" said Ben.

"For centuries—" said Daz.

"Crusty old dudes have been trying to decipher this! They think it's all about alchemists!"

As the on-screen Ben and Daz started up their double act, Berkshire was overturning boxes, looking for anything that might be useful.

"Or gods!"

"Or demons!"

"Or who cares!"

"We've taken the twelve most identifiable plants in here, and we're basing a salad on them."

"That's right! This week, we're making the Voynich Salad!"

"Don't forget to subscribe if you like what you see."

Annoyed with their voices, Argana turned the phone off and sighed, leaning heavily against the pile of boxes Berkshire had discarded. His search had turned up an out-of-date fire extinguisher, a gleaming red metal weight.

"*That's* the deal? A Voynich salad?" she said to herself.

"I won't even pretend to know what that was about," he said, "but I'm guessing those are the kids that Keeran hired the place out to."

Argana pulled her copy of the menu from her pocket and unfolded it.

"It's this. They've assembled a menu from the Voynich manuscript, a peculiar book from the 5th century. It is just possible that it was recipes, although most interpreters believe it was the work of alchemists."

Berkshire sat down, flummoxed.

"What has that got to do with the monster?"

"I think … I think Ben and Daz *summoned* it," said Argana. "They didn't mean to. I'm hypothesising that the Voynich manuscript is a how-to guide, and that they really messed up."

"I didn't see any…" Berkshire waved his arms in little circles, "um, occulty stuff. Magic circles, skulls, candles, that kind of thing."

"Exactly. Alchemists believed you could achieve magic with combinations of herbs. These two didn't even crack the code, they just picked plants from the pictures. Made up what they thought was a salad and – boom – they and all their guests are being eaten by first lieutenant plantboy up there."

"Hey," laughed Berkshire, "let's call it Seymour."

"That's ridiculous," she sighed. "That's like confusing Frankenstein with Frankenstein's monster."

A grinding sound made them both jump. It became louder, accompanied by wood creaking and then cracking, the mortar giving way. In the far cellar, above the air brick, the dryad was pushing roots through the ceiling, breaking it open. More tendrils dropped through and thrashed around, seeking them blindly.

Berkshire was on his feet at once, squaring up, baton in hand as he faced it. Argana tugged urgently on his shoulder.

"There's the other door, let's get out of here!" she said.

He grabbed up the fire extinguisher and she took the bauble wrapped in the coat and they retreated, pushing through the door into the third cellar. The thrashing monstrosity didn't come after them, but remained where it was, tearing up more planks.

***

The final cellar was the smallest and possibly oldest, reeking of damp and mould. It had a dirt floor that sloped steeply upwards, and above them only beams and the floorboards of the room above. They had hoped to be able to get out of the back of the restaurant, but if there had ever been a passage through, it had long since been bricked up.

"We need to get out of here," stated Berkshire as he started to search the underside of the ceiling with his fingers in the hope of finding another hatch. Finding none, he reversed the fire extinguisher and pounded it against the floorboard above.

"I've got to see what this is!" said Argana, ignoring him.

The coat was cold to the touch when she unrolled it, the bauble coming free. It didn't go far, instead wobbling to a stop on the uneven floor. In the dark it was even more mysterious, a quivering liquid evil that reflected little glimpses of Berkshire's erratic torchlight.

She poked it again, and the swirling cloudlike structure beneath its surface curdled. There was something below them, a human form bent all out of shape as if seen through the peephole in the door to her flat. As if this was not a bauble at all, but a portal that looked down into an oubliette.

"Give me your torch."

"I'g usig ib," said Berkshire, the torch gripped in his teeth.

"Give me your torch! Look!

This time he passed her the torch. While he went back to his aggravated property restoration, she shone the light into the bubble from several angles until one finally illuminated the interior properly.

What she saw made her recoil. A face stared out at her, a woman's face, mouth open and eyes wide, but still unconscious. Little bubbles of air broke away at her lips and nostrils, getting trapped in her floating hair. The fisheye distortion mostly hid her body, but she was wearing a tattered red dress, and her arms were outstretched in shock, crisscrossed with scratches.

"How does she fit in there!?" asked Berkshire, astonished.

Argana shook her head,

"The question is, how do we get her out? How do we get all of them out?"

"I know how *we* get out," said the policeman. "I can shift two of these planks. If we scurry up quickly enough, we can probably make it to the backstairs before it comes for us."

"You're suggesting we flee and leave these people in their bubbles?" said Argana scornfully.

"Heavens no!" he said, taken aback, before grinning and adding, "Down the backstairs is the storeroom. With the woodchipper."

"Oh yes!" she yelled. "The creature has to follow the wall, right? So, we can herd it to the stairway and into the chipper!"

There was a second thump, and a third, the sound of wood landing from a height.

Dropping through from the far cellar were rugby-ball shaped objects, gleaming brown and smooth with a point at one end. Seed pods. The closest one, rolling across the flagstones toward them, split as it came.

"Crikey," said Berkshire.

A green gas oozed out from it, flowing unnaturally toward them.

"Let's get out here!" he said, heaving on the boards from below. They popped open, pushing aside carpet tiles, and he threw the extinguisher up. He vaulted up after it.

"You don't have to tell me twice!" Already Argana could feel the strange gas closing her airways.

She jumped up, wedging her elbows over the edge. He grabbed her belt with strong hands and pulled.

* * *

Gasping for air, they emerged from the hole into an alcove at the other edge of the restaurant. The monster was eyeing them – if it had eyes – from the next wall. It moved the moment that they did. There was an explosion of white as Berkshire gave it both proverbial barrels of the fire extinguisher. It was repelled just long enough for them to make it out and run to the middle of the room.

It flailed at them, thorny cables thrashing just out of reach, but its crawling roots kept it fastened to the wall. There were traces of missing plaster all around the restaurant now, the tracks where its searching tendrils had dug in as it travelled.

"You distract it," said Argana. "I'll get the chipper."

"I'll get the chipper, I'm stronger than you."

"Distracting the monster is far, far more manly," she cooed.

Then, while he was still untangling whether he had been insulted or not, she pushed him between the shoulder blades.

"Here, critter, critter, critter," he said, accepting his new role.

Berkshire advanced on the dryad, empty fire extinguisher in one hand and baton in the other.

Argana scampered toward the stairs at the back of the restaurant, the ones that went back down past the toilets to the storage room and the woodchipper.

"Don't you even think about leaving the restaurant!" Berkshire yelled after her.

The thought had not crossed her mind, although it did now.

She took the steps two at a time and ran past the toilets. She flung wide the door to the stock room, and the chipper was still there, in all its glory. It was the height of a dustbin and cradled in a single loop of iron tubing that both formed a handle and provided a mounting point for two sturdy wheels. It squeaked and bumped as she dragged it back up the stairs.

Berkshire was keeping the monster at bay at the other end. The fire extinguisher abandoned, he held a stool in front of him. It lunged at the stool, wrapping tendrils around it, and the moment it did he struck with the baton, crushing and snapping them. But the thing grew new ones at a prodigious rate, the vines readying to strike again almost before he had the stool back into position.

"A little help here!" he called out.

Halfway up the stairs, Argana came to a halt, abruptly unable to move the chipper any further. Its orange cable was a taut line, caught on something in the junk room.

"I need more time!" she shouted.

"You haven't got any!"

Argana tugged furiously on the orange cable. The otherwise satisfying sound of metal scraping and things falling in the stock room just increased her anger. There was no time to go back down and see what it was tangled on. She braced her feet against the sides of the stairwell and put her back into it.

There was a scream behind her. Berkshire reeled backward from the creature, the stool abandoned, his hand up against his face.

The monster reached for him, straining, but he had fallen all the way back to the island bar and was out of reach. It screamed, or appeared to scream, the petals that made up its barbarous face opening wide.

Which is when it sensed her. At once its body language changed and it tucked its head in. Over and over it turned along the wall, a tumbleweed made of nature's barbwire, picking up speed as it came.

More plaster came away from the wall, splinters of wood lath, flakes of paint. A framed picture of a smiling woman holding prize marrows fell and smashed.

It had reached the apex of its path when the cable finally came free. Whatever last thing entangled it gave out and it burst from the storeroom, a striking orange cobra. Argana, who had put her entire effort into it, launched herself unintentionally into the room when the resistance gave.

She landed heavily. And then the plug hit her between the eyes.

The shredder stood where she had left it in the doorway. The creature hurtled toward it, and her, its first viny arms reaching for her, cutting her clothes with serrated thorns. The socket was at floor level, and she reached for it.

The plug went in. The monster reached the doorway.

The chipper started.

At once, all was noise. The furious grinding, the sound of a thousand axes being shaken. The scream of sap being rent from stem. Argana struggled free and paced backward, still watching the monstrosity.

Berkshire half-rose behind her, watching intently. Blood from a heavy cut above his eyes made him blink.

Chips of green wood spurted from the machine, ricocheting down the stairs while a mist of dust and sap rose around it. The deafening sound changed, and the choppy hack-hack-hack was replaced with a high-pitched whine. It was an excruciating sound, the promise of a jammed engine about to burn out.

Which it did, and when it blew, it took the electrics with it.

The Taste of Chandigarh was plunged into darkness.

* * *

They stared open-mouthed at the plant monster as it disentangled itself from the smoking machine. It was wreathed in darkness, the only source of illumination the yellow streetlight threading its way through the window blinds. It was half the size it had been, the walls splattered with dark liquid and strewn with chippings. Thorny limb over thorny limb, it dragged its ragged mass back onto the wall, pulling the chipper along behind it like the shell of a hermit crab.

Argana gathered up her chin, which had been hanging in astonishment.

"Well, that didn't work then," she said.

Already new leaf-buds were springing out on it as it regenerated, its ugly head turning back and forth searching for them.

"Now what? Run?" asked Berkshire.

"Run? Are you insane? It'll grow down the row like bindweed through back gardens. We've got to stop it. Anyway, your mates locked the front door, and we can't get past it out the back."

"And I suppose," said Berkshire, drawing himself up to his full height, "there are the customers to think about."

"Oh yes. And the customers," nodded Argana, for all the world as if she hadn't forgotten about them. The strange orbs lay quivering around the restaurant, individual diners trapped in their own suspended dimensions.

The monster was just watching them for now, making no move to attack. Withered and bleeding sap from a thousand wounds, it reached one creaking tendril for a red box on the wall. The fire alarm. The sprinklers activated the moment it broke the glass, and it turned green leaves toward the artificial rain.

As they watched, horrified, it plumped out again, regenerating anew.

"How long?" shouted Berkshire over the sound of the water pattering off every hard surface.

Argana was no expert on plants. Everything except the spider plant in her bathroom died, and she left the gardening to her landlady.

"Minutes. Minutes only. Maybe seconds," she shrugged.

Berkshire went back to the small bar, the island in the middle of the room. Optics and spirit bottles hung above it, and below them the mahogany bar sported abandoned detritus, a couple of overturned mugs and a chipped plate. There were tubs of vegetables, tins of herbs and spices, lumps of cheese wrapped in greaseproof paper. The bar was L-shaped and set in its shorter arm were a sink and a small stove.

"We could burn the place down," he said, his voice grim, though with the sprinklers on that would take some serious effort.

"No," Argana pushed past him, leaning over the bar and pulling out a book. It was a paperback reprint, very much familiar from the video they had watched. The Voynich manuscript.

"I'll prepare something," she said, determination in her voice. "If it can be summoned with food, it can be *unsummoned* with food too." She waved the menu at him. "If we can reverse this, we can send it back where it came."

Berkshire nodded, but he was rooting through the cutlery draw for big knives. He found a heavy cleaver and turned out a lighter too.

"What are you doing?" she asked him.

"Even if you're right … and I have to say, cooking a meal to defeat a monster is the most insane thing I've heard in a while. And that's with *you*. Even if you're right, it's not going to go down without a fight. I'll hold it off, or at least slow it up."

There was a cupboard to the side of the oven, and he flipped it open, rummaging frantically.

"Armour," he said. "Help me here."

Between them they turfed out a colander, a couple of baking trays and one of those curved, single-sheet cheese graters. Argana couldn't help giggling as she attached them to him with gaffer tape she kept in one of her many pockets.

The cheese grater made a passable vambrace on his right forearm, the colander protected his shoulder and the baking tray his chest. Lastly, she pushed the metal sieve onto his face and wrapped a strip of tape under his chin and over his policeman's helmet, narrowly missing the corners of his expansive moustache.

"Who' oo lughigb ad?" he asked, his jaw taped shut.

"My knight in shining armour," she said, her eyes twinkling.

"Cobb ogg idt."

"The Kitchen Knight is one of the *best* Arthurian stories."

She loosened the tape just enough for him to talk properly.

"So, this thing," he tapped the menu, "just how are you going to reverse it? I mean, if you just do it exactly the same, you'll summon another one of those, er, dryads, won't you?"

"I dunno – it's a salad, maybe the opposite is to cook it?"

"You're not much of a chef, are you?" he said, testing the knife and cleaver for wait.

"Swap salty and sweet? Bitter and sour? There's four basic flavours …" her voice rose in pitch, panicky.

"Umami. There's five flavours."

"Don't tell me that, Fred, don't tell me that!" She actually had her hands in her hair now, tugging aggressively.

"Look. We'll burn the place down, get as many of the bubble people out as we can. I know it's hard to stomach—"

"What?"

"It's a terrible decision to destroy it, it's hard to—"

But they were out of time. Fully regenerated, the dryad was reaching out from its wall, ready to go again.

"Berk, get over there and fight that thing. Just buy me five minutes," Argana said grimly.

Berkshire grimaced, looking over his shoulder at the spreading plant.

"You're my hero," she said, patting him on his lacerated face.

* * *

Poised in the tiny kitchenette, Argana opened the book, which was instantly soaked. Gruesome noises filtered through the sprinklers, and it took all her willpower not to just stand and watch Berkshire's life-and-death struggle with the monster. His only chance – their only chance – was for her to get this right.

Argana was a terrible cook. Her flat had only a single ring on the hob, and her two abortive years at uni had consisted of kitchens shared with Neanderthals and before that her stepdad had done it all. Fortunately for her, it appeared that the menu was salad. The Voynich manuscript, while fascinating when she flicked through it, was unintelligible. The best minds of the last century had failed to crack it;

even she didn't have the audacity to think she could do it in five minutes. The creature was visibly regaining strength.

But that was okay. Something Berkshire had sad gave her an idea and she set about recreating the original meal, as made by Ben and Daz, the 'Medieval Chefs'. She glanced nervously upward to check on the constable.

Given that combat gardening was not a traditional part of police training, he was giving it a damn good go. The dryad pushed him back, but he made it fight for every foot of ground that he relinquished. Vines grasped and clawed at him, scraping against the wet metal of his impromptu armour. With each swipe of his cleavers, leaves and brambles fell away. With each blow, his arms were heavier than before. He was running out of time.

Argana put the last touches to her salad, a pile of bay leaves, a pinch of coriander, a handful of pink star-shaped flowers that she couldn't name.

She picked up the plate and walked steadily toward the combatants, her bleached hair lacquered to her head by the sprinklers.

"You said I couldn't stomach it!" she yelled over the din.

"You're going to argue about that now? I'm going to die over here!"

Berkshire stumbled to one knee under the onslaught from the monster, its tightened stems growing under his arm and around his back. It pushed its face up to his, spine-edged leaves biting against the impromptu facemask. It was the only thing between him and a very short lifetime of disfigurement.

"No, it gave me an idea!" she yelled.

She shovelled more leaves into her mouth, chewing frantically. She could feel them sticking to the sides of her mouth.

"I don't need ideas, I need a rescue!" Berkshire called.

He was flat on his back now, the dryad towering over him. Its vines snaked around his legs and arms, curling tighter. It had his left arm too, bearing down on it with barky weight. Only his right arm was still free, and he hacked at the monster's face with the chopping knife. It was sharp, and the monster was vegetable, and sliced easily. Sap poured off it as leaves and petals came free, spattering the policeman in sticky residue.

"Almost – almost there," gasped Argana, between mouthfuls. Unsure how to make an opposite meal, she had made the same one again and hoped to whatever gods might be listening that it would not summon another dryad.

Berkshire was full on screaming now. Not in pain, but in terror. It had bound his remaining arm in fast growing tendrils. They curled around him, rolling him into a ball against his will. In seconds he would be entrapped, converted into one of those hapless bubbles and kept for a later snack.

"There's *another* way to reverse a meal!" Argana called.

A hunk of blue cheese was still on the sideboard, and she bit off chunks of it. It tasted good. It tasted of vengeance.

Berkshire's screaming had stopped, muffled by the layers of ethereal wax the monster was exuding. Already he was half-folded into an extradimensional space. Only his terrified eyes implored her.

Argana took four frantic steps toward him, closing the gap. The dryad turned its face toward her, a hissing sound rising in its – a hissing sound rising from it somehow.

The cheese did its job.

She vomited. A bilious, projectile, herb-infused vomit that cramped her in half and hosed the dryad down.

The dryad caught a face-full.

It flailed backward, retreating to the wall, its trails of thorns and leaves coming with it. It thrashed, bringing down the remains of the plaster and pulling out bricks. Its madly searching roots spread through the mortar with a terrible sound.

Argana hooked her elbows under Berkshire's armpits and hauled mightily, dragging him away from the outraged thing. He made choking, spluttering sounds in his semi-consciousness.

Something new was happening. Leaves fell from the dryad. Entire lengths of root and branch dried and withered, snapping off at the base. Even its arms and legs were peeling, the bark turning back and the wood below punking and crumbling.

Its face ceased its silent snarl and that too crumbled. The barrel of its rib cage was the last to go, springing apart into individual twigs and branches, the skin giving way like dried leaves in crisp winter.

A round and solid thing fell out of the middle of the remains, smooth and shiny, a deep waxy brown with a lighter brown saddle shape in it. A seed. As Argana watched, it seemed to roll into itself and disappear, returning to whatever realm it had been summoned from.

She sat down, exhausted, and wiped her mouth on the back of her sleeve. The sprinklers cut out.

***

The room was almost silent. The dryad had been so very noisy, full of creaks and pops, and its habit of continually eating the walls had only added to the cacophony. The walls had been stripped to the brick, sometimes further. The tables were smashed, the chairs overturned. There was water everywhere, damping the smell of plaster, decay, and blood.

The sphere encasing the constable was incomplete and became unstable around him. It ruptured, leaving him on the floor in a pool of slime and plant matter. He didn't move, hands clasped to his throat where the dryad had throttled him.

Argana looked at his wide eyes and his bluing lips, unsure what to do. She leant over him, readying to give him the kiss of life.

He swatted at her.

"Your – your breath stinks," he croaked, and sat up.

"You alright?"

"I will be," he said slowly, rubbing his red throat. The colour was coming back to his face. "How did you know to do that?"

"It was what you said, about not being able to stomach it. I literally reversed the meal."

He nodded, and she stood up and held her hands out to him.

"Let's get you up. You look like sh—"

The front doors swung open.

Outside there were lights. Trotterwell's only squad car had pulled up, and Sergeant Luciana Cianciolo stepped out of the driver's door, Argana's dog Max bounding out after her. He had not even ridden in the boot.

"Good boy," said the Sergeant, patting him.

"That's my line," said Argana jealously, but her heart was not in the rebuke. Cianciolo, even stern and cold as she was, was too welcome a sight.

* * *

While Berkshire lent against the island counter Cianciolo tended to his wounds, which were limited to many scratches. He pulled unmanly faces as she dabbed at him with disinfectant she had brought in from the car.

Argana cautiously approached the remains of the dryad. What was left was dry and crumbly, the fallen leaves curled and crisped, now a faded orange. Coils of brambles had also become dry and insubstantial, powdering at the slightest touch. Most of its mass had disappeared altogether, returned to whatever hell it had been summoned from.

Max was poking one of the baubles-with-people-in with his nose, and it wobbled like a bubble on the breeze.

"Come away from that!" called Argana.

The dog did not. Instead, he licked it.

All at once, the bubble popped. The red-dressed woman slithered out of it, covered in mucus like a calf in afterbirth. Scuffing at her face until it was clear, she took a deep, gasping breath as if half-drowned. She looked dazed.

Two more of the bubbles burst, spilling forth diners. And then another dozen, and then all the rest. Bewilderment reigned on their faces, their skin scratched, their clothes torn.

Cianciolo looked around in astonishment.

"You're doing the paperwork on this one, Fred," she said.

There were twenty or more of the mucus-covered diners strewn semi-conscious amid the wreckage. As none seemed to be on the verge of dying, and she could hear ambulances in the distance, Argana left them alone.

"How are you doing, Berk?" she asked.

He looked battered but unbroken and nodded slightly at her. Several cuts on the side of his face were held together by the sergeant's hastily applied medical tape.

"I'll be fine. Apart from the paperwork. You take off."

"What about Mrs Kapoor?"

"I'll ring Keeran and make sure she's okay. We'll take a statement from her in the morning."

Argana gave him a hug and left, Max padding at her side. Behind her, Cianciolo was directing newly arrived paramedics.

* * *

She ruffled Max behind the ears.

"So, let me get this straight," she said to him as they walked back to her car. "I told you to fetch – to fetch anything, and instead of getting the radio, you ran half a mile to the police station and brought the cavalry?"

Max gave her a big-eyed, tongue-lolling look.

"You're a total duffer," she said. "Salmon for your tea, I think."

She opened her door and he bounded into the back.

"The *police station*," she said, shaking her head. "That's the last time I let you watch bloody Lassie."

Wuff.

The End

Argana Zeit Stones the Solstice

"They've vandalized the bloody circle," said the man, pushing into the shop, ducking under the low doorway. Cold rain swept in behind him.

Argana Zeit looked up from the workbench at the back, where she was riveting small bells onto handmade leather cat collars. It was not her shop, but it was a flexible job and that was all she needed. The man who came in looked familiar, mid-thirties and muscular with sharp, flighty eyes like a carrion bird's.

"Argana Zeit?" he asked, squinting into the darkness.

"Mr Enoch?" she said. He appeared to be the self-proclaimed druid she had rescued from the mirror abyss in the late summer, although she had not expected to see him again. "You're looking, er, surprisingly well."

"Call me Ewan," he said, poking distractedly at rolls of leather piled on shelves. "There's a stone circle south of Bakewell they call the Noon Stones. Well, they call it Nine Stones, but that's not its name."

"Nine Stones? The Nine Ladies?"

"No, a different circle. It's more of a … well, you'll see when we get there. It's by a lumpy tor called Robin Hood's Stride. Neither is exactly a tourist spot, although they're marked on the map."

Argana, concluding that he was not going to buy anything, went back to lining up leather straps with a hole punch. She wished that the shop owner would come back; they had only nipped out for some change.

"Is this a solstice thing?" she asked. "I don't really hold with religious celebrations. I'm strictly on an ask-don't-tell relationship with all higher powers, both real and imaginary."

"It *is* a solstice thing," said Ewan, "but no, I'm not asking you to come to the celebration, although that is where I intend to see the sunup."

"You wouldn't catch me getting up that early! Not for some pagan nonsense!"

Ewan sighed.

"It's literally the middle of winter, Argana – the sun doesn't come up until 8.18! I can leave my alarm on at the normal time and still get down there and park up in time for some 'pagan nonsense'."

"Still not seeing what this has to do with me?"

"As I said, the circle's been *vandalised*."

"I repeat—"

"They've painted runes on the stones. You're a paranormal investigator, right?"

"I am. I'll charge a consultancy fee, you know?"

Ewan threw his arms wide.

"And here's me thinking you've got your little kingdom, making minimum wage selling cow peelings. Lock up the tannery, I'm going to take a drive and have a look at it myself. Come with me."

"If you're not buying anything, bugger off." Argana stuck out her tongue.

"Hmmph. I'll go alone. But you will take the job, to figure out what's going on. I'll meet you at The Crossed Spoons after work – it's the only café in Trotterwell without Wi-Fi."

"I know it, it's a gr—" started Argana, but he had left already without waiting for a reply, the door gaping behind him.

"Put wood in 'ole!" she yelled after him. It was December, after all.

* * *

The Crossed Spoons was a little place tucked under a railway arch, with blistered paintwork and a tired linoleum floor. Argana had walked over from the workshop, protecting herself against the cold by donning an enormous scarf over her customary body warmer and pushing her home-bleached hair over her ears. It was already dark outside by the time she got there, and she spotted Ewan through one of the steamed-up windows. He was alone at a table, only a handful of other customers dotted around.

As she pushed the door open it rang a little bell, for all the world as if the proprietor was not just two metres away, leaning on their aluminium counter. Argana gave them a smile as she pushed in, and her dog Max ambled in behind her, sniffing the air enthusiastically.

"Chicken salad please, Hilary, on a granary cob."

She pulled out the folding chair opposite Ewan, but he caught it with his foot.

"Turn your phone off before you sit down," he said, looking sternly at her.

"What?"

"There is a war on, Argana – a war for the soul of humanity. It was prophesied two thousand years ago, in the lore of the druids, and in your holy book too."

"It's not my book, I'm not a Chri—"

"We thought it was going to be a spiritual war. But it's not, Argana; it's a war of humans against the machines. The algorithm controls everything. The data they have on you, it's the mark of the beast. Turn your phone off."

Argana turned her mobile off and he let her slide the chair out. Max settled down at her side, his tail over her feet.

She stared at Ewan. "You've gone full Butlerian Jihad, haven't you?"

"Orange Catholic Bible; thou shalt not suffer a thinking machine to live."

"You know that book's fictitious, right?"

"All holy books are. But the gods reach us through their authors anyway, and since the bloody Romans destroyed the druid oral tradition in 43 AD, we'll take our meanings wherever we can."

"That's, er, a long time to keep a grudge for."

Argana sat back as the proprietor placed her food in front of her. They had a bowl of water too, that they set before Max. The dog lapped eagerly.

"While you've been hole-punching for the man, I've been out at the circle. I took some photos. It's pretty bad," said Ewan. He turned out his man-bag on the table, disgorging a collection of polaroid photographs and a crumpled hand-drawn map.

The pictures showed standing stones in an unmarked field, the nearest drystone wall intersected by a massive oak. Argana had expected something more majestic, or at least a circle with more than four sides.

"That's a *square*," she said indignantly. "I thought you said there were nine?"

"*Noon*. Noon Stones. Although there were more than four once."

She looked closer at the photographs. The drystone wall, although less ancient, was of the same gritstone as the 'circle', just in smaller lumps. One conspicuously large piece caught her eye, one that rose from the ground and protruded from the top.

"Is that a fifth stone?" asked Argana.

"Good spot," said Ewan, who clearly knew this already. "Yes. Might have been a fiddler stone, but more likely it got moved by lazy arses when they built the boundary wall. There's a house not far from here where they used one to brace the chimney."

"Henges in houses. If it's alliterative, it's true."

"It's a dangerous business, stealing leystones." Ewan shook his head ruefully, leaving her unsure if he was serious.

Some of the café's other customers had fallen silent, better able to listen into their conversation. It happened to Argana a lot. She ignored them, turning the photos the right way around for herself.

The grass was darker and greener around the standing stones, each of which was a different shape. One was clearly rectangular, another coned, another bulged in the middle and the fourth tapered out at its upper edge. All were heavily worn and lichened.

"Were they made in those shapes, or did time do that to them?" she asked.

"Look at the *symbols*," he insisted.

The graffiti was daubed on in thick beige lines, a mixture of sweeping and angular. In Trotterwell such sigils were invariably spray painted. It adorned shop shutters and end-walls and was always cleared off in the spring before the tourists came back. The work in the photographs was different; it had a dimension to it, it looked thick and sticky. It had been brushed on, possibly even spooned on.

"It looks thick," she said.

"It is. It's like congealed sick."

"Dude. We're in a *café*."

Hilary, wiping the counter front with a cloth, pretended they had not heard that. Nevertheless, a warning eyebrow was up.

"Are they even runes? They have a pictogram quality to them," mused Argana. But if they were pictograms, they were undecipherable ones. At least to her.

Ewan nodded absently.

"Look, I'm grateful for the money, but what is it you want me to do here?" asked Argana. "If I'm cleaning the stones, you can ring the council for graffiti—"

"Oh, It's too dangerous for the council. Occult runes?" He shook his head scornfully. "Anything could happen."

"Then you want me to work out who painted them?"

"Oh, I've got a good guess about that. I need you to work out what they are, and why. We've got three days until the solstice, and that's when we need to purify the circle."

"You *know* who did this?" she yelled.

"I'll tell you outside." Ewan took a last sip of his coffee, stood up and dusted the crumbs from his jacket. "Take the map and the photos. The map has my phone number on it, too."

Argana glanced around, and the other customers studiously didn't make eye contact. They had outstayed their welcome, so it was a relief to leave, but Hilary gave her a nod anyway as she left.

"Come again soon."

* * *

Outside, Ewan's Land Rover was parked on double yellows just down the road. Not one of the new, overpriced Tupperware box types, but the 80s variety, all flat metal right angles and parts that could be changed like a Meccano kit.

"Who daubed the stones, Ewan?" she said, following him impatiently.

He swung open the rear door of the vehicle. It was square ended, with a wooden bench down either side of the load bay, the footwell between them entirely congested with a tangle of jump leads, bungee cords, lighting rigs, digging equipment and a myriad of other bric-a-brac.

In amid it all was a mahogany box with worn hinges. She leaned in as he opened it up, revealing a selection of twigs nestled in gold cloth, each one with an edge scraped smooth and burned with ladderlike runes.

"Those are for divination?" she asked.

"Yes. You ask a question of them, cast them and read them."

"I know how—"

"I did it over the photos that I showed you. I asked them if the graffiti was, as I suspected, the work of Bronwyn Jones."

"Who?"

"Someone I hoped never to see again—" started Ewan, but already Argana was reaching for the box.

"Can I touch them?" she asked, grabbing a stick without waiting for an answer.

It was like she touched a live electric cable. There was a flash of light, and she was travelling through the air upside down. She slid when she landed on the wet tarmac, acquiring unflattering mud stains along the back of her body warmer and jeans.

That was not the worst of it.

Her left arm, the one she had grasped with, burned. She tugged the sleeve back with her other hand, and the surface of her skin wriggled. Wriggled and settled. On her forearm, where she had undeniably never had them before, were fresh tattoos of feathers.

"What – what the hell is this?"

"Anti-scrying shield, I suspect," said Ewan matter-of-factly, as if this sort of thing happened all the time. Not to Argana it didn't, and she had a stranger life than most.

"That's all? *Help* me!"

"You should have taken magical precautions, like I did. Don't they teach you anything at uni?"

He shut the box and closed up the back of the car, walking around to the driver's door. The Land Rover started up on the second attempt, grunting like a thing alive. A thing alive and *grumpy*. It left Argana standing muddied in the road, clutching her arm in a cloud of diesel fumes. Max pushed against her leg, whining mournfully.

* * *

That night, having failed to either scrub away the new mark on her arm nor find any description of it on the internet, Argana slept badly. She fidgeted and cried out so much that in the end Max took pity on her and curled up across her feet on the bed. She dreamt of dark wings, of cruel beaks, of things that fled in the light. Of luminous gold eyes, burning circles in the dark.

So it was that in the morning she was both tired and motivated, and that contradiction weighed upon her as she went to Tony and Paul's house.

Well, not exactly a house. Tony lived in a caravan on a plot of land that he had inherited. He and his partner had planning permission for a bungalow – supposedly – but what they had ended up with was a static caravan and a series of outbuildings that a generous soul would describe as sheds. Argana, who was less generous, thought of them as ramshackle ruins. And the chickens. Oh gods, the chickens. She would have to keep Max on a lead to minimise the mayhem.

"You be good now," she said to the hound. "We want to get invited back. No, I'm not sure what we're being paid for, either, but figuring it out is going to be the key to getting this mess off my arm. Paul knows about graffiti."

Argana parked her car at the top of the plot. She enjoyed parking at Tony's, because there was no actual tarmac and therefore, as nothing that was officially either road or not road, she couldn't get it wrong. Not that she cared, anyway.

"Tony!" she called out.

"Over here!" Tony was over by the beanpoles at the top of the allotment-like garden, which was fitting, as he was about the same shape. In his early forties, he looked far older, his face aged by too many summers and winters outside, just like boulders are.

"Hey Tony, is Paul in?"

"I'm glad you're here. I need to move the rain barrel on the south patio. Paul would do it, but he's thrown his shoulder."

Argana shrugged. It was always this way – no one could visit the plot without being roped into something. She didn't mind.

On the way to the south patio, they passed stacks of pictures against the edge of the caravan. Or at least what Tony and Paul thought of as pictures, as they bore the same resemblance to paintings that his caravan bore to a house. All of them – a mish mash of old boards, offcuts of plywood, kitchen cabinets, old car doors – had been spray painted in jagged lines.

"These are good," Argana said to Paul as he came to the window, as short and wide as Tony was tall. He wore several layers of dark hoodies, the outer ones studded with gothic logos, the inner ones bright and fluffy. One arm was in a sling that competed valiantly with all this bulk.

"Thanks. I'll put the kettle on," said Paul.

The water butt was full and therefore heavy, and they had to tilt it just a little and turn it against its lower edge to move it. Tony had a wiry, cablelike strength. Although Argana was of mostly average build, she was broad-shouldered for her height, the legacy of a youth spent rowing at Carsington Water. Even so, it took all the effort of them both. When they were done, her older friend led them both inside.

TeePee – Argana's power-couple name for Tony and Paul, a cunning play on their initials and their settled-nomad lifestyle – owned the kind of mismatched crockery that would have made Mad Alice proud.

"I'm not on a social visit, to be honest. I'm here for work," she said as she accepted a cup of tea.

"Come to drop by the latest leather catalogue? I've told you before, we'll come by the shop if we need anything."

"No, the *other* business." Argana was already trawling her pockets for her 'Astral University of Tibet' student ID.

Tony laughed. "The Paranormal Investigation? There's no such thing as supernatural."

"Then it's a good thing that it's Paul's expertise I'm after."

"Oh?" asked Paul, from behind a copy of Artist & Illustrator's.

"I've got these pictures of graffiti; I'm hoping you can make something of them. Like what they are, for instance." She produced the photographs Ewan had taken.

"Oh, go on, humour the poor girl," said Tony, going back outside with a power drill.

Paul leaned over the table, scratching his chin as he examined the pictures.

The simplest of the runes was shown on the south-west stone, the leaning one. It consisted of a circle that was open at the top, with a flattened oval in the gap. Something halfway between a capital O and a capital U, with a hat or accent.

Each stone in turn had a different rune. The next had an oval with a spiral on each side. Another had a sort of upside-down tree, all spiky lines. The fourth had a wide 'M' shape with two circles in the centre, and a V below those.

"They're not tags," he said, "and a *true* graffiti artist would use spray paint…"

"I think the paint mix is important," said Argana, "but you let me worry about that. I want to know what they say. Like, are they letters painted over one another? Or runes?"

"I don't know a lot about runes," he said, "but anyway, these aren't, they're *pictures*."

"Oh?"

Paul tapped the first picture with his finger, the one with an open-topped circle capped with a shallow oval. "That's a pot, I'd say. And this one's a lion."

He pointed to the next photograph, with an upside-down tree attached to a halo. Argana turned her head side-on and squinted. She could maybe see what he was talking about.

"And an owl, and a sheep – no, a ram, it has horns – and a …" Paul paused, before turning the last photograph toward Argana.

"And this one is undoubtedly a devil. Look, that's his pitchfork!"

"It's called a *trident*," said Argana, her pedantry hiding her unease.

* * *

Back in her car, Argana tapped Ewan's number into her phone. A Trotterwell dialling code marked it out as being a landline rather than a mobile, which made sense given his fear of computer chips. It rang a couple of times before it picked up.

Ewan's voice had a strange quality to it, speeding up and slowing down as it went.

"This is Mr Enoch, I'm not in. Please leave a message. Use a code word if you have to."

"Ewan, I've got the symbols identified. They're all animals – or almost all animals. I think our perpetrators are probably intending to summon ghosts of animals to the circle on the Solstice. I don't know what for yet – but I'm disturbed to discover that they also intend to summon a devil. If that's true we should seriously consider—"

A beep on the other end cut her off. There was no further communication, no electronic voice explaining what had happened, so she hung up.

"How rude," she said to Max, who shook his coat out in response.

Ewan's refusal to engage with modern technology was getting on her nerves. A tape deck answer machine, where had he even found such a thing?

* * *

The Joseph Wright Park in the centre of the town was bitterly cold and almost deserted. The runners had retreated to the gyms or decided that the end of year festivities were an acceptable time to take the week off and fatten up. The grass was dormant and muddy tracks marked out all the shortcuts between the official paths. The trees pushed bare, gnarled fingers into the grey and sunless sky.

Argana found her favourite thinking bench and settled onto it with a tub of noodles bought from the high street. Ducks waddled toward her, hungry eyed and sufficiently bored to risk a thorough herding from Max.

"Go on," Argana urged him. He obliged, coercing them to the pond in formation, down past the edge of the football pitch.

A well-wrapped man was down there with his two shivering, small-boy sons. The children looked frozen in their replica football kits and Santa hats, but the relentless enthusiasm with which they bounded backward and forward was keeping them just the right side of hypothermic.

The football got out of their control when their guardian booted it far too wide of the goalposts, and it rolled away toward Max.

"Is that your dog?" yelled the taller of the two boys. "Tell him to give us the ball back!"

The man behind him, staring resolutely at the ground with his hands in his embarrassed pockets, mumbled something.

"Please?" added the boy, retaining his volume.

The football rolled into the middle of the ducks, who would have liked to have scattered, but the collie would not let them.

Argana stood up.

"Bring the ball!" she yelled, praying to whatever god she didn't believe in that Max would not bite the thing. At least it looked like a proper football, not one of those sponge things that he would rip apart for his little doggie giggles.

Max bounded up toward her, booting the ball along with his snout after finding it too big to fit in his jaws. Behind him the ducks looked first relieved, then disappointed, and finally went back to sticking their bright beaks in the filthy mud.

"No, that way!" She waved in the direction of the boys. Max, whose experience of football had not been extensive, stopped with the ball between his front legs and looked pleased with himself.

Argana met him halfway, took the ball off him and booted it as hard as she could. It went somewhere. Not exactly toward the group, but thankfully not too far away either. The younger child was in fits of giggles, but the elder managed a patronising "Thank you, miss." Their owner – no, parent – gave an embarrassed wave.

Argana sat down again but carried on watching the boys. Both wore blue kits, and their sports bag by the parent was adorned with a logo, an antelope in a circle. A buck, kind of stylised. It reminded her of the animal graffiti.

"Hey!" she called, deciding that the ice was well and truly broken now. "What's the buck for?"

The man looked up at her, gave up on his British reserve and shouted up, "Oh, hi. Thanks for booting the ball back."

"No problem," she said, stealing Max's credit as she walked down the slope. "The buck?"

"It's for our football team, Buxton F.C. It's good to support local, unlike all those band-wagoners chasing Man U. There's shrines to them in India, you know. That's how local they aren't."

"Local? What about Trotterwell F.C?" asked Argana, slightly unsure if there even was a Trotterwell F.C.

"Them? They're two leagues below us!"

"I see," said Argana, without seeing anything at all, and left, bewildered, with her dog. Bewildered, that is, apart from an itching feeling that the pictograms were starting to make sense.

* * *

Argana dropped Max back her flat. She didn't like leaving him, but he didn't play well with Yasmin's cat. And Yasmin Nuri was who she needed to see next, a childhood friend who had grown up to become an uber-geek and often helped her out with technical questions. But today it was Yasmin's unlikely love of football that Argana wanted to tap.

Yasmin lived in a flat in a faux-swanky block of newbuilds suspiciously close to the floodplain, and Argana eventually remembered which one of the near-identical doors was the right one and knocked on it.

"Oh, it's you. Hello, Argie!"

Yasmin, mid-twenties, dark-eyed and wearing a shapeless, oversized hoody of a Japanese cartoon character, beckoned her friend into the apartment.

"Happy Christmas! Who were you expecting?"

"Someone else," shrugged Yasmin. "What do you want?"

Argana clocked the mistletoe hung above the doorframe.

"Well," she said, "if 'someone' turns up, I'll make myself scarce."

Yasmin nodded sombrely.

"So, er, you're into football, right?" asked Argana as she followed Yasmin through to her living room. They both flumped down onto the sofa, ignoring the suspicious glare of Yasmin's oversize cat Ramoth. The rest of the room was taken up with a giant TV and a proliferation of consoles, laptops and half-repaired computers.

"Kind of. They've got great thighs. Plus, there's a lot of money in betting."

"Betting?"

"Yes," said Yasmin, giving Argana an *I-told-you-this-before-and-you-forgot* look. Unlike Argana, Yasmin was famous for her memory. "I've been offering odds on bet trading websites, specialising in football matches for the last couple of years – that's where most of my money comes from. But it's trailing off a bit now; the margins are getting tighter."

"So," said Argana, feeling like the conversation was getting away from her, "I wanted to ask you about football mascots. Like Buxton has this buck, kind of thing."

But Yasmin was not listening, tapping away on her laptop.

"Here's something that you'll like, you spooky wench. I found it in my research, I thought of you. Y'know, it's like … that thing."

Yasmin cast her laptop to her 55" TV, displaying a badly compressed news stream.

In the video a funeral was taking place, a young teenager lying on his back in an open coffin, a procession of distraught and sombre mourners. He wore a striped t-shirt with matching shorts, and some of the mourners lovingly tucked items under his folded arms. A whistle. Some football programmes. Several scarves, all in team colours.

"Grave goods?" asked Argana, surprised. "Like when they buried ancient warriors with their weapons and torcs?"

"I know, right? What did you say you wanted?"

"I've got pictures of animals and things drawn on stones, and I want to know what football teams match each mascot." Argana showed her the photos, and explained Paul's interpretation of each picture.

Yasmin squinted at them. "They are hard to make out. You say that's an owl? Sheffield Wednesday have an owl."

"This one's a devil."

"That would be Manchester United," mused Yasmin. "Why those teams? I mean, Man U, I get that, they're huge. But Sheffield are a league below – they're still big, but there's thirty teams above them."

Argana thought for a moment.

"Bring up a map of the Peak District," she said, and Yasmin did.

The screen brought up the sparsely populated landscape, Trotterwell sitting on the Derwent to the east of the larger tourist town of Bakewell. Hills, woods and caves of interest were all marked with little symbols, inviting the click-happy.

"Has Bakewell got a football team?" Argana asked. "What's their symbol?"

"They're little-league – I don't bother with them, there's no liquidity in the betting market. It dried up a bit after I ran into an outfit who called themselves 'The Mallet', who went hard undercutting my bets and then arbitraging them if I moved them. It was uncanny."

"Yes, yes. But what's Bakewell's symbol?"

Yasmin stared at the ceiling, the way she did when she accessed the deeper corners of her memory.

"They don't have a mascot or anything; the club logo features a viaduct. It'll be for, y'know, because…"

Argana reached for the mouse. "Let me drive," she said, but Yasmin snatched it away from her.

"No one sullies my tech!"

Argana shook her head, "Well you zoom out a bit, then."

Now the view took in the whole of the Peaks, little towns joined by a handful of winding roads divided by moors and hills. Beyond the edges of the national park, much larger conurbations. First Buxton coming into view on the left and then Manchester, while on the right of the screen the zoom revealed Sheffield. To the south was the city of Derby, and to the south-west Stoke-on-Trent. On the western edge, Macclesfield Town.

"See what you want?" Yasmin asked.

Argana looked at the four cities that bounded the area, roughly forming the corners of a great square, and mentally overlaid the map

Ewan had shown her of the Noon Stones. She jabbed her finger at the monitor, making a temporary artifact in the gel-backed screen that had Yasmin glaring at her.

"These cities," she said excitedly, "they line up with the stones. Manchester in the north-west, like the stone with the devil on it, Sheffield to the north-east, as is the owl stone. And so on."

* * *

Sunday morning Argana was making scrambled eggs in her studio flat, heating a frying pan on the single hob and a pot of fresh coffee wrapped in a tea towel next to it. Her dog came over from the sitting area, a cheerful ringing tone emitting from his jaw.

"Give me," she said, stooping down and taking her phone from Max. He wagged his tail.

She wiped the phone on her sleeve and put it to her ear.

"Argana Zeit?" asked Ewan.

"What?" she replied. It was far too early on a Sunday morning for any kind of communication, in her view.

"Hello, Ewan," she continued, her voice creaky with sleep. "Gods, it's early. I'm glad you rang. We haven't arranged what we're doing tomorrow, for the solstice."

"I thought you'd figured that out. You count back an hour and a half, obviously. I'll come by yours at 6.48am."

"If you assumed that, then what are you ringing for?"

"You worked out what those symbols are for yet? I have to figure out how to get rid of them."

"I at least know what they represent. Hey, did you know that some football fans are buried with grave goods? I think maybe someone is trying to scry for them, to loot them. I guess some of the merchandise is collectable, whatever. You did pick up my message, didn't you?"

"Of course not. The playback function broke years ago. Listen, we're in danger. This Bronwyn Jones, she's heading up a splinter sect, the Hammer of Bori. They've turned their back on the green ways and pursue wealth now. I can't be having her messing up stone circles on my patch. Troublesome woman; we banished her from Anglesey a decade ago."

Argana rubbed her eyes one-handed, not sure she was still following this. She certainly didn't need Ewan to tell her the situation was dangerous. Her fresh-tattooed arm reminded her well enough by itself.

"Who is she, Ewan? This nemesis – a former student, turned to the dark side? A spurned lover?"

Her playfulness was returned only in silence.

"Nothing so personal, huh?" she ventured, stabbing at her eggs with a fish slice.

"You're trivialising our vows, Argana. Each druid is assigned one or more circles to watch over, and she abandoned her duties. That's why we banished her from the Order of Cuchulain."

"From who?"

"My order, the Ascended Order of Cuchulain."

"Gesundheit," said Argana. She couldn't stop herself.

* * *

An hour later, togged up against the cold, Argana was rooting through the scarf box in a charity shop while Max waited patiently outside. It was not one of the brightly lit, well-branded sorts, but a ramshackle affair with the feel of a jumble sale. She was not even sure what it raised money for. Shoes for baby monkeys, perhaps.

"Can I help you?"

Argana's shoulders twitched at the sudden voice behind her. Not the comfy old woman who normally ran the place, but someone younger, someone she knew.

"Hi, Alice," she said, with brittle friendliness, as she turned around.

"Argie! I didn't see you come in," replied Alice. More often known as *Mad* Alice, her massive hair was as scruffy as ever, face beaming with whatever inner illumination she was claiming this week. At least she didn't have an instrument within reach this time. Not unless you counted the three-stringed guitar on the back wall.

"I know I complained," Alice was saying, "but my smallpipes sounded a lot better after that priest took a look at them. Is he a musician, your friend McGillycuddy? How's Mr Lovegreen doing?"

"My uncle's doing fine," snapped Argana. "Now, about this help you offered?"

Alice blinked at her. Even her blinks looked like smiles.

"I need a football scarf. I bought a bunch online last night, next day delivery. Manchester United, Sheffield, Derby, Stoke, the lot. But I can't find Macclesfield Town F.C for love nor money. So, you know, last hope of the damned …"

"You didn't think to try eBay?"

"I need it now. Well, tomorrow, before sunrise."

"Ah, the solstice," said Alice. "We're having yuletide at my house, would you like to—"

"No, I've got evening plans," lied Argana. Unless not-being-at-Alice's house counted as a plan. "Have you got a scarf?"

"For Macclesfield Town F.C? You're in luck. Well, you are, they aren't. The poor team shut down this year; financial troubles. Some fans ditched their scarves when they moved on. It's so sad; I've been keeping them in the back instead of the bargains box. In case they, like, change their minds. It's their history, isn't it?"

She ducked through a bead-curtained doorway behind the counter and came back with a blue and white scarf with a lion in the middle of it.

"It's even this season's" she said, holding it out to Argana.

"Oh Alice, you're brilliant. How much?"

* * *

It was dark outside, the pillow was warm where Argana was snuggled into it and Max's occasional reassuring snuffle came from his dog bed as he twitched in his sleep. She would have happily stayed in this idyll were it not for the sudden onslaught of cheerful 80s pop. Late night Argana had believed that 'Wake me up before you go-go' had been the perfect alarm. Early morning Argana begged to differ.

Sadly, snoozing her phone was an exercise in futility as Max, awake in an instant and well-trained, gripped the corner of her duvet in his maw and tugged it away. Groaning, she tumbled out of bed.

"I wish you'd bloody make the coffee too."

Still, she scruffled him behind the ears before making her way to the kitchenette, putting his food in a steel bowl to soak and filling the kettle for herself.

Ten minutes later she was dressed, caffeinated and there was a reeking Land Rover Defender on the road outside, parked up with one headlight on.

* * *

Argana climbed up into the passenger seat, and Ewan gave her a nod.

"We've got a little over an hour to sunup," he tapped the analogue clock taped to the dashboard.

Max jumped up into the open back of the vehicle.

The ancient Defender took the potholes with leaps and bounds, eating up the road like a hippo on speed. It was surefooted, but the occupants were less lucky, careening from side to side. Behind Argana, her hound settled down into the footwell for safety. He had squeezed down back there between all the junk. He jostled for space with a couple of traffic cones, an endless supply of bungee straps, a spare coat, a sleeping bag, a toolbox and, incongruously, a tarnished trumpet.

"Tell me about the graffiti," Ewan insisted.

"I've figured it out. The stones are arranged in a square, right? If you put a compass rose over them they would be at the corners – north-west, north-east, and so on."

"Yes. Go on."

"It's about football teams. There's a devil scrawled on the north-west stone, and out to the north-west is the City of Manchester. The emblem of Man U is a red devil."

"Good work," nodded Ewan, taking his eyes off the road an unnerving length of time. "And the other stones?"

"There's an owl, for Sheffield Wednesday, a ram for Derby County, and a clay pot for Stoke City, whose team are referred to as 'The Potters'."

"And the fifth stone, the one buried in the wall?"

"Macclesfield Town F.C, whose emblem was 'Roary the Lion'. But they've shut up shop now."

The Defender lurched as they rounded another corner, cresting the brow of a hill and threading the narrow lane between high stone walls. The lights of Trotterwell were lost behind them. There were cold stars above and the moon was setting, meaning the only true illumination between them and a terrible, ditch-enhanced accident was the car's single working headlight.

She waited until they turned onto the B6001, a nominally safer road – it at least had centre lines – before she answered him.

"If your friend Bronwyn is trying to call ghosts… between them, there's over a million people in the graveyards of those cities. At least some of their spirits will be restless. She's gambling that some of them will be football fans."

"Stands to reason. The solstice is the time when the veil between worlds is—"

"Don't give me that veil is thin nonsense," said Argana. "I hear that for the solstices, the equinoxes, Halloween, Christmas Eve and the anniversary of every battle ever."

"What's in the backpack?" he asked.

"My Thermos. Oh, you mean the scarves? I've tracked down the scarves of each team as offerings to the ghosts. Those fans buried with grave goods, right, what's most important to them but – hey, are you listening?"

She was answered only by an unimpressed grunt.

"My turn. What's the trumpet for?" she asked, trying another tack.

"Before battles between rival tribes, Celtic war-chiefs hired Druids to go ahead of them and play instruments, striking fear into their enemies."

"Oh," said Argana, as if that made sense. Ewan seemed very much a loner to her, and in his waxed trousers and Gore-Tex jacket, about a million miles – or maybe two thousand years – from the image of himself that he evidently had in his head.

"You're proper worried about this Bronwyn Jones, aren't you?"

"She's greedy. Greed for power is perfectly natural for any self-respecting practitioner of the true arts, but greed for money? It's so mundane."

"Urghh, *sooo* basic."

"All the same, she can be dangerous. The bigger question, Argana, is why anyone would want to summon five ghosts to the Noon Stones."

She took a deep breath before answering.

"You're going to think this is crazy but—"

"Try me."

"I think maybe they're betting. My friend Yasmin had a run-in with a betting outfit who called themselves The Mallet – that could be this Hammer of Bori cult, right? What if they've got some way of binding spirits to their will, some way of getting information on future matches from them?"

There were streetlights ahead, and Ewan slowed the car as they passed through Bakewell's cottage-lined streets. Predawn, Argana felt that it should be deserted, but there were already plenty of people on the pavements. Shopkeepers going to open their stalls, early risers on their errands.

"Could be. She *is* motivated by money," said Ewan.

"There's a long history of mediums trying to use prophecy for profit. I'm not sure that it ever works. Can *she* do it?"

"We'll find out soon enough," said the driver, "and I don't think much to your scarves. I'll deal with the ghosts my way."

Beyond Bakewell was the A6, which at least had street lighting. Each light was ringed with a halo, a fog rising densely from the country around them, giving the night an encroaching quality.

* * *

The last leg of the journey was a narrow, unnamed road with lumpy grass verges and steep stone sides, climbing one of The Peaks' many untamed hills. The fog was even denser now, the Noon Stones invisible from the road but the convenient landmark Robin Hood's Stride forming a huge dark mass on the skyline.

"There's no visitor's centre or anything," said Ewan. "We'll just ditch the Landy up on the edge and hop a couple of walls and... oh, That's odd."

Already on the roadside ahead of them was a campervan, a long wheelbase transit coloured brightly but encrusted with mud. Its wheels had dug trenches into the grass verges, but all the same the back end stuck out far enough that Ewan struggled to inch the Defender past it.

"Someone's here. Bronwyn?" asked Argana.

Ewan nodded. He eased his vehicle off the road a few metres further on, crushing down frosty grass, the chunky suspension delighting in the tussocks.

Argana hopped down and let Max out, although he had to pick his way over all the junk in the back. Junk that Ewan was now hastily shovelling into an enormous canvas holdall, of the khaki variety that suggested he might once have been in the forces. Or merely *au fait* with his local army surplus.

While he was busy, she walked over to the campervan, put her hands against the window and peered in. Something in there had tiny LEDs on it, like those on phone chargers and laptops, but she couldn't make out what it was. There was no telling how far away the camper's owners were, who had probably heard them arrive, so she chose not to use her torch.

Several sets of fresh footprints led from the camper to the first gate. Max found those, issuing the lowest of barks and pointing with his nose. He was not a natural tracker, but the frost made them easy to see, even in the darkness.

"Bronwyn's got company," said Argana.

"Seems that way." Ewan had filled his holdall and hefted it onto his shoulder.

"How come you don't have acolytes?"

"A couple of hers will be genuine disciples. The others will be hangers-on, groupies drawn in by the lure of true magic," he said dismissively.

Argana laughed, considering Ewan's lack of charisma.

It took some time for the three of them to thread their way into the field, the fog crowding in on them and reducing their vision. The route took them first up to the tor over a stile, and then down through a gap in the wall into the field with the Noon Stones. All the time, he was lugging his heavy bag and she toting her smaller backpack.

The stones had a different atmosphere in the dark, looming in the unlit mist. In the daylight photos they had seemed an extension of the clear skies, the soul-warming hills. In the night, they took on the sinister occlusion of the fog around them, ancient testaments to a dangerous past, of druids and blood sacrifices.

There was something moving between them, too. Several somethings. People. Instinctively, Argana froze.

It was too late.

"Who's there?" came a woman's voice, Welsh and forbidding.

The stranger wielded a torch, shining it full in Argana's face from her position amid the stones, dazzling her. A few metres to her left, Ewan was unseen. As his pace slowed, he reached over his shoulder to loosen the straps on his holdall.

"No, who are *you*?" demanded Argana, standing her ground.

"You're in the wrong place, young lady," growled the woman in the circle. "Go home. No good will come to you this morning."

The woman's backup loomed behind her, moving with the unsteady rhythm of sleepwalkers and – unless it was a trick of the light – their eyes glowed. There were at least four of them.

Argana scratched at her arm – it itched horribly where the owl feathers were marked.

"Bronwyn?" she asked uncertainly.

"The same." She was close enough to see clearly now a determined-looking woman in her forties, thick grey hair falling in cascades around her narrow shoulders. Her eyes were hidden in shadows, but her nose jutted like a knife and her cheekbones offered no softness. But it was voice that was impressive, melodious, compelling.

"You'd like to go home now," Bronwyn said soothingly. What was Argana doing here? The sun was down, her bed was far away. She could hotwire the Landy if she had to.

Ewan was closer to the circle, the trumpet freed from his backpack and in his hand.

Argana put her hands over her ears.

"Hey, what are you—" started Bronwyn. Her pointy eyebrows drew in, an instant before her eyes widened in recognition of what was to come, but too late to cover her own ears.

The sound was a pulsing wail, an all-encompassing wave of power and emotion, a reverberating brass crescendo that stood Argana's soul on end. It was to a normal instrument what a demolitions explosion is to a back garden firework.

Ewan lowered the trumpet from his lips, and Argana, shaken, likewise lowered her hands from her ears. Bronwyn Jones and her retinue had scattered, disappearing at speed into the mist. Max was still with her, having taken his lead from his mistress, put his head down and flattened each ear with a forepaw.

"That was epic!" Argana shouted. "You terrified them! Who were they?"

Ewan shook his head. "Bronwyn and her cultists. Or hypnosis victims, who knows? We probably don't have long."

She laughed. "The Stonepeople are easily startled, but they'll soon be back, and in greater numbers," she misquoted.

"What?"

"Nothing. What are you doing?"

Ewan was upending his plastic box of trinkets in the middle of the circle, all the time checking his watch.

"Seventeen minutes to sunrise. I'm going to prepare a ritual here. As a non-initiate, you're forbidden to help. If you want to do something, you can get up on the rocks and give me a holler if the ghosts approach."

"They're not going to just appear here?"

"No, they'll have to come in from their resting places. They'll have started walking hours ago, through the night, timing it to reach the circle as the sun comes up. What is meant to happen then, Cerridwen only knows."

There were lines drawn on the ground in some powder, and as he talked, he scuffed them out, kicking the shape out of them.

"I'm here to help those ghosts, unnaturally disturbed, back to their resting places," said Argana, uncertain that they were on the same page.

"You do what you like. I'm here to protect the circle. And Bronwyn's here to thwart both of us, so we should work fast."

* * *

Max started barking. Legs braced, body wired, lips curled back from his teeth. This was not usual behaviour; he was a laid-back animal, not given to barking without due cause. Something far beyond the north-east stone was giving him that cause.

He ran back into the circle and tugged at the hem of Argana's jeans, or at least would have if they had not been stretch fit, settling instead for butting her in the shins with his forehead.

"I'm going, I'm going," she said, glancing around for refuge. The massive limestone block that was Robin Hood's Stride loomed on the hilltop, a black monolith in the fog. It seemed liked the fairest bet. Ewan was lost in his preparations, skipping from stone to stone with his herbs and twigs.

"You coming?" she asked him, without response.

"Just don't make me have to save your life again."

And with that, she was loping toward Robin Hood's Stride up on the hilltop.

* * *

Argana and Max left the field at the top end, picking their way through the fog. Already Ewan and the stones were only dimly perceptible behind. With Bronwyn still out there somewhere, Argana was grateful for Max's presence. He was good in a tight spot and, more importantly right now, had strong, sharp teeth. Some expensive vets' bills had proved that.

A gap in the tumbledown wall led them into the nettle-infested field below Robin Hood's Stride. The wide tor of grey gritstone was the shape of a particularly ugly, particularly squat castle, albeit much smaller. It was festooned with trees and finished off nicely with a stack of extra rocks at each end. The first rays of sunlight leant the tor its truest beauty, cresting the darkness to pick out the two boulder stacks. They alone glowed amber in the daybreak.

"Come on, Max," she urged him up the slope, occasionally having to lift him onto the next ledge and scramble up after. She panted with the effort, but it was worth it.

The view at the top was enough to stop her blinking in her tracks, briefly forgetting all the angst and turmoil below. She was in sunlight, spreading out all around her, having climbed above the fog layer. It had the look of a cloud deck seen from a light aircraft.

Max barked, breaking the moment.

"You're not wrong, boy. We've got things to do."

She fished binoculars from her backpack and swept them along the edges of the far field, catching an instant of movement. Staggering alongside the hedge, still shrouded in night, was unmistakeably a ghost. It gave her a little surge of delight to be right, and a larger surge of dread, tingles climbing over each other up the back of her neck. The ghost was limping, a crutch under one arm. It was that of a teenage boy in a tracksuit, translucent and grey, one leg terminated mid-shin. A scarf blew behind him in an unseen wind, trailing away from the knot under his hollowed-out face. He lurched as he came.

There was a bird flying above him, impossibly large. The ghosts had mascots with them, then, avatars of their allegiance. This was going to get complicated.

"He's got an owl; he's coming from the north-east. That'll be Sheffield Wednesday," she mumbled to Max, who was enthusiastically sniffing rabbit poo at the other end of the tor. "He will be here in about five minutes."

She turned to the south, again scanning the hills.

It took her a while to spot it among the herd, a sheep not like the others, a sheep where the lighting was wrong. A vast, oversized ram. It was trotting directly toward her, or rather, toward the circle behind her. It was only when she saw the ghost that it travelled with that its true scale became obvious. The spirit appeared as a middle-aged man, football shirt stretched over his pendulous beer belly, forearms black with ink. The ram came up to his shoulder, which meant it was the same height as him, on account of the fact that his head was missing.

"Even you wouldn't mess with that," she said to Max. "It's the size of the bloody Derby Tup!"

Argana shuddered, beginning to regret her recent life choices. She liked to be more of an investigator than a woman-of-action, letting Father McGillycuddy do the exorcisms or Fred Berkshire be her muscle. She was not sure could rely on Ewan the same way. Yes, she had saved his life once, but would he return the favour?

"Incoming!" she yelled down into the fog. "Five minutes, Sheffield and Derby!"

Lost in his preparations, Ewan said nothing.

Continuing to look around she made out two more – no, three more – ghosts in the night, all of them football fans, each converging on the circle from a different direction. Another teenager, this time from Stoke City, carrying an earthenware pot under his arm. The two after that consisted of a small girl from Macclesfield accompanied by a lion twice her size, and lastly a Mancunian, a tall devil dancing behind him.

A *devil*.

She gulped.

***

"We've got to get down there and help Ewan!"

Argana scrambled back down the rock pile, Max bounding behind her. The moment that they passed beneath the fog layer was abrupt, and beneath it, the cold clung to her skin and soaked his fur.

"Ewan! Ewan!" she shouted, without reply, as they ran down the field.

She misjudged their location and ran straight into a low stone wall. Well, not quite; she stumbled through the nettles first, which bit at her ankles. Which way was the gap in the wall? She couldn't see through the fog and couldn't hear the druid either. With a shrug, she turned left. Max, a resourceful dog, bounded in the other direction. She let him go – he could be called back easily if she found the gap first.

Something enormous and travelling at speed passed through the fog thirty metres beyond her, heading toward the roadside. She threw herself full length into the undergrowth, but the monstrous ram had not seen her. The ground had rumbled with its passing; it was far less ethereal than she had hoped. Mighty hoofbeats were replaced by screams. Out there in the night Bronwyn and her cultists were encountering the mother of all poetic justice.

Max was barking for her attention. Not his, '*oh my, intruders!*' bark, nor his carefully trained '*there's ghosts, miss!*' bark. This was his '*Come and look at this!*' bark.

She doubled back. He had found the tumbled down gap where broken stones pressed into the mud, and they crossed it. Abruptly, they could see through the fog. There was still a wall of it all around them, but a clear zone, like the eye of a storm if you somehow brought the storm to a stop, had formed around the stone circle, cleared by – by what? Ewan's magic? The convergence of the ghosts?

Convergence of ghosts, it seemed to Argana, would make a cracking name for a prog rock band.

The stone circle itself had shifted. The standing stones were in two pairs now, some thirty metres apart. She didn't like to imagine what kind of force it took, magical or otherwise, to drag such heavy stones so far apart. There were no furrows in the ground, and the grass still sprouted dark and unkempt at their bases, so perhaps it was the space between them that had changed.

There were other shapes too, completing the circle, shadows of the stones that had once made up the whole. If she looked straight at them in the half-light, she saw nothing, but with her head turned a little they were there in her peripheral vision. More standing stones. Another four of them, with the stone in the edge wall making up the ninth.

"Hey!" she called out again to Ewan, but he was still busy chanting and dancing, his sticks and paint forming ritual shapes on the ground.

Which is when the ghosts arrived.

* * *

The ghosts stalked out of the fog, one from behind each stone, matching their football allegiances to the daubed runes. The ghost child from Macclesfield passed clean through the stonewall on the edge of the field. Their footsteps left the grass uncrushed, and the fog curdled in wisps around their shimmering forms. The huge owl helped the Sheffielder along, and the Stoke City fan swung his pot, but of the other mascots there was no sign. She could hear the ram fighting the cultists in the dark, which left the lion and the devil unaccounted for.

The dead football fans ran at one another, whatever civility they had had in life stripped from them by the manner of their raising. Ewan screamed as they broke without effort through his wards, scattering charms and sticks and scorching the earth around his runes. The Mancunian launched a powerful haymaker at the Derbyite, that would have taken his jaw off if he had had one. Ewan crawled terrified between the feet of the warring spirits.

As Argana ran back toward the circle, she slipped her backpack off one shoulder, swinging it to the ground as she came to a halt. She jerked the top of it open and delved inside, pushing aside the scarves. Below them was a football she had brought in case, and she jerked it free.

"Play up, and play the game!" she yelled, and booted it.

Unfortunately, bunking off with her friends had always been a preference to PE lessons and it showed, the ball striking the nearest standing stone and coming back toward them. The duelling ghosts paid no heed.

Which is when Max intervened, running flat to the ground through the crunching grass, barrelling snout-first into the ball. This time it reached the place between the ghosts. Sheffield let go of Manchester's collar, Stoke stopped beating Derby with the earthenware. The small girl ghost from Macclesfield steamed into the football, scooped it into the air with her foot and headed it.

Ewan, now forgotten, crawled backward out of the circle, breathing hard.

Argana was not done yet. The ghosts were not dealt with, but they had at least stopped fighting. There were more pressing matters.

"Bronwyn Jones and her cultists are still out there, with the ram and the lion after them. Shouldn't we do something?"

"I'm not surprised," said Ewan, hauling himself to his feet. "Bronwyn messed up her protective circle."

"*You* messed up her circle! I saw you scuffing it!"

He just shrugged. "What she's summoned, she'll have to deal with."

"What if it kills her? What if it kills her disciples?"

Ewan said nothing. Not for the first time, Argana was reminded how little she really knew him.

The fog swirled, and for an instant she could see the struggle at the far end of the field, Bronwyn's group against the arcane ram. A teenage boy was tossed a dozen metres into the drystone wall, crumpling over it and lying unmoving, and the scene was hidden again. She couldn't just leave them to their doom.

"Right, you buggers," she snarled, running into the mist.

* * *

Above her, the sky was turning orange and peach as the sunlight ate the upper layers of the fog.

But the mist was not out of surprises yet. A tall, terrifying figure lurched out of the fog right in front of her, blocking her path. She yelped, and stopped suddenly, wishing Max was at her side. He was still in the circle, playing keepy-uppy with the ghosts. The spirit in front of her, blood-red, seven feet tall with a whipped tail and a trident was… was not as terrifying as she thought. Up close the devil, the mascot of Manchester, was not a devil as she knew them, but rather the cartoon variety, like a man in a morph suit, hopping from foot to foot and giggling.

It pulled a face and laughed at her.

"Have this," she said, pushing a scarf against its chest. Fortunately, it was the right red-and-white scarf, and the devil clasped hands across it. The creature started immediately to rise and drift, caught on the breeze and becoming more insubstantial with each passing second. She gathered up her bag and ran on.

The sound of laughter was behind her. The ghost football fans seemed happy, kicking the ball back and forth between them, the two pairs of standing stones now makeshift goalposts. The spectral owl held up the one-legged Sheffielder whenever he took his turn.

They might have made peace, but their mascots had not. The lion made its lunge, and the cultists scrambled up and over the wall. The slowest of them was caught by a leg and dragged backward, screaming, her ankle in the lion's mouth. Sods of earth and grass came up in her hands as she fought desperately to get away.

Argana, running full-tilt, let go her backpack and stretched out the Macclesfield scarf between her hands. She leapt. This close up, the Macclesfield Lion was a barbarous mess, huge and muscular, its shaggy mane dripping with dark, foul slimes. It let go the cultist and turned glinting, vengeful eyes toward Argana.

She collided with it, wrapping her arms – and the scarf – around its powerful neck, her eyes closed in terror.

It shrugged her off.

Argana, flung down in the mud, soaked instantly through her clothes, opened her eyes and looked up. The monster was filled with light, its tormented body language relaxed. Sparkles moved like fireflies within its translucent form as it turned its head skyward. It drifted with the mist, just as the devil had done before it.

But she didn't have time to enjoy her victory.

The giant ram, the size of a minibus and with the temperament of a rhino, was angling toward her. Her backpack – and the black and white Derby County scarf within it – were just out of reach. The wall was closer, and she tried to vault it. She strained a dozen different muscles just making it to the top – but not quite over – in time. The ram bent its head down, its massive flat brow striking the boundary with phenomenal force. The wall buckled, fragments of stone spinning away from the far side. A rock the size of a brick careened off Ewan's Land Rover thirty metres away.

"You're not helping," said Bronwyn from just the other side of the wall, her voice bereft of all its earlier smoothness. She was thin and scornful, an unfriendly cast to her weathered face, a score years older than her acolytes. Argana caught all these details in the instant that

Bronwyn raised her broom-handle arms and pushed her from the wall.

Although Argana twisted frantically to meet the ground as it came up, she still fell awkwardly. Her head bounced against a stone embedded in the mud, and a sharp pain in her wrist said that that was at the very least sprained. She groaned and rolled over, too winded to even stand. Back in the field with the ram, the wall might as well have been sixty feet tall for all that she could climb it now.

As for the vast sheep, that was circling back for another run at her. It bounced on all four of its sturdy legs at once, bent its head and charged. Horns the size of digger shovels and a head like a mini turned sideways. Strange way to die, thought Argana, as she threw up her hands in front of her face.

The sound of wings.

The ghost owl blitzed past her, turning its vast wings out at the last second as it cannoned talons-first into the Ram's face. There was a storm of feathers and a sound like a sack of meat falling into a mineshaft. The monstrous sheep turned away.

Then the owl was on Argana, huge golden eyes like portholes into another world, beak like the jaws of life. Talons the size of pythons grasped onto her wrist. Her skin squirmed, seemed to bubble under the surface. The tattooed feathers marked on her, the ones caught from the divination box on the first day, flowed off her and onto the owl.

The force of its wings, three metres across, knocked her to the ground as it took off again. As it swooped past her backpack, one of those unimaginable talons scythed it in half, dextrously picking up a blue scarf in the same motion. The words on the scarf – 'Consilio et Animos' – were the last thing she saw of it as it vanished into the sky.

With a courage that she didn't feel, Argana picked the Derby scarf from the ground and approached the ram. It leant against the wall nearby, apparently dazed, bleeding from wounds like ploughshares might inflict.

"There, there," she said soothingly, every atom of her will keeping her voice even.

The creature shook its massive head, focused its eyes. It snorted, its lungs the bellows of a massive furnace.

She hooked the scarf on the very tip of the creature's horn.

The sun finally pierced the fog, touching the stonewall, splashing beyond it to the Noon Stones, cutting through the fog like a lighter through dandelion-heads. It burned away with supernatural speed. No longer shrouded in darkness, the land looked free and unthreatening in the amber light.

Tucking her wounded wrist under her armpit, Argana looked around. Of the ghosts and spirits, there was no sign. The ground was trampled, the stone wall shattered. The teenage casualties were still there – the boy against the wall, still unconscious, the girl clutching her savaged ankle and crying loudly. Bronwyn and her other companions had fled to the campervan, which started up and pulled away. A surly-looking young man in the passenger seat gave her the finger as it went by.

Ignoring the wounded, Argana walked back toward the circle. The four Noon Stones had returned to their original arrangement, mere metres apart, and Ewan was packing his druidy paraphernalia back into the box.

* * *

Only the ghost from Stoke-on-Trent remained in the circle, motionless now that the other fans had gone, clutching his clay pot in front of him. Argana walked up to him, taking in his young face, wide nostrils and short, curled hair. Most of all, the lost look in his eyes.

"I think you want this," she said, placing the last of the scarves into the pot. A smile lit up the boy's face, and he and the pot became just more threads of the dissolving mist.

"What happened to the other ghosts?" Argana asked Ewan. Max was nonplussed in the centre of the ancient monument, one paw over the football, looking around for his vanished playmates.

"I banished them," said the druid triumphantly.

"The buttocks you did! I gave them new scarves, to replace their outdated grave goods. They change the kit every season. I placated the ghosts! I laid them to rest!"

"You just pratted about over there with the ram. I did the real work." Ewan shook his head.

The sun finally broke through to ground level, fully cresting the eastern hills. It ate furiously through the remaining fog, illuminating the stones, the roadside and the Land Rover.

"What about them?" Argana pointed to the moaning girl by the field wall.

"Forget them. You saved their lives, that's enough. They can pick up the pieces."

"I'll ring them an ambulance." Argana thumbed the buttons of her phone.

"You turn that thing on, I'm going home without you," said Ewan gravely, fearing the electronics more than he ever feared any ghost.

"Pay me first," she snarled, calling his bluff.

He thrust a heavy pouch full of something that clinked into her empty hand and walked away.

She looked between him and the fallen cultists, grumpily making up her mind.

"Damn it all."

She dialled 999.

* * *

The Land Rover ground its way off the verge and off down the sunlit lane, carrying Ewan away and leaving Argana behind in the field. She had moved the teenage boy, still unconscious, into the recovery position and left him. The girl's face was wet with tears, but she was silent as Argana applied pressure to her bleeding ankle. The scraps of her shredded backpack made a passable tourniquet, tied in place with its own straps.

"You got a name, love?"

"Where am I?" asked the girl.

"You don't *know?*"

"I – I thought I was asleep. But it hurts too much."

"The woman who was with you, the dangerous-looking one…" started Argana, running out of ways to explain easily what had happened.

"Who?"

Argana shook her head in surprise and disappointment. Amnesia explained the strange light that had been in the cultist's eyes – probably brainwashed, but it left her with no one to question. If she was honest with herself, that had been half of her motivation to stay and help them.

"The paramedics will be here soon."

The girl wept tears of relief.

Argana sank down with her back to the stone wall, suddenly exhausted. Max came over from the Noon Stones at a gentle pace, nudging the football ahead of him, and settled down next to her. Unless the ambulances would give them a lift too – and it seemed unlikely – she and the hound would have to walk the limestone trail as far as Monyash and flag down a bus. It was going to be a long day.

Was it all worth it? The pouch that Ewan had given her was heavy as she turned it over in her hands. Cheeky sod, paying her in change. She tipped a few coins out. They were tarnished and earthy, and most definitely not metric. The profile of an emperor was revealed when she thumbed the dirt away. She smiled, despite her anger with the old druid.

Max barked once. In the distance were sirens, and she stood up to better able to flag down the paramedics.

The End

Argana Zeit Rings the Other World

"Is this a video of you?" the message read, apparently from her friend Yasmin.

Argana, who was frying breakfast in the kitchenette of her Victorian studio flat, shuddered. There was a video clip attached with a blurry thumbnail. Was it her? New Year's Eve yesterday had been both epic and hangover-inducing, and it was depressingly possible that someone had recorded her dancing to *Timmy Mallet* in the small hours. Still, at least she might find out how she bruised her elbow.

She thumbed the phone, and the video clicked through to another menu. When that asked for her password again, she reflexively tapped it in.

"Ah, ratfish!" she cursed as her brain caught up. "It's a phishing scam! Max, why didn't you stop me?"

Her usual guardian and protector in times of peril merely raised an eyebrow. Dear Max, all he really knew about phones was how to find one if it was lost. He blinked lazily at her from his dog bed, awaiting a moment when she might be sufficiently caffeinated to take him for a walk.

Her phone screen froze, with an official looking pop-up over the top of it, informing her that a Microsoft operative could help her through it. How she was meant to ring the helpline when her phone was locked was anyone's guess – as too was what exactly it was that Microsoft could do to fix her Android phone. Still, she scribbled the number down on a piece of paper to look up later. It even started with 09, the UK prefix for premium cost services, an obvious scam.

"I'm such an idiot—"

When she didn't click further, the malware disposed of its prompt screen. Every app closed, replaced by ominous numbers ticking down in plain, green text. 15,342. 15,341. Some kind of countdown... 15,340.

The screen did nothing when she jabbed angrily at it. She tried turning it off with the side button and, when that was ignored too, settled for banging it against the counter before removing the battery.

"Well, that's torn it," she grumbled. "We'd better go see Yasmin."

Behind her, the hash browns burned.

* * *

Argana got all the way out into the street, car keys in hand and dog bounding along behind, before she had a moment of startlement.

"Bloody car's not there!" she exclaimed. Her battered Nissan Micra was normally pulled up on the wasteland at the end of the cul-de-sac. If only Max could play fetch with vehicles.

Max barked softly, uncertainty in his brown eyes.

"Oh yeah," Argana giggled, slightly embarrassed. "I left it two streets over."

On Boxing Day, on the way back from her parents, she had chanced the fuel light to its limit. The car had run dry minutes short of her home and she had simply left it there. She had meant to go and rescue it before now, of course, but had never got around to it.

So it was that she walked to Yasmin's place. Fortunately Trotterwell, all stone cottages and hilly streets, is a small enough town that it can be traversed on foot. At least Max enjoyed the journey. The pavements were thick with January's joggers, who would be back in front of their TV sets come February when their resolutions wore off.

Yasmin lived in a new build in the centre of town, a set of boxy flats that had sprung up in the grounds of the old mill. The apartments in the mill itself were swankier but, as Yasmin often pointed out, also much colder.

* * *

"Hi, Argie. I'm surprised you're up; I heard you got obliterated at The Green Dragon."

Yasmin, garbed in a huge fluffy dressing gown and dragon slippers, stood in the doorway with a game controller in her hand. A tubby white cat peered from around her legs.

"Nah, I was fine," lied Argana, although it was true that the walk over had been the kind of bracing that could optimistically be thought of as curative. "No, my phone got hacked this morning. From *your* phone. I thought …"

"You thought maybe I could fix it for you? I'm just your go-to techie, aren't I?"

"I thought you might want to fix *your* phone," objected Argana, "although it would be a total bonus if you could do mine at the same time."

"Are you sure it was sent from my phone?" said Yasmin, looking puzzled as she closed the door behind them and followed Argana into the living room.

"Yeah. Hey, this is cool, is it new?"

Yasmin's largest television screen – she had a selection – sported the frozen image of an epic battle, a tentacled monstrosity in a warehouse vs a little dude in a lab-coat, sporting green hair and cornucopia of steampunk accoutrements, all in cheerful blocky colours.

"It absolutely is," beamed Yasmin. "Christmas present to myself. *Bandit Infinity*. It's brilliant; I've been playing it non-stop. It's written by Jackson Moore, you know, the RPG guy. Wrote that eldritch sourcebook. Anyway, this little guy slides between worlds stealing treasures—"

"Awesome, has it got co-op?"

"No co-op mode, sorry. But I have got a new toy to show you; this will blow your mind!"

"What about my phone?" asked Argana mournfully, but her complaint went unnoticed.

Yasmin steered her friend to a bench with a proliferation of cables, a black box or two, a couple of hard drives and an incongruously antique greenscreen monitor. They beeped satisfyingly as she booted the jerry-rigged system into life.

"Ta da!" she exclaimed, standing up from her work. The tiny monitor lit up, a black screen with a flashing green cursor.

Fragmascope, it read, ©*2020 Yasmin Nuri. V 0.87*

"Retro, much?" observed Argana, staring at it.

"It uses an AI to complete sentences. I fed it on a diet of news articles, but with a twist. Try it out."

It was a rare honour to be allowed to touch Yasmin's computer equipment, so Argana seized the moment.

'*My phone is still broke.*' she typed.

The cursor flashed a little before the machine spilled out a reply.

'*You probably think of your phone as indispensable, especially after this year, but ask the question, what is it really doing to you? Is the social contract between human and machine broken?*'

Argana clapped her hands. "That's so cool!"

"That's the least of it," said Yasmin, sounding more excited than Argana had ever heard her before. "This AI is simulating headlines from, y'know, a divergent reality. OK, so you can consider the data acquired here to be a matrix, a massively pan-dimensional matrix…"

Argana's ears picked up at that.

"Other dimensions?"

"Yes. No. In the mathematical sense," said Yasmin. "Stop interrupting me when I'm doing the exposition! The thing about a matrix is that you can apply a uniform transformation to it and get a new matrix. In 2015 there was an accident with the large Hadron Collider—"

"That's a sort of universe-destroying doughnut, isn't it?" interrupted Argana. "I remember there was some wacko trying to get the courts to shut it down. What's it got to do with your toy?"

"There's a theory going around that it *did* destroy the universe. Or at least, cause a moment of divergence, and I was curious about what the differences might be. So, I took my dataset, trained it on ten million news articles in our world, and applied a transformation for the other world. Now the AI produces fake stories from a different reality!" Yasmin picked the cat up onto her lap and stroked it slowly in a frankly sinister fashion. "I'm sure you're wondering how I got the transformation?"

"No, I'm wondering if it's got a name. I think you should call it Hal. I'd call it Hal."

'Would you like to be called Hal?' she typed.

'This computer is called Hal has a special friend called Dave is afraid of Hal.' it displayed back.

"Your AI speaks fluent Garblish," she told Yasmin, who was not listening.

"… well, that's the transformation, that's the clever bit," Yasmin was saying. "The LHC team release much of their data publicly, so I started looking for anomalies in the information. I mean, I didn't, I had second box using hidden Markov models to look for … anyway, there was a discrepancy at 5.35 pm on the 1st June 2016, between the expected weight for … that thing … and I used the discrepancy to build a matrix that I postulated formed a measure of divergence between our world and theirs …"

"This is amazing," said Argana. "I gotta talk to it some more."

'Hey Hal,' she typed, *'what is it like in your world?'*

"I need to emphasise, Argana, this isn't real – it's a simulation. Most of it's not even plausible. I got it to generate headlines! Remember that local outbreak of pangolin flu China had a year ago?

In their supposed timeline it went worldwide. The Yanks haven't even had Jeb Bush as President this last four years, either."

"I liked the older Bush, he's sort of grandaddyish," mused Argana.

"Maybe, but it's not right for a political dynasty to exist in a republic."

'My world is cold. It is darkness.' The words flickered up from the black box.

"That's bleak, Hal," said Argana.

Yasmin put the cat down again. "Go on, give me your phone. I'll hook it up to something."

Argana passed it to her, and Yasmin took it between finger and thumb as if it were something that her cat had brought in, half-dead.

'Why is it so dark in your world?' typed Argana.

'This is death. We are death.' came Hal's response.

"I'm not sure this is right."

"What? Give me a minute, I'm, y'know …" Yasmin prised the sim and SD card out of Argana's phone and inserted them into slots in an adaptor.

"There's someone in the machine," insisted Argana.

"Hold up, OK, Argie, I'm trying to think. I'll need to reset the firmware on your phone too, in case … well, in case. And you say got this from me? Impossible. I'm running double virus scanners."

Argana stood irritably away from the keyboard.

"Oh, for god's sake, why don't you just check your messages? You'll see that you sent me it. Then will you believe me?"

"Alright." Yasmin unfolded her phone, the screen popping back into shape, black, glossy and uncreased. "No, see, no messages to you …" she trailed off, consternation on her face.

"No messages to anyone," she said, "for three hours this morning, when I definitely texted the vets. OK, Computer. Cross-reference phone memory with yesterday's backup, compare residual file structures in empty areas."

"Affirmative," soothed her main computer in a digital-but-still-seductive Irish voice.

"Gods. It's like Star Trek!" gasped Argana.

Yasmin rolled her eyes. "It is *not*. We have literally had off-the-shelf speech recognition modules for over a decade; you don't even have to be able to code to use it. It's child's play. I didn't even write Hal – the A.I – from scratch. It's mostly open source."

"You've got a god complex."

"I do not!"

"Imperator Nuri," interrupted the computer, putting Argana instantly into stitches, "3 megabytes of files were created and deleted between seven and nine this morning."

"Frak it," said Yasmin, moving to a different terminal and started typing. "You're right, Argana."

"About your god complex, *Imperator*?"

"No, about the virus. Whatever it was, none of my scanners caught it, which means it's still in the system somewhere. I don't need you under my feet while I sort it out; you're as bad as that cat."

"Charmed. Well," she looked hopefully at the PlayStation, "I could try out Bandit Infinity?" Argana picked up the controller and started poking buttons at random.

"It looks likes the infection somehow started in Hal and spread to the rest of my systems. Right," said Yasmin with a sigh, "make yourself useful, will you? You and your quadruped go check out the other people who got virus messages from my network, make sure they haven't been hacked. So that's Akira Pixels – he's the YouTube guy who lives out at Brink Hall – and Dr Jonah Harp, a science journalist and, well, there's no name on this message. But I apparently emailed something to the leadership team at the scout hut. You know where those are? You can call me when you've, y'know."

"How am I going to call you? You've got my phone!" objected Argana.

"Use your *other* phone." Yasmin was now up to her elbows in cables, linking small boxes together or pulling PCI boards out of the back of desktops.

Argana threw her arms wide in exasperation. "What kind of person has more than one phone?"

Yasmin pulled open a draw full of stubby phones like miniature calculators, still in their blister packs.

"Burners," she said. "Take one of these." She tossed it to Argana.

"Sometimes I worry about you."

"Let yourself out," said Yasmin, without looking around.

Argana took a last look at the green CRT screen showing Hal.

'I'm coming for you.' it read. That didn't seem to read like a newspaper headline to her.

* * *

Argana retrieved Max from outside the flat, a little cold and sorry for himself, and checked the list. The scout hut was down near the river, quite a way off, and Brink Hall would require the car.

"We'll visit Dr Harp first, buddy," she said to Max. "He's in walking distance. That'll warm you up."

Dr Harp's place was also conveniently close to the Co-op petrol station, so she could swing by and grab some fuel for the car before going on to Akira and the scouts.

Max came to heel, and they walked off through the crisp winter air.

"So, my phone," she told the dog, conversationally, "got hacked by a virus from Yasmin the same day she built a box that talks – or pretends to talk – to other dimensions. Coincidence? I say thee nay!"

'Rowwp,' said Max speculatively.

"Just so, my furry amigo. It makes a nice change not to be the one doing the investigating, just doing Yasmin a favour …"

'Rowwp.'

"No, I don't believe myself for a moment, either."

There was something more going on than a mere computer virus. She could feel it.

***

"And how is little Yasmin doing?" asked Dr Jonah Harp, having trailed through the obvious introductions, Argana explaining whose friend she was. They were in Dr Harp's study, a room heavily burdened with books and papers enclosed in an outbuilding behind his thatched cottage. A heavy sediment of old pipe-smoke hid the slight mouldering that insufficient heating had lent the documents. They sat either side of his desk, he in a heavy coat and she with Max curled over her feet.

"Not so little anymore," said Argana snidely. "She's doing well. She works as – I'm not sure, but she seems to make quite a lot of money doing it."

Dr Harp nodded. "One of my brightest postgrads. I had high hopes, but she always had her head in some anime or another."

"Manga. You read manga, you watch anime."

"She did awesome coding, awesome, but never on the projects I set her." As he spoke, he tugged thoughtfully at his goatee.

"You want a drink? I don't think you were ever in any of my classes, were you?"

He tugged open a felt-lined draw containing a pouch of tobacco and a hip flask.

She answered him with an out-turned palm. "I'm driving, thanks."

He nodded but poured himself a measure in a steel. She was beginning to realise that his red nose was not entirely to do with the cold.

"It is funny you should come asking," he said. "I got an email from young Yasmin this morning, as it happens."

"Oh gods, did you open it? She got hacked by a computer virus overnight; you could be infected."

He guffawed as if this was the funniest thing in the world, the tar rattling merrily in time in his lungs.

"As if I wouldn't check! No, it was fine, but she did ask me to dredge a bunch of academic papers out of the uni system."

"Yes?" asked Argana, leaning forward.

Dr Harp swung his monitor around, mounted on a cantilevered arm that was a feat of engineering. A whole bunch of windows were open, the most prominent of which was an obituaries column.

"Dr Marianne Torus," Argana read, "beloved daughter of blah, blah, well-respected and so on … magnetic field specialist at CERN. She died in a car crash, 3rd June 2016. Isn't that—"

"Three days after a major Hadron Collider incident," Harp finished for her. "There's always been talk of a cover-up, that maybe she was injured in the incident and the car was a cover story."

"You believe that?"

He shrugged. "There's nothing in the traffic incident reports for that day, and no photos on her social media of her ever having owned a car. But conspiracy theorists are considered 'noises off', and investigations tend to ignore them."

Argana scanned the rest of the screen. Dr Torus had pride of place, the only obituary with a photograph. The others were just text;

a couple of schoolteachers, some teenagers who had died in a possible suicide pact. A lot of people, it turned out, could die in one day. Beyond these were science papers, each of which Dr Torus had authored or co-authored. The topics were beyond Argana's ken, all Monochromatic Knots, Multipoles and the like.

"Can you print these for me?" she asked.

"Won't take a moment."

The printer hummed and chirped, extruding crisp sheets of paper. As she took the topmost, Argana was struck by the photograph of the dead scientist, a woman with excitable eyes and a squirrel-like pose and recalled Hal's words. *This is death.* An idea started to form.

"You're a scientist—" she started, slowly.

"*Scholar.*"

"You're a *scholar*. How possible is it that Dr Torus died in this incident? That the incident created a divergence between two universes and her soul ended up trapped in the gap between them?"

Dr Harp laughed long and hard, choking briefly on his whisky. "You kids and your antics. I can't imagine Yasmin believes that for a second; what a wind-up."

* * *

Back outside, Argana walked back toward the town centre, Max trotting alongside. Trotterwell was gloriously silent, its population nursing their hangovers and breathing a collective sigh of relief that 2020 was done with. Just as she reached the petrol station, she pulled the burner phone out of her pocket and called Yasmin.

"Hi Argana, what's up?" replied her friend.

As she talked, Argana selected a 5-litre fuel container from the forecourt. She waved it at the cashier in what she hoped was a signal that she was going to fill it up first and then pay for it.

"I've been out to see Dr Harp; he's convinced you asked him to download a bunch of science papers. It wasn't you though, was it? It was whoever hacked your phone."

"Papers on A.I?" Yasmin asked, the alarm registering clearly in her voice. "Oh god, it's the singularity! That thing where, y'know, with the computers."

"No, no, no, it's not that," replied Argana, without having the faintest idea what the singularity might be. "No, it's ghosts. Not papers on ghosts, you understand, but a paper by a ghost. Marianne Torus, a doctor at the LHC, who got offed in an accident at the same time as your anomaly. I think she's trapped in the system."

There was a loud sigh from the other end of the phone.

"That's lovely, Argie. Just go and find out what the other two got."

"… or it could be these suicides," said Argana. "There's a Terrence Findern. That'd be a local name, wouldn't it? There's a Findern village just south of Derby."

"Listen, just don't run any of your weird theories by the others. Don't, y'know, make me look stupid in front of …"

"Really, you're soft on Akira Pixels?" Argana laughed. She now had the phone clamped between her chin and her shoulder while she attempted to get a petrol nozzle into the plastic container. When she squeezed the handle it just clicked, dispensing no fuel.

"Leave it alone," Yasmin was complaining on the phone. The station attendant was complaining too, waving at Argana through the window and mouthing something that she couldn't make out.

"Bye!" said Argana, concluding that she didn't have enough hands for all her tasks and wanting to end at least one of them. Max was making circles around her feet trying to work out how he could help. In this instance, he couldn't.

"Wait!"

"What?" asked Argana, breaking the habit of a lifetime by not hanging up before the end of the conversation.

"The infection has reached my primary computer. It's saying something. Hold the phone by the speakers."

"10,742," said an Irish voice, clipped and modulated. "10,741. 10,740…"

"That's a *countdown*," said Argana, and this time she did hang up.

She looked at the station attendant and pointed at the empty container.

"It's not working!" she yelled.

The attendant, rolling their eyes, pointed at the red sign on the wall next to them. Please turn your phone off, it said.

* * *

The Micra was waiting for her where she had left it, and Argana decanted the petrol into its tank. It was not a lot, but it would be enough for a round trip to Brink Hall and the scouts, maybe even all the way back to the Co-op for a top-up after.

Once at Brink Hall, unable to call ahead, and thoroughly unconvinced that the gate intercom would work, Argana parked up on the road and walked on into the driveway. Max padded at her side. The main gates were stoically shut, but the foot-gate to the side was unlocked, so they entered that way. There had been changes since she had last been there; a few more flash cars in the driveway, a few less rusty campervans. Scaffolding covered one wing of the house where new windows were going in. The vast oaks and beeches that had been lush in the summer were skeletal now, pointing twisted branches at an empty sky.

The stone lion in the doorway was still there, copper buzzer its mouth, although someone had seen fit to gaffer tape a police helmet to its head. Argana pressed the buzzer and waited. On closer inspection the helmet was, to her relief, a fake.

It was not Akira Pixels, however, who opened the door. Instead, a grey-haired woman in the final years of middle age flung it open and stared up at her, her pointy nose and thin limbs giving her the appearance of quizzical bird.

"Hello, love," she said. "You don't look my son's type, have you got the right house?"

"Hi, you must be …" Argana flailed around her mind for something useful without finding it, "Mrs Pixels?"

The supposed Mrs Pixels let out a hearty cackle that was not altogether friendly. All the same, her crow's feet crinkled a little, and she ushered Argana in. The mansion was toasty, giving Argana some cause to regret the heavy layers she had donned against the winter.

"Oh, son of mine!" the woman hollered into the depths of the mansion. "There's someone to see you, a girl with big stupid hair.

Doesn't look rich enough or weird enough to be one of your usual lot."

"It's genetics," objected Argana, putting her hand uncertainly to her head. "I have to use a lot of product…"

"Oh, no offence, dear."

"None taken," said Argana chirpily before snarkily adding, "*beaky.*"

The old woman cackled again.

At the end of the long hall, with its wood panelling and original Victorian tiled floor, a door opened and a thirty-something man appeared. He wore red trousers and a designer variant on checks, which was a waste of good checks if you asked Argana. Akira Pixels, a little shorter than he looked on his YouTube channel, but no less flamboyant. A boyish face, designer beard, artificial blue-black hair.

"Angela!" he said, thrusting his hand out.

Argana shook it. "*Argana,*" she stressed.

"Of course, of course, us unusual name types should stick together," Akira said, mock-seriously, and put and arm around her shoulder to guide her into the next room.

"Weird names?" blurted his mother. "When I had you christened you were called Anthony!"

"Not now, Mum!"

She shrugged and headed off in the direction of the kitchen, and possibly the gin cabinet. Argana watched her go, wondering what she herself would be like at that age.

The next room that Akira drew them into was the extravagant hall that Argana had seen on her previous visit, moose head and Edwardian fittings and all. It was in better condition, no longer filled with confused nerds on stepladders or piles of tools. It was supposedly finished, although Akira's taste in repainting the elaborate corbels in neon was open to question.

"Anything weird happen today?" Argana asked him.

"I woke up without a hangover, which was honestly surprising! I got my hundred thousandth subscriber, too. We're planning a series on moles; we're gonna mark out a giant roulette table on the croquet lawn. If the little buggers come up in a square you've bet on, you get the takings. Neat, eh?"

"That wasn't the kind of weird I was thinking of."

Akira put his hands on his hips. "Well I'm sooorrrrrryyyy. Look, if you're going to be a killjoy, you can make like rain and go away, come back again another day."

"Anything from Yasmin. Yasmin Nuri? The geeky girl who never finishes her sen—"

"I know her," interrupted Akira, smiling. "She comes to the monthly tech meetings."

That stopped Argana in her tracks. It was hard to imagine Yasmin in social settings.

"Oh yes," Akira was saying, "she's very talented. Remarkably quick on the uptake with new ideas. She emailed me a blueprint this morning, for me to make on the 3D printer. I set it running; I haven't taken a gleg yet to see if it's finished."

"Can I see it?"

"Sure. Come up and see what's on the slab."

He led the way to his office up on the next floor.

* * *

Akira's study was magnificent, or had once been so, before the wood panelling had gotten the avant-garde paint job. The stone framed windows still commanded an impressive view over a back garden elaborate enough that it was no doubt properly referred to as 'the grounds'. Inside, monitors covered antique mahogany desks, a proliferation of technology born not out of obsession, as Yasmin's was, but out of efficiency. There were dashboards ticking up views, comments and memberships on his various channels.

As for the 3D printer, that was a bright orange affair that looked like the surprise offspring of a forklift truck and a lava lamp. "Let's see what we've got," said Akira, opening the load-doors at the front.

Argana nodded, although she was not watching. She was still staring out of the window, taking in the winter trees, the ha-ha, the uneven croquet lawn. Akira was right – there were a *lot* of moles.

"Well, this is a surprise." intoned Akira, in such a monotonal voice that she supposed that he must be telling the truth.

She peered past him to see what was going on. The hatch to the printing bay was open but he had not gone so far as to move what was lying there. She could see why, too. It was unmistakeably a gun.

"What does Yaz want with a gun?" asked Akira, astonished.

"Yaz?" Nobody Argana knew called Yasmin that. "Yaz doesn't. I keep trying to tell you, she got hacked. The hacker's getting you to make weapons, presumably because Yasmin's printer is offline."

"This model's got a larger bed than hers."

Akira gathered his courage and gingerly took the gun out of the machine. It was a sort of waxy colour, with an obvious seam down one side. With decorative emblems, two barrels and an oversized sight, it didn't look purely functional. He snapped open the stock and poked a little at the trigger mechanism.

"It's the real deal," he said. "When I bought this place it came with a whole raft of shotguns in one of the barns; we spent a while shooting paint tins with them."

He scratched a little at his designer beard. "What kind of hacker wants me to print a gun?"

She hesitated for an instant, aware of how this was going to sound, but she couldn't stop herself. "I think you got hacked by an undead scientist the Hadron Collider unleashed from another dimension."

It was minutes before Akira stopped laughing at her.

"Argana, you're a card. Remind me to invite you to one of my parties."

* * *

Twenty minutes later, Argana Zeit was at the East Street police station. She went in, carrying the handgun in a brown paper bag. The station had that small-town station feel, a single-storey building that had gone up in the 70s. It was all red-brick and concrete, with iron grids artlessly bolted over the windows. The interior was no less dated, and she found the reception unattended.

"Hello?" she called, hammering a buzzer.

A policewoman appeared, about a decade older than Argana with a slight frame, Mediterranean eyes and an instantly wearied expression. Sergeant Luciana Cianciolo.

"Ah, Miss Zeit. With the greatest reluctance, what have you got for us today?"

Argana smiled artificially and bumped the paper bag containing the gun onto the counter.

"I found this," she said. "Do you want me to sign anything?"

Cianciolo opened the bag with a pencil and peeked in. Her face stiffened.

"Found it where?"

"Not actually found, more, a friend gave it to me after they were conned into printing it out."

"Your friend could be in a lot of trouble. Tell them not to skip town, OK? I'll get on with a firearms unit from Manchester, see what they can tell us."

"Thank, Luce. Listen, I got things to do, I'm outta here—"

"Hold, on! Constable Berkshire has your number, right?"

"Yes, of course," said Argana breezily, before remembering the burner phone, "which is to say er, no, my phone's out for the count. I'm using this thing."

She read out the number to the Sergeant, who was looking askance at the device.

"Well, there's nothing at all dodgy about that, is there?" said Cianciolo sarcastically.

"Nothing at all." Argana skipped out of the police station.

* * *

On the way to her car, Argana's phone rang. It was, of course, Yasmin, the only person whose number was in the contact list.

"Hey, *Yaz*," she said.

"What?" said Yasmin, slightly too fast. "Did you, er, did you see Akira?"

"Yeah, it's worse than we thought."

"Darwin's beard! His computer's infected, isn't it? He'll never talk to me again!"

"No, he got emailed a blueprint. For his 3D printer. For a gun, Yasmin. For a *gun*."

Argana opened the rear door and Max jumped in the car.

"He didn't … did he?" Yasmin sounded aghast.

"Oh, for sure. I've taken it down the police station, I'm waiting on a callback from them after the firearms team take a look."

"Oh. Does he blame me?"

"*Blame* you? Yasmin, Akira sees everything in life as an adventure. He's too rich and too naive to imagine that printing a gun can get him into any further trouble."

"A gun, though. Argie. Why a gun?"

"Well, I thought Hal was picking up signals from the ghost of Marianne Torus. Now I'm not so sure; now I think it's the ghost of a criminal pretending to be Dr Torus." As she talked, Argana tugged the papers from Dr Harp out of her bag and onto her lap. "Maybe someone in this suicide pact. But anyone who makes a gun expects someone to use it, right? Who were they sending it to? It doesn't make sense."

"Well, you keep on with your weird theories. My scans are halfway, and that bloody countdown won't stop…"

"Have you tried turning it off and on again?" asked Argana, as she inserted her keys into the ignition.

"Dear heavens, Argie, do you think I'm an amateur? It's the first thing I tried, but it's in the firmware!

* * *

Last on Yasmin's list of people the virus had contacted was the local scout group, not any specific individual, but instead their info@ email address.

The scout hut was a half-brick, half-timber building on the edge of the recreation ground, down near the river. It had a little gravel car park of its own, but Argana avoided it, as she always stalled the car trying to start up on such granular surfaces.

She knocked on the barnlike door. It was exactly as she remembered it from her childhood before she had been thrown out of Brownies for insubordination. Or, as she preferred to think of it, for being too adventurous. Miss Troublestone had run the outfit back then, and Argana hoped that she no longer did. Some history was better left unstirred.

So, she was relieved when it was a woman about her own age who came to the door, tanned even in winter, with short practical hair and kind eyes.

"I'm looking for the Scout leader," said Argana. "My name's Argana."

The woman opened the door just a crack, the sound of children's voices behind her, chanting.

"That's me, Tricia Notts. But I'm kinda busy right now."

Argana craned her head to try and look into the space. Whatever the children were chanting, it was not in English, and she had the feeling they were not working on their Spanish badge either. The only child she could see was about seven, gripping a black candle earnestly in his hands.

"What, er, exactly are they doing?" she asked.

"They're practicing for their occult badge … now if you're not a parent, I'm going to have to ask you to leave. Right now." Tricia's threatening tone was only slightly undermined the chirpiness with which she peeped over her shoulder. "You're doing fine, children, keep going!"

Argana, who didn't like the situation at all, tried to push past the scout leader. Tricia was shorter but faster and blocked her. When she reached for the door, she found her wrist caught and turned in a powerful grip. Tricia had her in an armlock. Max growled, baring his teeth, ready to get stuck in, but Argana shook her head and he backed off, whining.

"Emma!" Tricia called out, "You know how to ring the police, don't you? Go ahead, love."

From her adjusted vantage point – mostly doubled over – Argana had a better view inside the scout hut. Seven children, a mix of boys and girls of primary school age, stood at the points of a heptagram drawn in salt, clutching candles and trying to avert their impressionable gazes from what appeared to be a human skull in the centre of the rite.

The eldest girl, who she took to be Emma, was wavering between continuing the chant and going to find a phone.

"Wait!" screamed Argana, reaching across her body with her free arm. "I'm a guest speaker!"

She flipped out her ID in support of her hasty lie.

Without letting go of Argana's wrist, the scout leader took the ID and read it out loud.

"Argana Zeit. Parapsychology Diploma. Astral University of Tibet. You needn't phone anyone, Emma."

"I'm sorry about that," she continued, releasing Argana and passing the wallet back. "You can't be too careful."

"I'm sure," said Argana, rubbing her aching wrist.

Tricia faced the cubs and clapped her hands. "That's enough, children! We've got a guest speaker, Miss Zeit. Come and pay attention!"

"Hello boys, hello girls!" said Argana, with much more bravado than she felt. Small children struck terror into her in a way that eldritch horrors never managed. "This is my assistant, Max. Say hello, Max!"

Max, who had no such qualms about infants, was immediately at home, wagging his tail and enjoying the hands crowding in to pat him.

"That's a very … it's very well-drawn, your circle. Er, well done," said Argana. Their heptagram and circle were, fortunately, amateurish, and the runes within them drawn badly. Close up, she was relieved to see that the skull was a plastic replica. Less reassuring was the smell, enough ozone to tell that the ritual had not been completely ineffective.

"So," she continued, desperately trying to think of a way out of the situation, "just before I start, have you all, er, got your parental waiver forms with you?"

"Our what, miss?" asked Emma.

"Parental waivers. For, er, astral travelling."

The children stared either blinkingly at her, or at her feet.

"Never mind, perhaps we can do it next week?" she said, brightly, and then to Tricia Notts, "I'm very disappointed with this set-up. Can I have a quick word with you?"

"Of course," said Tricia, a look of consternation on her face. "Brown Badger, you deal with the troop for a minute."

"Yes, Grey Eagle," said a teenage boy Argana had not noticed, who was watching from a chair in the corner. An assistant leader, judging from his greater age and more badge-encrusted uniform.

While Max stayed with his new fan club, Tricia went with Argana into a side room, a sort of vestigial office.

* * *

Certificate-covered walls looked down on a plain desk with a phone and an ancient beige computer. Beyond the desk, heavy bags of salt were stacked against the wall. There were boxes labelled as black candles, even a brace of dead birds hanging from a clothes hook.

Argana looked at the computer, and next to it a dot matrix printer and a couple of pieces of paper with red pen all over them.

"I think you may have misunderstood the instructions," she proposed. "This occult badge, it's not entirely normal, is it?"

Tricia looked uncertainly between her and the computer.

"The email is from headquarters," she insisted.

"I don't think so. Show me the email."

The scout leader turned the machine on, and Argana spent the time it took to boot up counting the artifacts, or their empty boxes. 666 kilos of road salt – presumably a cheap substitute for table salt – 17 black candles, 5 game birds, possibly pheasants, and one ersatz skull.

"See, it's here," said Tricia, having found the email. "The instructions say to mark this out with the salt before starting the performance. The word performance is in quotes, even."

Argana took control of the mouse and hovered it over the email sender's name. Purportedly 'Scout HQ' – this revealed the actual source as Yasmin's email address.

"You've been duped. This whole thing's a scam," she said bluntly.

"A practical joke, perhaps?" said Tricia. "But it must be an expensive one! I got the message this morning saying that they're introducing a witchcraft badge. I know it's a little odd, but some in our community are wiccans or neopagans, so maybe that's … I thought it was from HQ." She shook her head. "I don't know, but what I do know is that a pickup arrived this morning with bags of road salt, black candles and game birds. It said we should do a practice run."

"My friend Yasmin got hacked – her phone sent out a bunch of weird messages this morning. This was just one of them."

"Why would anyone want children to … hey, did you say Yasmin? As in Nuri Yasmin?"

"You know her?" asked Argana, surprised. She always thought of Yasmin as a well-kept secret, and it was becoming disconcerting that so many other people knew her.

"Of course. Miss Nuri comes down and helps out with the tech badges."

"The A.I that hacked Yasmin's – I mean Nuri's – account ordered all this stuff, sent you a fake mail to try and get you and your pack to act out a ritual."

"What am I going to do with all this?" Tricia gestured at the enormous pile of salt bags.

"Pray for a snowy winter and send all your little helpers out to grit driveways," said Argana. "In the meantime, give me that printout of the email, would you?"

When she left, it was only with reluctance that Max tore himself from the adoring children.

* * *

Argana was back outside, putting as much distance as possible between herself and any possibility of having to work with children, when her temporary phone rang. As the number was not in the single person contact list, she just had to chance it.

"Hello, Argana Zeit, Paranormal Investigator?" she answered in her most formal voice.

There was an only-just-stifled giggle on the other end, followed by, with exaggerated pomp, "Yes. This is Constable Frederick Bikram Berkshire of the Derbyshire Constabulary, Trotterwell south street station."

"Hi, Berk. What's up?"

Argana reached her car, readying her keys in her non-phone hand. Max, normally eager to hop in, was padding with exaggerated slowness from the scout hut.

"You love the attention don't you, you silly boy."

"What?" said the phone.

"Sorry, nothing."

"That gun you handed in – thanks, btw – I got a specialist to have a look via video link. He doesn't think it's a real weapon; it seems to be a cut and paste of two different designs. The exterior is from a toy, a knock-off of a weapon used in a sci-fi show. Your kind of thing, I'm sure. The interior is from a proof-of-concept 3D printed weapon that was circulating in the States."

Argana finally cajoled Max into the back of car and went around to the driver's door.

"So, it's still a gun, on the inside?" she said.

"Not exactly. Derek – that's the specialist – he said that it had been cut down to fit, not in a proper way, but like with a digital cookie cutter – and it looks like not all the parts are complete. Anyway, the base design is American and relies on you being able to nip out and buy ammo at your local grocery store. Which, you may not have noticed, is not a significant feature of life around here."

"It's a fake then – intended to look like someone 3D printed a gun?"

"That's my guess, Argana. I thought you'd want to know."

Argana belted up and put the phone on the passenger seat.

"I'm putting you on speaker phone. What show did he say the gun's from?

"I think Bandit Infinity, something like that."

"That's a game you duffer, not a TV show," retorted Argana, who only knew herself because she had seen Yasmin's copy that morning. She turned the ignition, the engine coming to life with all the finesse of an asthmatic tractor.

"Hey, Ms Zeit, while you're on the line, is it true that at New Year's you—"

"That's ridiculous!" she said, hitting the accelerator as she did so. The phone tumbled off the seat and into the back with Max, effectively ending the call.

A toy gun. This A.I was *trolling* them.

* * *

"You can't, y'know, stay away, can you?"

Argana was back at Yasmin's place, Max this time waiting in the car. Yasmin still had not changed out of her dressing gown, but there was something cooking in the kitchen, That Argana could hear boiling on the hob. There was another sound too, the Irish machine-voice counting. 341. 340. 339.

"Virus still going, then?" asked Argana.

"Come on in. Yep, tragically. I've spent all day sourcing some cleaners from my Russian contacts. The standard virus scanners are all based on white hat research, y'know, but sometimes you need to go to …" she shrugged.

"I want to talk to Hal again," said Argana. "I have a hunch I need to check out."

"Um … you can't."

"What, you think I'm not technically savvy enough?" Argana put her hands on her hips, elbows out.

"No! No, that's, er, Hal is on the stove," said Yasmin guiltily. "After I, y'know, the scanners couldn't … well, better safe than the other thing."

Argana peered into the saucepan, bubbling merrily away on the induction hob, empty apart from two litres of agitated water and a hard drive.

"Old school," she said, both approving and annoyed. "Gods, I hope you never had a Tamagotchi."

"Cup of tea?" said Yasmin playfully, crossing to a corner cupboard.

"Not from that!"

Yasmin broke out a couple of cans of energy drink and some chocolate biscuits. They sat down at the kitchen unit, where her cat Ramoth circled them like a house-shark waiting for crumbs.

"So, what's up? What did you find at the scouts?" asked Yasmin.

"Hal is not an A.I at all – he's something communicating from the other world, the one you linked the box to."

"I told you before, it's just a simulation. Everything's an unspeakable astral horror to you, isn't it?"

"Well, everything's a technical problem to you," objected Argana through a mouthful of biscuit.

"So far you've told me, y'know, Hal is the soul of a dead scientist, then you told me that he's a criminal trying to pass between worlds—"

"It wasn't either of those things," insisted Argana, who ploughed on before Yasmin could interrupt again and claim victory. "It was something else, pretending to be a criminal that was pretending to be a scientist."

"Ah, niche."

"You joke, but I've got to send this thing back to its own world."

Yasmin checked her watch. "Well, my system purge is still running, so while it's doing that, you can entertain me with your maverick whatsits. Theories."

Argana stood up and started pacing. "It was all hidden in plain sight. The gun at Akira Pixel's place – it never would have worked. It was a fake real gun, if you see what I mean, based on the one in Bandit Infinity. And Bandit Infinity is about—"

"A world-sliding bandit, I know. I've only been playing it for six days."

"Exactly. Hal's trolling us. They wanted to throw us off the scent, but couldn't resist laughing at us at the same time. Which is how I know who it is."

Argana shook a raft of papers out of her backpack. "Hal sent Jonah a raft of documents, right? And we thought they were about Dr Torus, but that was incidental."

She turned the printout over, the computer still counting down in the background. 115, 114, 113.

"Also in the obituaries were these suicides? Hal's one of those. It wasn't research, it was a vanity check. That's who we're really looking after. You know who makes suicide pacts?"

Yasmin shrugged. "Star-crossed lovers, if my GCSEs are to be believed."

"Cultists. That's who. Hal is one of those cultists; he must have killed himself in their world too. In fact, this is three days before the Hadron Collider accident, so I guess it *was* our world then. Either way, I dug around their local paper a bit, and there's not much to go on. The usual statement of surprise, about how they were quiet kids who kept to themselves, loners…"

"*Four* loners," said Yasmin, reading the printout. "Lazy journalism! I'm surprised there's not a whole bit on who they were metalhead roleplayers with their, y'know, emo music collections."

"There was. I thought I'd spare you that bit. Anyway, I couldn't separate them much. But I got to thinking, what did they want the scouts to summon? That level of Bandit Infinity you were playing, with all the tentacles, what was that all about?"

"That's easy. Heinrich uncovers a Nazi plot to summon a Silithosquatch, an emissary of the elder gods, a tentacled monstrosity that—"

"Have you got the d20 sourcebook for eldritch horrors? The one written by Jackson Moore, the game designer on Bandit Infinity?"

"It's just over here," said Yasmin excitedly. As far as Argana could tell she never actually played any of her tabletop RPGs, instead getting her pleasure by memorising them.

"Do remember though, this is fiction," insisted Yasmin, as she got the book down and opened it.

"It is fiction. But even fiction has roots, right?"

Yasmin had gone white, which was impressive given her starting point.

"What is it?"

"There's a dedication in the front. For my dear friend Terry Findern, gone too soon. Isn't that one of the names from that thing?"

"Well, hell's bells," said Argana, hastily scanning the paperwork she had from Dr Harp. "Terrence Findern was one of the suicides just after the Hadron Collider incident. Is there any more about him?"

"He's listed as one of the play testers." Yasmin flicked anxiously through the pages.

"See if there's something in there that matches the instructions sent to the scouts," instructed Argana. "They were asked to draw this symbol, see? In a circle, about twenty feet across. That warped pentagram, that's the elder sign – everyone knows that – but I don't recognise any of these others."

"It's this. It matches the summoning rules for a Silithosquatch."

Yasmin opened the glossy, full-colour manual to a page featuring a ton of minor statistics and an illustration. The tables included words like 'abomination', 'hungry' and 'transdimensional'. The image featured something halfway between a giant squid and a mammoth, with altogether more eyes than either.

18. 17. The countdown droned on, nearing its end point.

"I'm going to talk to Hal, to Terrence Findern, the ghost," insisted Argana.

"You can't, in case you'd forgotten," said Yasmin, pointing at the boiling pot.

"I've still got the number. How many minutes have these burners got?"

"They mostly come with a fiver on. You're seriously going to ring that scam number? You'll get a minute tops before you run out of credit!"

"I'd better be concise, then."

Beeeeeeeeeep!

They both jumped.

"Captain Nuri," purred Yasmin's pseudo-Irish computer, "scans complete. (1) malware removed."

Argana relaxed, sinking back into the sofa a little.

In the kitchen, something exploded. Water erupted from the saucepan, a violent geyser that drenched the ceiling and worksurface. It continued to bubble, boiling the hard drive. Both women looked at it in surprise.

* * *

"That's – not normal," said Argana.

"Nonsense, my cooking does that all the time."

Now slime and ichor were being vomited from the pan, which contained far more liquid than was physically possible. Yasmin ran from the flat, leaving Argana alone and staring. As she watched, a three-pronged claw emerged from the pan, as if the pan were a portal to another world. Which, right now, it almost certainly was.

The claw groped around, water continuing to froth over it and pooling on the kitchen floor. It took a chunk out of the worktop and a tentacle emerged behind it, green and mottled, with eyeballs where its suckers should be.

Argana, backing up, tripped over a stool, and tumbled gracelessly onto her rump.

Scared to get up, she pushed herself foot-over-foot into the corner as she dialled the scam number. It stopped ringing, but nobody answered it, not as such – there was just breathing, irregular and rattly, the sound deadened as if its owner was in an infinite space.

"Terry Findern?" asked Argana. The breathing caught slightly, but no words were uttered.

"This is Argana Zeit of, er, of Earth One. We are sorry that your death was so traumatic; you have become confused. You cannot summon a Silithosquatch – you invented it with your friend Jackson Moore. It doesn't exist; you can't make it exist."

The tentacle, which possibly begged to differ on the question of its existence, was turning this way and that, trying to get a fix on her. Pushing open a cupboard door, she crawled out of its line of sight.

The breathing became louder, taking on a snorting, angry quality.

"You tried your best, but you failed. The scouts don't have what it takes, no matter how prepared they may claim to be."

There was a shower of sparks as the electric hob shorted out under the onslaught of water, and the apartment was plunged into darkness. Only the pallid green light of her phone lit Argana's face.

"You've fallen into the gap between worlds, Terry. Just step to one side or the other, find the light and go into it. Or if you prefer the dark, go quietly."

"You don't..." croaked Terry, his voice haggard by lack of use. And, for that matter, lack of vocal cords. "You don't understand. It's here, it's coming for me. If I don't let it into your world ..." he trailed off into heavy sobbing.

"You need to move on," she insisted.

"It – It's here, I—" the voice abruptly became a scream before cutting off into wet gurgling and crunching. The sound of something slithering. That ethereal music, its not-quite harmonics latching onto Argana's mind, resonating uncomfortably in her psyche.

It was whispering to her. The whispers were overlapping waves of sound, incoherent and burbling. She screamed, and found she was unable to let go of her phone. The thing had a hold of her mind, and her mind had a hold of the phone.

"Help meeeee!" she screamed. The sound drew the attention of the monstrosity still working its way into the world through the saucepan. In the distance she registered another sound, the flat door opening, Yasmin returning.

Which is when the credit ran out.

The phone shut off abruptly. The monster retreated squealing from the world, leaving the saucepan boiled dry and the kitchen in chaos, fire belching from the underside of the cooker.

Argana stared at the phone, open-mouthed, fear dancing on her spine.

Yasmin carefully took the phone from her, holding it pinched between thumb and second finger as if it was unsavoury, and dropped it unceremoniously into the saucepan. Even she looked disturbed at the way the call had ended, but she kept it together long enough to find a fire extinguisher and blasted the fire out.

The two friends slumped together on the sofa in the next room.

"I'm out of shape," Yasmin puffed.

"You've never been in shape."

Argana's eyes adapted a little to the darkness. It was not as gloomy as she first thought; from the next room came the light of Yasmin's computers, which had their own backup power supplies. Ramoth the cat padded in past them and searching the floor hopefully.

"Poor Ramoth," cooed Yasmin, "that's not mummy's cooking this time. That mess is on aunty Argana!"

"Are you for real?" objected Argana. "I might well have just saved the whole of Trotterwell from being eaten by the elder gods!"

Yasmin broke into belly laughs.

"Poor, dear Argana. No, you got a virus on your phone and I fixed it for you. You're welcome."

The End

Argana Zeit Collects Snow Toads

"How can you even see where we're going?" Argana Zeit's teeth rattled so hard they garbled the question. It was not the cold making them do so, but the cantankerous progress of the SUV, fighting its way into the blizzard. Given enough snow the Peak District became nigh-on impassable, and this was more than enough. Farmer Turner said nothing, gritting his teeth and gripping the wheel tighter. Constable Berkshire in the seat next to him and rocked with the car's uneven motion, one hand grasping the ceiling handle.

"... the paramedics called it in," the policeman was saying. "They've taken the fatality away already, but I need to see the scene of the accident before it gets any more messed up."

Argana leaned forward to better make herself heard over the grumpy suspension.

"What's that got to do with me?" she yelled.

"Well, that's the thing, the paramedic said that—"

Bdduunnnk!

Something hit the windscreen, making Argana shriek. Turner put the brakes on very gently – doing anything else would risk a thrilling heart-to-heart with the ditch – and slowed his oversize pickup to a halt.

"What the hell was that?" demanded Argana.

"Snowball," said Turner. "Stupid kids."

"Hard to imagine what they'd be doing this far out of town," said Berkshire.

The road reached a flat point beneath a steep hill. They were in the countryside three miles north of Trotterwell, investigating an accident near Yellow Rose Cottage. A blizzard covered everything, the sky a grey-yellow colour that promised more of the same.

Argana pulled her fur-lined hood up to her ears, obscuring everything except her broad cheekbones and green eyes, and opened the door.

"Ladies first," said Berkshire.

"Are you kidding? A yeti could be out there, for all I know!"

But she jumped out anyway, accompanied by her dog Max, who had been in the footwell. Berkshire got out his side and came around.

There was a single house in sight, a stone-built cottage in the field below the road; a shingle drive, and a paddock behind it. Diagonally across the drive entrance was a Subaru Forester. Even through the swirling snow it was obvious something was terribly wrong with it. The bonnet was bent up and the grill had been staved in. A side window was shattered where something the size of a fist had punched through.

"I'll stay here, if it's all the same to you two," ventured the farmer, bravely.

Berkshire nodded at him.

"Thanks for the lift. We won't be ten minutes."

After the call had come in, it had been all too obvious the squad car wouldn't make it this far out. Which is when Turner had volunteered his four-wheel drive vehicle. Argana and her uniformed friend crossed the road, the fast-falling snow crunching beneath their feet.

"This is where Bernard Keeper died, Ms Zeit. You don't need to see it," said Berkshire, reaching the car first.

"What, you think I'm some wallflower, I—" Argana stopped abruptly. Everything underfoot had so far been either icy or made the satisfying crunch-crunch of deep, fresh fallen snow. But her boot met something new, something that made a sound like a haunted whoopy cushion when she trod on it.

There was a toad glaring up at her, entirely white except for eyes like red gems. It shook itself back into shape and hopped over her other boot. Now that she had her eye in, she saw that there were more of them, two under the crashed car, three more hopping away toward the drift-encumbered hedge. A dozen more were already escaping into the snow.

"These toads, are they why you brought me out here?" she asked.

Berkshire, however, didn't answer, being preoccupied with the car's interior.

"Hey! Duffer!" she yelled, scooping some of the softer snow from the ground and moulding it between her mittens.

"Yes?"

As he popped his head above the doorframe, she let him have it. The snowball impacted softly with his forehead, just below his domed helmet.

"Someone died here Argana, have some respect," he said grumpily.

Argana made a grab for one of the toads, but it was too fast for her.

"What, you thought we'd bring you along for an RTA? Yeah, it was the frogs you were called out for. They're weird, eh?"

"Yes. Not least because they're *actually* toads."

Berkshire came around to the front of the wreck. The grill was concave, the wheels folded in toward each other. It had run into an obstacle fast and stopped hard. Implausibly, the snowball that it had run into was still there, a meter across like the lower half of a snowman, a lump of snow and ice.

He crouched next to it, pressed two leather gloved fingers into its icy surface.

"Pretty strange that it didn't get destroyed," he said.

"You think he didn't see it? White object in a white blizzard…"

"I think it rolled into him," said Berkshire, pointing over to the far roadside, at the bottom of the slope. "See there, these indentations, you subtract a couple of hours of snow … that was its path down. Someone rolled it down from the hillside, timed it perfectly."

"That's murder," said Argana, with an equal mix of excitement and horror. She had never been called out on a murder before.

"Or a prank gone wrong, which is manslaughter at most."

"I can't see any more toads," she said sadly.

"Never mind those, you can deal with them in a minute. He must have been turning into his own drive when the accident happened. The back end of the car is still in the road; I don't want anyone to run into it."

"Who the hell's going to? Nobody is going out in this weather!"

"There's always some idiot thinks a heavy snow is the best time to push their 4x4 to the limit. We'll get Turner to tow the car, we'll need to shift this boulder – this snowman, whatever – first."

"I've got a quicker method!"

Argana took a short run up and jumped feet first into the snowball, a sure-fire method of disintegrating the things learnt from a childhood spent irritating her elder brother. Her Wellingtons left prints alright, but rather than neatly crashing the snowball in half her ankles twanged and she skidded onto her rump. Max bounded over and snuffled at her.

"Are you – heh – are you, I say, are you OK?" asked Berkshire. Argana hoped his tears of laughter would freeze on his stupid rectangular face.

She got up and dusted herself down.

"It's solid," she said.

"You don't say! It took out a car! Help me roll the damn thing down into the ditch."

Berkshire braced his broad shoulders against the iceball and Argana leaned into it mittens first, and between the two of them they got it moving. It groaned as it went, crushing the fresh snow under as it accelerated suddenly into the ditch below the road. There was ice at the bottom, which it smashed, throwing up a gout of almost-frozen-dirt-and-mud with an accompanying stagnant stench.

Berkshire waved at the farmer. "Get over here, Turner. Need a hand towing this wreck!"

In the five minutes that it took Turner to meticulously turn his truck around and get it close enough to the car for Berkshire to hook a line up, Argana went back to searching for toads.

She followed the path of the snowball down into the brackish ditch. Dead reeds hid beneath the snow, making her unsure of her footing. Where her feet crunched through, they made dark portals into the rotting vegetation below, and an albino toad sprinted into one of them. She lurched for it, but her feet skidded out from under her, leaving her face down in the snow.

"Cut it out, wouldya, Zeit! We're busy, don't you know?" Berkshire was yelling somewhere above her.

"What?" she called back, poking her head back above the ditch, thankful that she hadn't slid quite all the way into the stream. Turner had the pickup backed up and Berkshire was clipping the tow cable up to the front of the other car.

He looked startled at her.

"What are you doing down there? I thought you were up on the hillside. I thought you threw another snowball at me!" he said, with a mixture of irritation and confusion.

"As if I—"

A projectile whistled out of the blizzard on the hill above them, a snowball so dense that it hit like a cannonball when it missed Berkshire and careened off the car bonnet.

Berkshire instinctively ducked. All the same, the next snowball hit him in the head and knocked him to the ground.

Argana grabbed it as it rolled toward her. Still in one piece, hard as ice. Harder, maybe. She stuffed it into one of her oversized pockets.

"I don't like it!" Turner was yelling as she pulled Berkshire to his feet. Blood ran from his face where his angular cheekbones had taken the brunt of the impact. He mumbled and gestured at the tow cable, still dangling on the ground.

Argana went around the back and undid the line, chucking it over the rear hatch into the cargo area. Another one of the snowballs narrowly missed her, crashing into the pickup and leaving a dent with a ringing sound.

"Get in! I'm out of here," shouted Farmer Turner.

"I'm not leaving the crime scene!"

There was the sound of glass shattering. The passenger window of the pickup truck was gone, and the farmer panicked. Foot to the floor, all four wheels spinning, the pickup went sideways for a moment, then took off down the road toward the town, leaving Argana and Berkshire behind on the roadside.

"We're in the open!" yelled Berkshire, grabbing her wrist and dragging her behind the stricken Subaru. Its hull boomed with another impact. They were still under attack.

"I'll stay with the crime scene," mimicked Argana. "Fine plan, Berk."

***

They crouched behind Mr Keeper's broken car, the dog huddled between them.

"That's torn it," said Berkshire. "I thought Farmer Turner was made of sterner stuff. His family have been in these valleys for generations!"

"Don't you think that Farmer Turner is an odd name?" mused Argana. "I mean, you don't meet someone and call them Shopkeeper Harris, or Plumber Miles. It's not like it's a title. Why don't we just call him Mr Turner?"

"Hi, I'm Constable Berkshire," said Berkshire, holding out a hand for a mocking handshake.

The moment, like the windscreen, was shattered by the next snowball from above. Tiny cubes of safety glass covered them.

"They're moving along the ridge, getting a better angle," said Berkshire, pointing, all humour gone from his voice. "Whoever's up there, they're mighty pissed off."

"You think?" said Argana. "We can't stay here. Got any bright ideas?"

She considered the ditch, but it was too shallow to protect them properly from the high angle of attack, and the hedge behind it was threadbare in winter. The projectiles would pass right through it.

"Ideas, no," said Berkshire with a secretive smile on his face as he jangled something from his pocket. "Keys, yes." He opened his hand, revealing a car key, and two more for yale locks and one for a mortice. "They were still in the ignition; I figured better to take them than leave them to be stolen. One of these must be the front door, we can – hey—"

Argana was already sprinting down the front drive, frosty gravel crunching furiously underfoot, Max loping ahead of her.

"Wait for me!" yelled Berkshire, scrambling clumsily out of the ditch.

***

She ran toward the cottage, the safety of its grey-yellow stone walls. It was low and old, with a misshapen roof and red-tinged ivy climbing at either end. There was no proper porch, but a central door of braced and painted oak was flanked with stone buttresses that held an extended lintel against the weather.

Unable to open the door, she pressed herself against the edge of the stones. Max crouched behind a faux wheelbarrow, one of a pair that lined the entrance sporting hibernating rose bushes. Two snowballs came out of the swirling sky at speed, one crashing into the door hard enough to flake paint, the other exploding against the stonework by her head. Fragments of ice blasted into her hair.

A toad croaked at her from by her feet, apparently dazed, milk-white with red eyes.

"Hello little fella," she said, but when she reached for it, it hopped away, and she didn't dare leave the security of the buttress.

Berkshire arrived, leaning into the other side of the shelter. He sifted the keys frantically until he found one that opened the door. Argana barged it open and they threw themselves inside. Heaving it shut again just as quickly, Berkshire locked it and for a moment the two friends leant against it, slumped and breathing heavily.

Being an old cottage, the front door opened straight into a quarry-tiled kitchen with oak table, rustic cupboards and a monumental, heart-of-the-house fireplace. There was a narrow staircase and a doorway to the sitting room.

"I want to see what's in one of these things." Argana pulled the snowball she had picked up earlier from her pocket. The outer layer has scuffed or thawed away, but what was left was an iceball the size of a coconut, and just as hard. She placed it centrally on the oak table.

"Pass me a cleaver," she said.

"I'm not your aide-du-chef," complained Berkshire, but he pulled open a draw and passed her the implement anyway.

"Hold on," he added, "I'll get you something to chop on…"

But while he was looking for a board, she belted the iceball as hard as she could, splitting it in half. The cleaver stuck in the table, quivering.

"Daaaamn," said Berkshire. He wasn't talking about the oak.

The two halves of the snowball rolled apart, each hollow, each studded with dense crystals. A toad tumbled out of it, shaking out its sticky limbs and blinking. After struggling the right way up, it took an almighty hop toward the table edge.

"Oh no you don't!"

Argana grabbed a glass jar, upended it to shake out the cashews it contained and slammed it down over the amphibian.

"Got you, you little vermin!"

Berkshire looked at the spilled nuts, the split table, the fragments of ice.

"You certainly gave this place the Argana Zeit treatment," he said, deadpan.

"Never mind that. Look that this! A snowball geode! That's amazing, right, and with a toad in it…"

"Now you've caught the thing, let's sit it out until Turner comes back," said Berkshire, going to the window and checking for any sign that their unseen assailants had followed them down from the hills. "I got all the photos I need of the, er, accident. We can fall back to Trotterwell and figure it out."

Argana put the top on the toad jar and tucked it into her satchel. "Forget that! I'll have a look around," she said.

"We don't have a warrant," he objected.

"I think that ship has sailed. You're the one who let us in here!" said Argana as she started speculatively opening cupboards.

There was plenty of fresh veg, strings of onions, much of it in the slightly warped shapes expected of market rather than shop bought goods. Mr Keeper owned a pestle and mortar set, a substantial one. Moving on, the refrigerator revealed decent cuts of meat and at least eight pints of milk. Tins and cartons were all branded.

"Mr Keeper certainly liked his grub," she said.

"I'm not seeing anything out there," said Berkshire, still at the window. "I think we're in the clear. What do you mean? It's not like he was overweight."

"No, I mean this kitchen – it's well-stocked."

She checked the bins. A scraps bin, presumably for compost. They hadn't seen the garden clearly, most of it being around the side and hidden by snow anyway. A general bin too, and a recycling bin. Over half its content was semi-translucent four-pint containers, crushed down with their lids on to take up less space.

Max checked the bins too, although his motives were more gastronomic.

"He got through a *lot* of milk," Argana said.

Berkshire was laughing, causing her to turn around abruptly.

"All that poking around in food, and you missed *this*?" he said.

In one of the small, low windows was a rig of twigs and cotton, a saucer, a candle, all tied together in a spiderweb pattern. Argana blushed at being mocked. She wanted to be angry, to blame him for blocking her line of sight, but the truth was she'd simply missed it.

"It's a dream catcher," she said, "or an offering, or …"

"Well, that's your department," said Berkshire. "I'm going to check upstairs, see if I can find a desk or something. There might be financial records, blackmail letters, incriminating documents. We get a lot of those kinds investigating murder victims."

"You've decided it *is* murder, then?"

"Of course," said Berkshire over his shoulder, his boots disappearing up the staircase that creaked with every step. "What else do you call it when someone crashes a car with a giant snowball?"

She gave up on the kitchen and moved through to the sitting room, the only other room on the ground floor apart from the lean-to bathroom at the back. A single armchair was pressed up against a small TV set in the corner, a high coffee table next to it supporting a couple of books and a sidelamp. But that was by far the least interesting aspect of the room. Every inch of the wall was covered in maps, certificates, framed photos and small, erratically placed shelves bearing corroded scraps of metal.

"This is more like it!"

"What have you found?" called down Berkshire from the floor above. The exposed beams meant he was easily heard, only the floorboards themselves separating them.

"I've no idea!"

"Then look harder! You are meant to be an investigator!"

"A *paranormal* investigator! The only spooky sounds in this place are your oversize boots."

Still, the room was inciting her curiosity nicely. The twisted lumps of metal on the shelves proved, on closer inspection, to be corroded iron and brass objects. Buckles, broaches, combs, tool handles. Even, in pride of place, a sword hilt with a stub of rusty blade sticking out. They had the look of provincial museum exhibits, each one tagged with a handwritten note.

"Button, 8th century, field north of Youlgreave," she read aloud.

"What?" called Berkshire who, from the scuffling noises in the room above, had found a chest of drawers to rifle through.

"It's all stuff from a dig, or multiple digs!"

Moving on to the photographs, she found that several of them were of groups of metal detectorists, often standing with their detectors in one hand and their newfound loot in the other. The certificates matched this story, some being formal permission slips to explore particular fields or woods, others prizes from contests or attainments of qualifications. One was a membership note from something called *The League of Collectors*. There were newspaper cuttings too, stories of gold nuggets and treasure hoards found, although none of the names in the headlines were Mr Keeper.

Berkshire's heavy footsteps moved across the ceiling and down the stairs, and he reappeared, a raft of papers tucked under one arm.

He looked around. "Busy fella, wasn't he? He's got piles of Union Jacks upstairs and down here. What is this stuff?" he said.

"Yes, busy. Here, look at this." Argana tugged a newspaper cutting off the wall, catapulting a drawing pin to the carpet. "I've found one which is actually about him, for a change."

"Charges dropped against local treasure hunter," read Berkshire. "Bring it with us. I'll get onto the computers and see if I can drag up some details; it could be important."

"Well done, Argana," said Argana, in a sing-song voice.

"Yes. Well done, Argana," he grumbled.

Max was barking from the kitchen. Not an alert bark, but a look-at-this bark, so they both went through. He had pushed one of the bins over and was nosing through it.

"Greedy hound," laughed Berkshire.

"I don't think so; that's vegetable scraps."

Those scraps were on the verge of rotting. There were bits of paper and cardboard too. Max was nosing large, rare-looking leaves, a little like carrot tops but bigger. They crumbled between Argana's fingers and had a complex smell that reminded her of apples and vanilla.

"These are mandrake leaves," she said. "I wonder what Mr Keeper used the roots for? They're poisonous to humans."

"There's a receipt too," said Berkshire, leaning past her. "Looks like groceries."

She took it from him. It was in the purple, mechanically stamped ink of an old-fashioned till, with a rubber-stamped logo at the top. *Lovegreen's Greens*, read the logo, causing her to smile.

"Hah! Whataya know, he shopped at my uncle's place!" Her uncle, Vincent Lovegreen, ran Trotterwell's most respected independent greengrocers.

A crunching from the gravel drive, along with the sturdy note of a diesel engine, interrupted them. Outside there was a break in the clouds, the sun shining down onto Farmer Turner's returned pickup truck. A white-clad calm had replaced the chaos of the blizzard.

The farmer wound his window down.

"You two in there?" he called out. "Come on 'en, I'll give you a ride!"

He didn't have to ask twice.

* * *

One hair-raising journey later, the farmer dropped them both back at Trotterwell's East Street station, one of the smallest police stations in Derbyshire.

They reconvened in a cramped room at the back, breeze block walls lined with metal shelves and lit harshly with a single light. There was a fold-out catering table to work at; Argana sat one side and Berkshire the other. His superior officer, Sergeant Luciana Cianciolo, stood behind him, poking at his scalp with a pad of cotton that reeked of TCP.

"So, what do we know?" asked Berkshire, holding back a wince.

"Oh, don't be such a wuss," snapped Cianciolo, "and you, hitching along for the ride," she said to Argana, "did you get any of your frogs?"

"*Toads*. Sure." Argana undid her go-everywhere backpack and turfed out the glass jar from the cottage. It was empty of toad, instead containing only a slushy liquid.

"Um. He's melted."

Cianciolo rolled her well-decorated eyes.

"Well, Bernard Keeper is still dead. The paramedics took the body away before we got there, but I have photos of the scene of the crime," said Berkshire.

"A crime? This weather's terrible, Fred – there's no need to blame an accident on any more than that. It's still a tragedy," said Cianciolo. She threw away the cotton swab and closed the first aid kit.

"No, someone rolled a snowball down the hill, like a flipping boulder, took out his car. Mr Keeper wasn't seatbelted; he headbutted the dashboard and split his noggin."

"That's quite the accusation."

Berkshire cast his phone pictures to the monitor and clicked through them. The caved-in grill, the boulder-sized snowball, the path from the hill, the blood on the dashboard. The Sergeant leant palms-first on the table for a better look, nodding.

"And I need you to see this," said Argana, showing her own photo of the cracked open snowball, with its hollow and crystals.

"What that?" asked Cianciolo.

"There's a common folklore that geodes – that's the round stones with amethysts and the like on the inside—"

"I know, they sell them in tourist spots all over the county."

"Sure. There's a common story that these hollow rocks are often found with frogs or toads inside. The dissipation of gas preserved them while the rock forms around them—"

"Plainly ridiculous," said Berkshire.

"It is, Berkshire – that's why it's more likely to be magic. Regardless, someone threw a geode made of snow and ice at you today and there was an albino amphibian inside. And judging from the number of toads that were on the ground, you weren't the only victim. If that isn't paranormal, I don't know what is!"

Cianciolo clicked back through to the picture of the car, the holes punched in its windscreen and side windows.

"These holes," she said carefully, "they *could* have been made by snowballs. If they were dense enough. But who the hell can throw a snowball hard enough to take out a car window though?"

"Really angry children," said Berkshire, "but as I told the farmer, hard to imagine them being that far out. We need to find out if Mr Keeper had any enemies – or … I don't know, these amphibians mean something."

"We need a plan," said the Sergeant, straightening up, "or at least, you two do. I'm washing my hands of this."

"They took the body up to the hospital for a postmortem," said Berkshire. "I'll take the squad car out that way in the morning and see what they've got. You look into these frogs, Argana."

"Toads," Argana stressed. "I've got a few leads. I can follow up this receipt with my uncle, but first there's a geologist I know out Dronfield way. Maybe she can shed some light on the geodes."

* * *

The next morning the roads to Dronfield were snow-and-ice encrusted, but not as bad as the ones out to the cottage had been. The naked tree limbs above the hedge rows were capped in white and would have been stunningly pretty had Argana not had to divert all her attention to the act of driving. Successive cars had worn a pair of tracks down through the ice to the tarmac and, as long as she stayed within those, she was fine. Fortunately, the closer she got to the town and its neighbouring city, the better the roads became.

Max, normally oblivious to the perils of her driving, kept his head low and his eyebrows high.

"Here's the deal, boy," she said to him. "Mrs Gurtwidge used to do the occasional guest spot at my school, in geography. I was a bit of a pain, so with luck she doesn't remember me, but my old teacher used to talk highly of her."

Mrs Gurtwidge lived in a detached 70s style chalet house in its own garden. Her gates were sided with lumps of gritstone, and boulders decorated the edges of the drive. In fact, as far as could be seen under the snow, her entire garden was one big rockery.

Argana took Max with her, the dog sporting a natty green jacket that her gran had knitted for him, and rang the doorbell. A substantial man in his 50s, with a tweed blazer and a welcoming expression, opened the door.

"Hello?" he said in a gentle voice, "Argana, is it? You'd better come in, love."

There was a small lobby that served as an airlock against the cold, and he ushered her in, where she stomped the snow from her boots and Max shook his coat out.

"Thanks. You'd be Mr Gurtwidge?" Argana balanced precariously trying to remove one Wellington, gave up and offered the heel to Max in the hope that he might grip it. The dog looked at her incredulously.

"That's me. And don't worry about your boots, the house is paved all through the ground floor," said Mr Gurtwidge.

"Helen, love, it's that Argana girl come to see you," he called through the house. "I'll be putting the kettle on."

He was not kidding about the paving. The entire downstairs was floored in a mosaic of different stones; travertine, slate, verdite, a myriad of shades and surfaces. Max's claws clicked against them, making a subtly different sound on each variety. The rest of the décor would have been unremarkable, being in the 70s style of the Gurtwidges' formative years, were it not for the fact that every shelf and display unit was covered in stones of all sizes, shapes and colours. Many of them, Argana was pleased to notice, were polished geodes, cut in half with their interior crystals gleaming.

"Hello love," said Mrs Gurtwidge from a semi-minimalist armchair with wooden sides. "Excuse me if I don't get up, my knees aren't what they were. Do pull up a pew, Dunc will be back through with some tea in a minute. I trust you'd like a cuppa."

She was as small as her husband was large, with closely set brown eyes and dark curly hair going grey at the temples. Argana sat herself on the leather sofa opposite while Max, assessing their host as dog-friendly, went to avail himself of a good patting. Mrs Gurtwidge obliged him thoroughly, cooing a "Who's a good boy then?" for good measure.

"I'm helping Trotterwell's finest with their investigations of an accident that happened to a Mr Keeper," said Argana, flipping open a notebook from her satchel.

A look of sadness crossed Mrs Gurtwidge's face. "Ah, poor Bernard. It was a terrible thing."

"You knew him?" asked a surprised Argana.

"Oh, we knew him. We're holding a funeral, did you know; he didn't have much family to speak of, just a sister, but they were estranged. We'll have to wait for the coroner to release his body, of course, but before then there'll be a wake on Friday. You can come if you like, but be respectful."

As if I'd be anything else, though Argana grumpily. But she didn't say so, aware that she had a certain undeserved reputation.

"That's you and Mr Gurtwidge, is it? Throwing the wake?"

"Certainly not," said Mr Gurtwidge forcefully, entering the room with a tray of three mugs and an occupied tea cosy. "That's The League of Collectors – it'll be at The Miner's Arms, Buxton. Near the pavilion if you know it."

"The League of Collectors? I saw that on one of Mr Keeper's certificates, but I don't think I—"

"They'd be the Peak's most unheard-of secret society," said Mr Gurtwidge with a laugh.

"We're not a secret society," complained his wife unconvincingly.

"But nobody's ever heard of you, have they, love?"

Mrs Gurtwidge leaned forward and looked earnestly at Argana.

"We're like a rotary society, but for collectors. We can have only one of any one type of collector, and we support each other across the lines, as it were. There are plenty of stamp collecting societies, or sci-fi paraphernalia, or film prop groups. We're a collection of collectors."

"Sugar?" said Mr Gurtwidge, ignoring the explanation.

"Yes please," said Argana, and he poured and passed her a cuppa. The chipped mug had a Wookie Hole logo on it, while the other two bore the logos of Blue John Cavern and Abraham Heights.

"I used to work up at the Heights, you know," said Mrs Gurtwidge, who had caught Argana's gaze. "That's where I came across geodes for the first time, where we sold them in the shop. I was a geology student already, but it wasn't until then that they became my passion."

"And now we have a house full of them," said Mr Gurtwidge.

"I was collecting rocks before I collected you!"

"That, darling, is because I am your rock," he soothed.

"How does a geode work, anyway?" asked Argana bluntly, feeling unsure whether oldish people should be allowed to demonstrate this much emotion without a licence.

"Oh!" said Mrs Gurtwidge, so delighted that she made a little clapping motion with her hands without actually bringing them together. "They're when a gas bubble in a rock is replaced with crystals. When the rock is formed, often by a volcanic process, with a void – because it's a bubble, that's why they're most often round – and then water carries minerals through that get deposited on the inside. You think of stone as waterproof, don't you? But it's not really – water can seep through it, just ever so slowly. It takes millions of years—"

"I found some with toads in," said Argana, picking her moment to change the direction of the conversation.

"You hear about that a lot," Mrs Gurtwidge nodded solemnly, "and I believed it for years, but it's hard to get any evidence. You see the one on the mantlepiece, over there, with the mummified frog in? It's a hoax, of course, but even hoaxes have historical value."

"You don't think it could happen?"

"There's plenty of theories about the animals being in perfect hibernation, about the combination of gases preventing their decay and the like, but the crystal and void formation takes ten thousand years and what's the frog going to do then, just sit still and wait? He's got flies to eat; he's got lady frogs to be a courting! No, no natural process could do it. Spirits, maybe."

"Like magic?" said Argana, pleased for once that someone else was suggesting it.

"Seems the most likely, doesn't it? But no, I think they're a hoax. I've lived here my whole life; I know there's boggarts in the marshland beneath the tors, I know there's fairies on some of the high hills, even spirits that think they're devils in some of the crags, but I've never seen anything that could put a frog inside a stone."

"So, the thing is," started Argana, shifting uncomfortably, "I found a snowball geode. More than one—"

"Oh yes, they're very common, although more often in the States; it tends to be quartz that gives them the colour."

"No, I mean an *actual* snowball. Made of snow. With ice crystals on the inside…"

"That's amazing!" squeaked the collector, hopping out of her chair despite her dodgy knee. "I wonder … I suppose, it would have to be a cloud formation effect, a sort of inside out snowflake."

"The size of a grapefruit," Argana said, standing up as she warmed to her topic.

"This merits further study. Where did you find them?"

"Out by Yellow Rose Cottage, Mr Keeper's home."

Mrs Gurtwidge paled slightly, the exuberance draining from her under a glare from her husband.

"Ah, so this is all connected to Bernard. Well, are you going to ask me about him?"

"Oh yes," said Argana, blushing, and sat back down again. Max made a couple of disappointed circles on the rug and did likewise.

"Constable Berkshire and I saw his house, after the accident – he's got a lot of metal detecting equipment and the like down there. Flags, too, did he collect those?"

"The flags? No, they're not a collection. He just likes – liked – to think of himself as a patriot. He'd hang the stupid things at the end of his drive for any occasion: the Queen's birthday, the first night of the Proms, a change of government. Even Brexit."

"That's not what he collected, then?"

"Exactly. The metal detection equipment, that was his passion. He turned up all sorts of coins and things through over the years."

"Did he – I don't know, is it a competitive business, metal detecting? Did he have any enemies?"

Argana's question again brought out an unreadable glance between the old couple.

"What is it?" she asked.

Mrs Gurtwidge opened her to say something but left her words unformed.

"He wasn't a popular man," Mr Gurtwidge came to her rescue. "Mr Keeper rubbed people up the wrong way. We've known him a long time, and it's not easy being his friend. He couldn't stand children either; there was a big palaver down The Green Dragon a few months back when he tried to get some family thrown out of the bar so he could drink in peace. I forget who."

"It was Patty Scholes and her brood," filled in Mrs Gurtwidge. "She rang The League to see if we'd do something. But what can we do? We can't throw a member out for being an awkward git."

250

Argana scribbled the name down in her book, but she didn't have to – Patty was well known around Trotterwell, for both better and worse. Patty herself was big-hearted, but whether her family consisted of pesky delinquents or the high-spirited go-getters of the future was largely a question of who you asked.

"Anything else?"

"Tell her about the hoard, love," said Mr Gurtwidge, still sipping his tea.

"Well, I don't want to get Bernie into trouble."

"He doesn't care now, does he? He can't be in trouble where he's gone. And it might help the detective here figure out what happened to him," he said.

"It was about five years ago … so, he found a hoard – technically, that's a treasure. Not of gold, which is what he'd always wanted, but of Iron Age buckles, and a knife. Well, it turns out he didn't declare it, as the government could have forced him to sell to a museum."

"That sounds a touch shy of legal," said Argana.

"He was trying to find private buyers in the Far East, via a middleman. Your Constable Berkshire won't know about it, it was before his time, but that Luciana Cianciolo from the station might remember. Of course, they didn't find any of the items."

"Quite right," said Mr Gurtwidge, with an impatient expression, "on account of the fact that he'd reburied them up on the hill."

"He never dug them up again?" said Argana, surprised.

"Not as far as I know, no."

* * *

Once they were on their way back from the Gurtwidges, Argana full of tea and cake and Max well-fussed, she called Berkshire on the hands-free.

"Hey, Ms Zeit," he said cheerfully as he answered her call, "any news on the geodes?"

"Well, kind of. They're definitely supernatural. Stroke of luck, though, the Gurtwidges—"

"The who?"

"The Gurtwidges, the geologist and her husband – they knew Mr Keeper. For years, apparently."

"Good work."

She fought the steering for a moment on a long right-hand curve. It was a good thing that it wasn't a video call, or Berkshire would have had her license.

"That's not everything," she said. "You know Patty Scholes?"

The groan at the other end of the phone was all the answer she needed.

"Keeper had a run in with her and her kids at The green Dragon, just before Christmas. You don't think …"

"They're trouble, that lot," mused Berkshire, "but they'd ever kill someone."

"Not on purpose," said Argana bluntly.

"I'll look into it."

"You do that," said Argana, the call ending abruptly as she drove under a railway bridge and the signal cut out. She glanced at the dashboard clock. Even accounting for it being an hour out, there was still enough time to get down to Mr Lovegreen's grocers' before the market shut up for the day.

* * *

The market was built around the market cross near the centre of town, consisting of an assortment of stalls. T-shirts – incongruous in winter – a burger joint, smelling of onions and grease, more traders selling off their leftover Christmas tat. Her uncle's stall was in a building just to the edge of the market, with vegetables downstairs and a tiny, three-table café upstairs that was only open Fridays and Saturdays, of which today was neither.

Mr Lovegreen smiled when he saw her across the market, winking at her past the customer that he was serving. By the time she and Max had reached him, the customer had gone. The store was open-fronted and freezing – Mr Lovegreen was all togged up to keep the cold out, with his collar turned up against his rotund cheeks.

"Uncle Vince!" squeaked Argana.

"My favourite niece! Look at you!" said Lovegreen, pulling her into a hug. He gave Max a fuss too, the dog wiggling and battering his wagging tail against the wooden vegetable crates.

"Business or pleasure? You're more often down on a Wednesday."

"I wanted to ask you about one of your previous customers," said Argana. "A Mr Bernard Keeper; he had a receipt with your name on it."

"Doesn't ring any bells. But a lot of people I don't remember their names, only their faces."

Argana passed him the receipt.

"There's a very unusual ingredient on the list," she said.

Lovegreen ran his finger over the scrap of paper.

"Potatoes, oranges, bananas, sultanas ... and mandrake? Yes, now I know who you're talking about. Alright, is he? Mandrake roots. I know your pagan friends get very excited about them sometimes, so I like to get a few in. He – Mr Keeper, did you call him? – he didn't seem the type, if I'm honest. More your wax jacket and comfortable Wellies sort."

He turned around and fished a box out from under the cabbage rack. With the word 'mandrake' scrawled on the front in black marker, along with a similar skull and crossbones, the box was conspicuously empty.

"I usually keep them here – they're not on public display, because the stupid things are poisonous, and I wouldn't want an average punter to do themselves a mischief. People have to book them and ask for them especially."

Argana looked at the empty box, disappointed. She had been rather hoping to see a mandrake. They seemed such quintessentially mystical things that it was odd to be able to just buy one from a grocer.

"You're all sold out?" she asked.

"I didn't have a single one to begin with, Argana. I have to buy them in from Europe, and this Brexit malarky has messed up deliveries the last two months. They sent me a refund and everything, but they're not going to resume shipping until the border settles down, maybe in April."

"What did Mr Keeper say?"

"Well, that's it, he came on down and had a proper go at me. It wasn't on, you know. Started ranting about little people. After that, I wasn't really going to sell him any more. I wondered about calling your boyfriend, that constable—"

"He's not my boyfriend!" objected Argana, blushing. Berkshire was far too dependable to be boyfriend material. No, Jason, widely referred to as 'that feckless biker', was much more her jam.

"Well anyway, Keeper going on about feeding little people, and mandrake being poisonous, I wondered if he planned to make someone sick. I had half a mind to dob him in."

"Why didn't you?"

It was Lovegreen's turn to look abashed.

"I can't go down the station, Argana. Not after what happened. With the haunted pipes and Mad Alice and everything."

Argana gave him a warm smile and squeezed his arm, remembering the incident. She had not hung around while her uncle was exorcised, but she had seen Father MacGillycuddy in action enough times to know that it was never pleasant.

"It's OK, Uncle Vince," she said. "I'm sure he didn't hurt anyone."

But she wasn't sure. There was the business with Scholes' kids. What if their feud had escalated, he'd failed to poison them, and they'd followed him out to the cottage and snowballed him?

* * *

As soon as Argana was back in her top-floor flat, she turned the hob on to make hot chocolate. The ancient Victorian building, once a three-storey terrace before it was subdivided, leaked heat like a perforated tent. This was both a good and a bad thing; while her flat lost heat through its rickety windows, it also gained it rising up the communal stairwell from the rooms below. It was the guy in the basement flat she felt sorry for.

As Max padded past her and curled up on his dog bed, she got the milk out and poured it into the saucepan. When she put it back in the fridge, her single bottle of blue top stood in stark contrast to the many bottles she had seen in Mr Keeper' house. The thought was interrupted by her phone, the noise of which made max prick up his ears. The caller was, to her not much surprise at all, Constable Berkshire.

"Hello, Fred," she said cheerfully.

"Ms Zeit. So, Patty Scholes and her kids, we haven't been able to talk to them – they're out of town. The neighbours don't know where they are."

"Wow! They've fled the country! They done it!" exclaimed Argana.

"Let's just keep an open mind on that, shall we? As for Mr Keeper, I've turned over a few rocks with the department—"

"Anything exciting?" She stirred the milk one-handed to stop a skin forming on it. She would have made it in the microwave, but that still smelt of kippers from the previous night.

"Not the kind of exciting you're thinking of," he said. "A caution for trespassing in his younger days, and a succession of speeding tickets. Booked for not wearing a seatbelt. Spent most of his life only a couple of points short of losing his license."

"We could have guessed that," said Argana, thinking of the Mr Keeper's mangled Subaru.

"I'm setting the scene, Ms Zeit, that's all. Because the meat is this, that newspaper cutting you found. Mr Keeper got into trouble for allegedly digging up and hiding treasure."

"His house was full of trinkets, that's what they're all looking for. Hold on, I'm putting you on speakerphone, I've got something on the boil."

"There's digging things up, and then there's digging things up. Some of it you have to report to the authorities. Gold, silver, ancient artifacts, that kind of thing. There was a to-do that he had dug up a treasure hoard near Ashbourne without reporting it. There was an investigation, but nothing was ever proven."

"The Gurtwidges were telling me about that. How long ago was it?" Argana put the phone down on the kitchen counter, lined up a Welsh dragon mug and deposited hot chocolate powder into it. It smelt good coming out of the tin, dry and promising.

"2012. So, what, eight, no nine years back."

"If he had an illicit treasure hoard, what would he do with it?"

"Sell it on the black market, I suppose. There was a description of the supposed articles, so he couldn't have done it through regular channels. An Inspector Sheerwater had his house searched, although he's no longer on the force; he emigrated."

"Say again? I was just pouring my drink."

"Inspector Sheerwater," said Berkshire in an exasperated tone. "He looked into it, but he moved to Spain."

"Oh! Can I go meet him on expenses?"

Max stirred on his bed, hearing the sudden excitement in Argana's voice.

"Absolutely not!" cried Berkshire, although there was laughter beneath his outrage. "Luciana would have my badge for approving that."

"Doesn't hurt to ask. Anything else?"

"The League of Collectors put up his bail money. Mrs Gurtwidge signed for it."

"I didn't think she liked him. So, did anything come of the postmortem?"

"No, it was just what it looked like. Fractured his skull on the dashboard, probably never regained consciousness. Oh! I've got to go. There's someone at the front desk—"

"Wait!" she demanded, afraid that the conversation was over.

"What?"

"You *know* I always get the last word," she said, and hung up before he could reply.

* * *

The next day Argana took the bus to Buxton for the wake, watching the landscape scroll by, the snow having retreated from the green valleys but still adorning the hilltops. Max, in the window seat, gazed with a primal longing at the sheep roaming free, if chilly, over the heather. They taunted him with their un-herdedness.

About midafternoon they alighted at the market square, a kind of triangular space lined on two sides by three-storey terraces and shopfronts and capped by a market cross that over the years had become an imposing square building. Although larger, the centre of Buxton was much the same as her own Trotterwell. A short walk to the pavilions shattered that illusion, a park of such obvious grandeur that it cast Trotterwell's Joseph Wright Park very much in the shade. The River Wye ambled primly through flat grass spaces, set off by formal gardens and exotic trees that, even in winter, exuded the civic pride of a bygone age.

Family groups, togged up against the cold, dragged their dogs from the water's edge or meandered on the ornamental bridges. Max and Argana passed them all on their way to The Miners' Arms, taking a shortcut past the pavilion itself, a palace among greenhouses, all bolted Victorian metal and vaulted windows.

The Miners' Arms proved to be a less grandiose affair, first built in an earlier era to service copper miners, its ceiling low and its entranceway sunk below the road so that she had to descend three steps just to get in.

"Hello?" said a barman in the largely deserted lower room as she came in, blinking slightly against the light that followed her.

"I'm with The League," she said confidently.

"You look a little young for that," he said, with a wink. "Go on love, they're upstairs."

* * *

There was a presentation going on in the upstairs room. How someone had found a slide projector in 2021 she had no idea, but they had, and a silhouette in front of a wonky picture of Mr Keeper was talking about him. There was a buffet, and at least twice as many chairs laid out as the twenty-odd people who had come for the eulogy. She sidled unnoticed into a chair at the back. Max took his cue from her body language and slunk in between her boots.

"We may not have known him well," Mrs Gurtwidge was saying, who it turned out was the silhouette, "but we knew him a long time and he was our friend. I hope some of the stories that we've shared of him have helped, and now I invite you all to have some snacks or get a beer from the bar downstairs."

Argana was relieved to have timed it so well. She could not imagine a one-hour sermon on the life of Mr Keeper being interesting.

Gravitating to the food table, she looked around, trying to guess the individual obsessions of the collectors, who were of all ages and appearances. Stamp collectors? Model soldiers? Serial killer memorabilia? At least one of them had to be a secret militaria expert, collecting illicit Third Reich material, she thought snarkily.

"I haven't seen you; you're not a member of The League. You're a, what, a long-lost daughter?" a man's voice startled her out of her daydream. She almost dropped the celery with prawn mayo dip that she had been guzzling. The newcomer was a weaselly fellow in his thirties, with restless eyes and far too little sense of personal space.

"Ha, no. I'm Argana Zeit, paranormal investigator."

"That's a relief. I don't much like the idea of Bernard having children; he'd have been a terrible father. Would have been a brilliant scandal, though."

"And you are?" she asked, taking a step backward.

"My dear girl, I forget myself! Name's Lowedges. Teddy Lowedges." Lowedges held out a hand in greeting, but Argana tactically had hers full, one with a plate and the other with a stick of celery, and just smiled diplomatically. Teddy struck her as an awfully old-fashioned name for a man only on the cusp of middle age.

"It's a bit odd though, isn't it?" he went on. "Mrs Gurtwidge doing the eulogy?"

"Oh, why's that?"

"Well, they fell out, didn't they? And – you didn't hear it from me – but she had an affair with Bernard about a decade ago, though it came to nothing."

Argana's eyes flicked involuntary to Mr Gurtwidge, standing away from the group, picking at a plate of vol-au-vents.

"That's right," said Lowedges conspiratorially, "he knew. I think it would be better not to rub his face in it, don't you?"

"What is it that *you* collect?" she asked him.

"Me?" he chortled. "Oh, I pick up gossip. There's nothing finer." He made a chef's kiss with his fingers.

"Lovely," lied Argana. She was about to flee the conversation when she thought of something else, "Hey, do you know Patty Scholes?"

"Everything," cackled Lowedges. "That woman and her family are a delight to me. So much trouble!"

"Any idea where they are?"

"Oh? They've been away for two weeks, jetted off to the sun." He leaned in far to close. "I think maybe she got a new fella to pay for it…"

He straightened up and looked appraisingly at her. "But one good bit of information deserves another. Why don't you tell me a little about yourself, eh?"

"I'm on bail for punching nosey people," she said smartly, turning on her heel before he could learn anything more about her. She made her way over to Mr Gurtwidge, leaning against a chair and brooding.

"Hello, Angie," he said.

"*Argana*. Hi, Mr Gurtwidge. Are we the only non-League here?"

"No, there's a few more. Mostly the W.A.G.A.H.A.Bs, like me. Let's see, there's Tim and James over there, Tall Kate and Margo, and Little Kate. Tim and James love their football, but I can't abide the stuff. What did you think of the eulogy?"

"I didn't catch it."

"You didn't miss anything. No one will come out and say it, but Bernard was a jerk. Most of them are just bloody awkward, but he was flat-out selfish."

"You didn't like him?"

"Don't beat around the bush, Argana, I saw you talking to Teddy Lowedges, I'm sure you know about Bernard and my wife now. Water under the bridge, I say, and we moved on – it's just that this meeting dredged it all up."

"You're mixing your metaphors."

"I'd rather be mixing my drinks. Let's go down to the main bar and I'll tell you all about Mr Keeper."

* * *

The downstairs bar was not quite as quiet as she had left it; several of the other non-League members, having bored of the conversations about dealers and price gouging, had quietly retreated from the function room. All the same, Argana and Mr Gurtwidge found a mahogany-clad alcove that was private. They had a pint and a whisky chaser each, making Argana glad she had taken the bus. Max, who didn't share his owner's interest in clandestine conversations, went first in search of a bowl of water and then table to table begging a scratch behind the ears. And maybe some crisps too if he was lucky.

"It's a shame," said Mr Gurtwidge, "that you didn't meet Yorick, who collects folklore. You'd have got on well."

"Never mind them, I'm trying to figure out what Keeper was mixed up in. I thought maybe he'd fallen afoul of a feud with the Scholes family, but they've been out of the country. So he has enemies out there, possibly with supernatural powers, and all I've got is a ton of speeding tickets and this business with the treasure hoard. Which you must know about. What am I missing?"

"Oh, I know alright," he said darkly, taking a deep gulp of his beer. "That was the year, you know. The year when – I knew they'd gone up the hill, that they'd taken a picnic with them. He never was good with computers; dozy bugger sent me a message on Faceache that he meant to send her, didn't he?"

Argana leaned back, nursing her pint, letting him take the time he needed to tell his story.

"Anyway, and I know it wasn't right, but I followed them up there. My wife had the car, so I had to get the bus to Trotterwell and take the footpath out over the hills. Took a while, I'll tell you."

Argana nodded. Being in a National Park, Trotterwell had a plethora of routes that took you up out of the town, and she had walked many of them with Max. The farm was further out though, a good three miles, and although she had gone that way a couple of times, she didn't remember it well. There were copses of wood and small abandoned quarries, in as far as she could recall.

"And you found them – you …" she trailed off, having decided that all possible endings of her sentence were tactless.

"That's just it – it wasn't a picnic at all. Before you say it, it wasn't the other thing either. No, when they carried their hamper up it looked heavy, and when they unwrapped the teatowels it wasn't any sandwiches in there. They buried it up at the top of the hill. The treasure, lumps of iron it looked like. I don't know, I'm no specialist. Let the ground keep its secrets, I say; it does no good to poke it."

"He was hoping to dig it up again later?"

"I assume so. There's always talk of changing the treasure laws. Perhaps he was waiting for a better time."

"And you're sure it was the hill above Yellow Rose Cottage?"

"Absolutely."

"I've got an idea. I'm going to have a talk with Farmer Turner."

"Do you need to go now?" asked Gurtwdige, a little sadly.

"No. Same again?"

Several hours later, after it had got dark, she got the last bus home. Max had to wake her up when they got there.

* * *

The following morning Argana Zeit drove over to see Farmer Turner. He lived in a traditional farmhouse with his main barns right alongside, a stretch of hardstanding out the front stained from years of being piled with silage and manure.

After she rang, he trudged up from one of the barns, clad in a boilersuit and green wellies, and me them at the gate.

"You can't bring tha' dog of yours down farm", he said, in lieu of an actual greeting.

Max looked nervously between them.

"Why not? He *is* a sheepdog."

"Is he well-trained?"

"No, but he's clever and he's kind."

Turner sucked air through his teeth.

"Very well then. But if the cows 'av you, tha's on you."

The gate groaned on its unoiled hinges as he swung it open to admit them both. Despite his reservations, he couldn't resist giving the dog a resounding pat on the way past.

"We'll be inside though, won't we?" asked Argana.

Turner's laugh didn't entirely set her on her ease.

"Nah. You want some of my time, young lady, you're going to have to trade me some of yours in return. There's plenty of jobs need doing around farm."

That is how the conversation went. Which is why, a half hour later, Argana was out the side of the cow sheds with a tub of hammarite and a paintbrush.

"It'll be calving season come the end of month, I need the barn to be ready."

"You've lived here forever, haven't you?" Argana asked him.

"Do I look that old? That's working hard for you. I'm thirty-seven year, if I'm a day."

"I meant," she said hastily, "the Turners have been on the land here."

"Oh tha's right, since before there were even town of Trotterwell. All these fields you can see, the copse of woodland, the small lake that feeds into river. We're the custodians of it. When those stone walls were young, my family were old."

Given that Trotterwell market cross had stood for a thousand years, she took Turner's claims with a pinch of salt. Still, exaggerated or no, his family had clearly been around for generations.

"What do you know about Peak District sprites? Fairies and such? Mrs Gurtwidge mentioned them."

He paused in his painting to nod solemnly.

"When the 'orses get to twitching, run down the hills, that's the boggarts tacking them. Young city girl like you wouldn't—"

"I was born in Trotterwell!" she objected.

"Well, that's a town now, isn't it? All I'm saying is I'm surprised at you, being interested in such things. What about your Nintendo, and your makeup?"

With her tangled hair, puffy coat and wind-blasted skin, that made her laugh. Nothing more exciting than moisturiser had been on her face since New Year's Eve. It was not that Argana was averse to makeup, but she needed an occasion, and investigating murders was not it.

"The boggarts?" she prompted, after she was done laughing.

"The swamp lights. Sometimes they come up and pester the animals; there's all kinds of ways of getting rid of them. Old wives' tales to a one of 'em, but it pays to listen to the old wives, doesn't it?"

That chimed with Argana's own research of boggarts, at least so much of the concept has had not been trampled on by popular films. But it was the fairies she was interested in.

"Fairies?" reflected the farmer when she asked him. "My nan used to talk about those, reckoned there was some up on the hills. Boggarts in the valleys, faeries on the high points, she used to say. You'll know about faery circles? The rings of mushrooms?

"Of course. I *am* a paranormal investigator, you know."

"Well, it takes all sorts to make a living."

"Is there a faery circle on the hill above Yellow Rose Cottage, where we were?"

Turner looked both ways as if he expected to be overheard, but there were only cows. They watched uncomprehending with their huge wet eyes.

"Oh yes, there's faeries in those hills. They move around, from time to time – you got to look for their circles. We've always had to know about them; they play havoc with the animals every generation or so."

"How do you deal with them?"

"Hah! Mostly you don't. A few of my ancestors tried making deals; but who do you even find to broker a deal like that? Would you?"

"I could!" started Argana, firmly trusting in the 'fake it 'til you make it' school of doing things. In this case, faking it didn't make it further than that single statement.

"You wouldn't. You're no hedge witch, I can tell."

Argana shrugged shamelessly and carried on painting.

"No," said the farmer, "by and large we go for the simple approach, and when the going gets hard and the eldritch forces come down from the hills and the elves are a knocking on our doors, the Turners of Trotterwell do the only sensible thing is to do."

"Oh?"

He put down his paintbrush and paused dramatically, commanding her full attention.

"We put out a saucer of milk for them," he said.

"I've got to go!" she said abruptly.

"What?"

"Thank you!" she called over her shoulder, already running back up to her car. The farmer was left behind with the half-painted shed and a look of consternation. Argana had a plan, and she had to call Berkshire.

*　*　*

A half hour later, Argana was explaining her theory to Berkshire as he drove them back out to Yellow Rose Cottage, this time taking the police car.

"It's really simple," said Argana. "Bernard Keeper was a metal detector. Detectorist, I mean. Right? He dug up some old Saxon buckles and had to hide them from the law. You'd know about that, right?"

"Right. Obviously, I'd know about an obscure law that's only going to be invoked once in Trotterwell in my whole life. That doesn't explain who killed him."

"I'm getting to that. What he dug up, it would belong to the crown as part of a hoard, so he reburied it up on the hill above his house. But that hill's been a faery haunt for centuries, and there's a mushroom ring up there, a faery ring."

"With you so far."

"He offended the fairies. They're not big fans of iron, as I'm sure you know."

Berkshire grunted. "That one time that Yasmin persuaded me to play Mazes and Minotaurs, when we were all teenagers, there was definitely something about cold iron. I thought that was elves, though."

"Same thing."

Berkshire stopped the car at the top of the cottage drive. The Subaru had gone, towed away, with only a confetti of broken glass to show where it had been. Argana let Max out and started off toward the cottage, while Berkshire got a riot shield out of the boot.

"In case they start with the iceballs again," he explained, waving it at Argana. He banged its Plexiglass surface for good measure.

"Cool. I'm going to grab one of his metal detectors from the shed; we can go dig up the treasure and put an end to the faerie feud."

Berkshire followed her, hustling Mr Keeper's keys out of his pocket as he walked.

"If I'd offended a whole bunch of elves – and happened to believe in them, too – I think I'd have just dug it up again," he said, unconvinced.

"I'm not sure he could. Disturbing elves is like poking a wasp's nest. Maybe he couldn't get back; they may have confused him every time he tried. Anyway, he found an alternate solution. The saucers we saw at the house?"

"Yeah?"

"He was preparing a paste of mandrake and milk in them, putting that out for the fairies. Fairies can't get enough of that stuff. I think he'd been placating them for years. The Turners have been putting out just milk for generations, but I don't think Keeper had their negotiation skills, which is why he needed the mandrake too. When he stopped, they got irate. I doubt they meant to kill him; they're more the pranking type."

"Why'd he stop feeding them?"

"Brexit. He couldn't get his mandrake supply anymore."

There was a shed at the side of the house, and it was full. Mr Keeper had collected metal detectors the way golfers collected clubs. The instruments were clean and well-maintained, and Argana took the simplest looking one. It was kind of broom-shaped, except made of metal with a plate shaped disk at the bottom and a box of electronics at the top.

"You know how to work that?" asked Berkshire.

"I've seen it on T.V."

"Is your driving by any chance the same approach? There's this American show where…"

"If you start calling me Michael Knight, I can live with that."

"I was more thinking *Wacky Races*, Penelope."

* * *

They left the house behind them, crossed the road and started up the hill. In daylight it was obvious where the giant snowball had come down, as it had smashed a hole through the hedge. They passed through it. On the other side, the foot of the hill was green and muddy, but the higher it went the more ice and snow it had.

"You notice anything about the sky?" said Berkshire.

"Still there, is it? No, I'm looking at the ground, aren't I?" Argana swung the metal detector in a steady arc in front of her. Contrary to her earlier statement, she had used one before. One summer as part of the well dressing festival they'd buried cups out the back of The Green Dragon. For a quid, a punter could have ten minutes with a detector and a shovel. If they dug up a cup, they won something with the raffle ticket inside.

"It's snowing again," Berkshire informed her, breaking her reverie.

Moments before the sky had been blue and clear, now it had the off-yellow look of a blizzard brewing. Tiny flecks of white were already drifting like willow fluff, the harbingers of more to come.

"Which is odd," he carried on, "because the weather forecast is flat-out dry."

"Those things are always wrong."

The hill got steeper. They were following a sheep trail now, too narrow for a human stride width, a meandering path of shorter grass between the longer, browner stuff. It was hard to get a decent footing, the thaw having turned the ground to mud. Except the closer they got to the top, the more it crunched underfoot. It was frosting up. The trees were stranger too, twisted, leafless things except for those evergreens draped like collapsed drunkards. Max slunk ever closer to Argana, his tail tucked between his legs.

"How do we even find a faery ring? It's not like there will be mushrooms out this time of year."

"There'll be a circle of darker, healthier grass. The fungus gives it nutrients."

"I shoulda brought a thicker coat," grumbled Berkshire, who was already wearing a greatcoat over his uniform.

"It's alright, you're thick enough!"

Berkshire turned up his collar as Argana smirked at him. The snow was falling fast now, fast enough to settle, sticking to her furry hood and sliding off the steep sides of his police helmet.

There was a whoosh and something darted past Argana's cheek, making her look up. The horizon was gone, lost in what was rapidly becoming a blizzard; even the gnarled trees were barely visible. Between them indistinct figures were moving, the height of children, exuding both menace and grace. She could not see them clearly, but the motion of one of them was clear enough. They were throwing things. Max's forepaws were braced and his hackles up as he emitted a low, continuous growl.

"I was hoping we'd have more time before they got riled!" she said.

"Duck!" yelled Berkshire, shoving her shoulder down. A heavy snowball missed her.

"Hurry this up," he said. "It's always the same with you, isn't it? Plant monsters, interdimensional horrors, even bloody elves. I'm always your human shield!"

"That's a polycarbonate shield, you wazzock. Maybe you should carry it more often."

They processed further toward the crown of the hill, him in front of her with the riot shield, she awkwardly swinging the detector around his feet.

"I think, I think we're here," Argana said finally.

"How can you tell? I can't see the grass anymore!" Berkshire scuffed experimentally at the snowline with his boot.

"I'm getting that vibe. Plus those fae urchins have completely surrounded us."

"I do love the word surrounded," said Berkshire doubtfully, readying his truncheon in his other hand.

They were at the crest of the hill – not the top of the whole thing, but the top of a foothill, a point where the ground sloped away from them on each side. Hominids stepped from their places of concealment amid the trees, visible for only an instant before the blizzard swallowed them up. Just three feet tall, they had grey robes of moss, onyx eyes staring out of smooth featureless faces with the oily texture of newly husked seeds. Almost at once they were hidden by the swirling curtain of snow, threatening figures indistinct in the mist.

Argana stopped what she was doing and stared open-mouthed into the maelstrom.

"I wish we could see them properly!" she said.

Berkshire batted away an incoming snowball with his truncheon, pivoted over his foot and stepped across to the other side of her, catching the next one on his shield. It rang like a drum.

"We don't have time for your sightseeing! Find the iron, or we'll get out of here."

"You don't fancy being brained by a snowball full of toad, then?"

"They killed Mr Keeper!" he shouted.

This argument-in-waiting was headed off by the rapid beeping of the metal detector.

"I've got something!" squealed Argana.

She knelt, the snow soaking her knees through her jeans, and threw down her satchel. Her folding spade – acquired from the army surplus in Ripley – made short work of the ground. She gripped it two-handed, putting her whole body into the hacking motions.

More snowballs dinged and thudded as Berkshire spun around her, blocking and swatting, shield in one hand and truncheon in the other like a particularly well-dressed barbarian. One cannoned into Argana's shoulder, making her wince. An explosion of snow and ice, a white toad tumbling into the bucket-sized hole she was excavating.

And then a spark. Metal on metal. She thrust her gloved hands into the dirt and twisted.

"Hurry it up! I don't know how much longer I can do this!" insisted Berkshire.

She pulled an iron bracelet free, followed by a couple of arrowheads.

"Ow!" yelped Berkshire. His helmet bounded past her down the hill, knocked from his head by the latest attack.

Last was a broach, beset with mud and rust, that appeared to have a long-eared face on it.

"That's it."

"Really?" Berkshire sounded incredulous. He caught another snowball with his riot shield.

"Really."

The snow was thinning again. Argana stood up tentatively and looked around. The attacks had stopped and, after a minute or so, the more cautious Berkshire relaxed his guard too. He straightened up.

"Where are they?" he asked.

"Look."

As the blizzard lifted, they could see again the circle of faeries surrounding them, seven pairs of liquid dark eyes. They seemed smaller now, their body language less threatening. Argana and Berkshire remained motionless, holding their breath as the silence dragged out. The creatures stared back, their expressions unknowable. Their hands were twisted and many-fingered, and their shoeless feet were root systems digging their gnarled toes into the soft soil.

They had what seemed to be a leader, wearing a crown of woven snowdrops, who inched a little closer to the humans, their toes rippling with the movement. She – or he, Argana couldn't tell – dipped their chin in acknowledgement. In the instant that Argana blinked the fae disappeared, replaced by twinkling lights that faded in seconds, drifting on the wind, leaving her with the sensation that she had simply stood up too fast.

Max bounded to the place where the leader had been and pawed at the ground, turning in a confused circle.

While Berkshire stared wordlessly into the distance, Argana gathered up the relics.

"I think they're happy. Let's go, leave them to it."

He nodded. "I'm in no hurry to do the paperwork on this one, but still, I'd rather be back in Trotterwell with a stiff cup of tea."

They returned to the squad car, Argana as always climbing into the back with Max.

"There's one thing I don't get. This business of fairies and cold iron, what's that all about?"

"You wouldn't believe me if I told you."

Berkshire raised a quizzical eyebrow. That eyebrow said that after they had been through together, Argana should trust his credulity.

"OK," she said, "it's like this. You think that faeries are magical creatures, and that's true, but it's not the whole story. They're also elemental creatures. Their metabolism is fusion-based, and that's the thing about iron. It's the element at which fusion reactions break down; you can't push them any further. They don't like iron because they can't consume it."

"Wow. That doesn't explain how burying it in their circle harms them, though."

"Who knows? Maybe they're just grumpy gits."

"Takes one to know one," said Berkshire, starting the engine up.

The End

Acknowledgements

There's a whole bunch of people I'd like to thank.

Firstly, there's my sometimes editor, sometimes proof-reader Alex Davis, who's help, encouragement and occasional tutoring has been invaluable.

And of course, there's my beta-readers and back-up proofers, ever ready to haul me up on a character inconsistency or plot hole. These folks are stars, every one of them, so big thanks to:

Jack Aidley, Alex Beau-Martin, Paul Beau-Martin, Andrew O'Connor, Kate Durrant, Vipul Gupta, Jay Hart, Nigel Holmes, Emma Hurst, Tim Ingham-Dempster, Jessica Jermain, Pat King, Jen Lewis, Cal Lugosi, Ant Newby, Hobbit Newton, Kate Sayers, and Lesley Taylor.

A Note from the Author

It was the summer of 2020 when I started writing these, which wasn't a great time in our world. I wanted to write something fun and escapist in response, and what's more escapist than hauntings and eldritch horrors? They say write what you know, but I don't know anything, so I dusted off a character I originally made for a comic's pitch and set her loose. The rest, as they say, is history – except that what it actually is, is this book in your hand.

If you enjoyed Argana Zeit – and you're reading the end credits, so I'm going to pretend you did – then I warmly invite you to join my mailing list at https://www.owainoakwood.com/subscribe/ I'll send you an alert when there is new Argana Zeit material out, along with news of my other projects and occasional musings. I hope to see you there.

All the best,

Owain.

Printed in Great Britain
by Amazon